FINDING MY ENDGAME

A Winter Springs Duology

CLARA MOON

TO MY HUSBAND

for putting up with my shit and loving me anyway. Thank you for telling me my stories are worth writing, even if it was a way to get me out of your hair so you can work on the derby cars.

TO MY FOUR BOYS

for being better people than I am, even if you talk about bodily functions daily. Just don't read this until you are older, much older.

TO ME

I did it!

CONTENT WARNING

This book contains a character talking about being abused in his home and told to kill himself.

This book contains a character talking about an ex that controlled them and then verbally abused them after found cheating.

This book contains a character mentioning that they had a miscarriage.

This book contains a kidnapping and physical abuse while kidnapped.

This book contains descriptive sex scenes.

This book contains strong language.

Saige

Mid-April
Friday

"Auntie Saige!"

I look ahead and smile when I see my nieces Phoebe and Paige running towards me. They jump into my arms for a hug, and I lose my balance. We topple over onto the floor and laugh together. Having the girls in my arms and hearing their laughter in person is some sweet music to my soul.

I look at their faces and no longer recognize the toddlers I last held five years ago. They are seven-year-old identical twins and it's still hard to tell them apart, other than Paige having a heart-shaped birthmark on her jawline below her left ear. Their chubby cheeks have thinned out and their freckles are more pronounced on their creamy skin. They both have the same long blond hair that ends in ringlets. Their caramel-colored eyes are the same as their fathers and their right sided dimple comes from their mother.

My brother River and his wife Ginny stand behind them staring down at us with the biggest smiles on their faces.

"I told you she would come." I hear my brother say to her in only what he thinks is a whisper.

"Of course, I came. Someone thought they should call me and tell me that I know deep in my heart that I should be back home to celebrate the Bicentennial with my family."

Now that I'm here and feel the warmth of love fill me, I know it was the right move to get out of the city after all. "Thanks for the push, Bub."

River laughs. "You're welcome."

He helps me up off the floor, and we exchange a warm embrace. I meet a hard chest, telling me my brother has been working out. His once dad bod is flat, and his arms have filled out with muscle.

"Look at you all pumped full of muscle. Work must be good for you."

"Isn't he hot? Look at his new haircut." Ginny pulls me into her arms.

"Yeah. Yeah." He rakes his hand through his brown hair. He's cut it into a military fade.

I turn to Ginny to embrace her as well and I'm always so amazed at the total opposite Ginny is to my brother. While River is six foot one, tan, with dark hair and caramel eyes, Ginny has a cream-colored skin that burns easily in the sun. She is only a few inches taller than me, and she has blue eyes the color of the Caribbean Sea. Her once long, luscious locks of blond curls are now cut into a bob.

We grab my luggage and leave in their new minivan.

The drive back to my brother's house is filled with laughter and the twin chatty Cathy's telling me everything they have learned since our last phone chat. I have just enough time to get in a few words before they are back to talking nonstop.

Once we make our way into the town the girls are giving me a play by play of our historic home and talking to me like I'm a tourist. In a way I sort of feel like one since I haven't been back in five years, but I notice the town hasn't changed a whole lot. There are some new people they are telling me about and some new shops that have opened, and I just try to keep track of it all.

~

As we pull into the drive, I look up at the house. It's a white two-story colonial home with a yellow door and dark blue shutters. It's my brother's home now, but at one point in time my mom owned it when we were all growing up.

She sold it to my brother when he got married and started a family for himself eight years ago. She always said the house was just too big for her. "What do I need a five-bedroom house for?" were her words.

So, my brother gladly took it over and mom moved into a one-bedroom ranch style home down the road. I think she was thrilled to finally have a place to call her own that was perfect for her and wouldn't take days to clean.

This will be the first time in five years that the entire family will be together to celebrate the Bicentennial. Finn comes home periodically when he isn't gone for work, so it is me who hasn't been here since I was twenty.

As I start to get out, I see movement out of the corner of my eye. The one person I wouldn't think to see has come back for the town celebration. Declan Wolfe is standing in his parent's driveway and I can't look away.

He was the stereotypical star quarterback in high school and only dated a certain type of girl. You know the type. Skinny, long legs, and blond. Let's not forget that they also had to be a cheerleader.

At five foot three with long wavy brown hair and brown eyes, I was nowhere close to what he wanted. I never thought of myself as ugly. I knew I was pretty, but because I was plus-sized many guys were turned off. I felt like a short, way less glamorous version of Ashley Graham.

Declan was no exception. He didn't give me the time of day, except when he came over to the house or when he would just call me 'little Saige' anytime he saw me out and about only because he knew I hated the nickname. That still didn't stop me from having a crush on him and hoping he would notice me just one time.

I put my leg back into the van and shut the door. "How long is Declan here for?"

River looks at me through the rearview mirror and studies me. "He moved back a year ago."

"I didn't know he moved back. So, he's living with his parents now?" I glanced out the window at him.

"No. They passed away two years ago in a car crash during his last year of law school."

"That's horrible!" I covered my mouth with my hand, feeling sorry for Declan. I know he didn't have the best relationship with them, but no kid deserves to lose both parents at once.

"Yeah, it was sudden. The house sat empty until last year. He couldn't bear coming back to the house until then. He opened up a law practice in town at the old bank."

"Is he okay?" I ask.

"I think so. He's been spending every moment when he's not

at work, working on the house. He's come a long way. Why do you ask?"

"No reason. I just didn't know any of this." I say.

"You're not still into him, are you, Sis? I mean, I know you had a crush on him back in high school, but that was years ago."

"Yeah right! He was a pompous jerk who thought he was God's gift to women. I don't care whether Declan is here or not. Besides, he left for school seven years ago, and the last time I saw him was the last time I was home. I'm way over him. I'm just surprised that Finn didn't tell me any of this."

"Uh huh. Just remember you are a different person than you once were in high school. And I'd even venture out and say he has changed too, with his parents being gone and putting himself through seven years of school for a law degree."

"Well good for him. I am washing my hands clean of men at the moment, no matter how good looking they are." I look through the rear window at the beautiful man getting something in his truck. He turns quickly to look in our direction again. He smiles like he is looking at me, and I can't help wondering why my heart keeps fluttering and why I can't look away.

"Good looking, huh?" I turn back around to look at River.

I roll my eyes. "Even though I'm not still hung up on him, I'm not blind. I didn't think he could look any better, but I was wrong."

River laughs. "Well, that's good to know because he is heading this way." I turn around again, and sure enough Declan is walking up the driveway. It's like watching a movie in slow motion as he makes his way over.

I open the door to the van and get out with as much confidence as I can gather. Out of the corner of my eye I see Ginny and the girls walking into the house, but River is lingering by the porch pretending not to eavesdrop. I roll my eyes again, but I am silently thankful that he still looks out for me.

My heart starts to flutter when I walk to the back to get the luggage out of the car, hoping he will ignore me. I grab one suitcase and go to turn around and run right smack dab into his hard-as-rock chest. I slowly lift my eyes up to his, and he gives me his megawatt smile. My heart flutters faster and harder this time, and I lose my breath completely. His gorgeous piercing green eyes are staring right into my soul, sending heat to my core.

"Little Saige. Is that really you?" He looks my body up and down. "Wow! You are all grown up."

His voice is like sex, the good kind. And I want to melt into putty just from hearing it, but I can't give him the satisfaction. I back up from him to give myself space. "Declan Wolfe, as I live and breathe."

He looks my body up and down again. "You look beautiful," he says.

I look at him trying to decide whether he is making fun of me, but he doesn't give me any hints in his facial expression. I have always been plus size my entire life, and after high school I learned to embrace my body. But my ex destroyed all that confidence.

I can already feel my body shut down and my defense mechanism kicking in. I shrug at him.

"Well, you look like the same ole same, Declan."

But then I do a bad thing. I check him out.

In high school he was the hot bad boy and a walking wet dream, but this man standing in front of me is a Greek god! He is the epitome of strong, powerful, and ripped. He has defined, well-built curves that are visible through his shirt. His chest, shoulders, biceps, and forearms strain against the fabric. The once shaggy black hair is now shorter and styled. He has grown out a beard that gives off a hot lumberjack feel. It isn't unruly though, instead trimmed and cleaned up.

I tell myself to stop staring at him. I won't get sucked in by another guy that is gorgeous, even if this one is like a present wanting to be ripped open and explored. All he will do is rip my heart out again like the others. I need to keep him at arm's length.

I rip my eyes away from his body and find him staring at me. His eyes give me a sign that he knows I checked him out and he gives his half smirk and winks. "See something you like?"

"N-no."

He walks closer to me and brushes a stray hair back. I shiver and he catches it. He leans down to whisper in my ear. "I know you do because of the way your body is reacting to me. Don't worry, you are doing the same thing to me."

My eyes drift down to the bulge in his pants and I take in a quick breath.

I push him back to give me space. "I don't know what you are talking about."

"Whatever you want to tell yourself. You know you are glad to see me, Little Saige."

"It's Saige, not Little Saige. Saige," I cross my arms. "Still blowing up that ego with all the girls fawning over you?"

"Not every girl, if I remember correctly. There was still one girl who couldn't care less."

"Oh, I'm sure there was more than one girl in high school who didn't fawn over you." He raises one eyebrow. "I was just more than happy to be the leader of the group of girls who were not affected by your charms and could see through your bull. We had better things to do than swoon anytime you walked down the hall thinking you were God's gift to the female population."

He smiles and opens his mouth to say something, but right then my brother Finn pulls up into the drive. I sigh in relief.

Finn is my older brother by two years. He is one of my best friends. He was a popular football player like Declan, but he was a social butterfly. He was the one that was friends with everyone no matter who they were or what they looked like. He also was willing to help anyone anytime. He was my rock and shoulder a lot during high school and the years afterwards. I always knew that if I called him, he'd drop everything to be there for me.

I run to him, and he gathers me in a hug. "Smalls! I've missed you!" His hug is so comforting that I wouldn't let go if I didn't have to.

"I've missed you so much!"

We both step back and take a good look at each other. Finn is also tan like River and me. He is as tall as Declan, so I have to stare up at him to see his face.

"You cannot be gone for years on end again! If you leave me alone with River for much longer, one of us will go missing," Finn says jokingly. He looks up at River with his ice blue eyes and smiles.

River walks down towards us and he and Finn hug. "Hardy-har-har! You know you love me." River then messes up Finn's blond hair that is styled in a messy side part kind of way.

"You know I do, but you aren't my dad, and if I wanted someone to tell me what to do with my life, I'd have stayed with Mom." River winces and Finn freezes.

Our dad divorced our mother when I was a freshman and just took off. River changed his life for those four years to help be the man of the house. He moved out of his apartment and moved back in to help mom, and he tried to be a father for Finn for two years and me for four until everyone was eighteen.

Automatically knowing he has said something wrong, Finn tries to apologize. "Riv, you know I didn't mean it like that. I just like living the carefree, single life and you like being a father and husband. While there is nothing wrong with your life, I just wish you would know that that life isn't for everyone. And I like my life the way it is."

"I know you didn't mean it, bro." River throws his hands up. "You're right. I'll back down."

I throw my arms around both of their waists. "Looks like I came back in the nick of time," I say.

"By the way," I say, "I love the beard." I let go of Finn's waist to give his beard a little tug and then place my hand around his waist again.

"It grows out on trips. I'll trim it up a little later."

"I don't think you need to trim it at all. I like it," I add.

Finn turns his attention to Declan. They have been best friends since middle school when Declan's family moved across the street and they both joined the football team together. Those two had been thick as thieves ever since, even when they both moved away.

River and I let them catch up. We finish grabbing my luggage out of the back of the van. He catches me stealing glances at Declan and gives me a raised eyebrow.

Knowing I've been caught, I try to downplay the situation. "Bub, don't worry about me. I am just trying to figure him out."

He looks at Declan and then back at me. "As long as that's it, Sis. You haven't had a lot of luck in the romance department, and I don't want to see you hurt again by any man."

"I know, but it's not my fault that every guy I've ever dated turned out to be a huge tool." I cringe.

"Okay." He gives me a hug and walks towards the house with my luggage.

I look at Declan once more and walk towards him and Finn. "I'm going to head inside and let you two catch up." I turn and start walking up to the house.

"Wait Smalls, I'm coming in with you." Finn yells to me so I stop and turn around. He looks at Declan once he knows I stopped for him. "I'll talk to you later man. Let's grab a beer tonight. Say, Sherry's at nine?"

"Sounds good." If I wasn't looking at him, I wouldn't have noticed that he did a quick glance at me. "Want to make it a group catch up? We can invite a few of our old buddies. Hell, you can even invite Little Saige if you want to." He gestures to me.

I roll my eyes. "Saige. And no thank you. I've done more catching up than I plan to do with people from high school."

"You wound me." He hugs his hand to his chest and laughs. I roll my eyes, motion for Finn to walk with me, and we head to the house. I'm about halfway up the drive when I hear, "I'll be seeing you soon." I turn around just as Declan's eyes raise from my ass to my face. He gives me another smirk and then he winks before turning around to head over to his house.

Finn looks back and forth between Declan and me. He settles his gaze on me. "Well, that was interesting." Finn says as he slings his arm around my shoulder and walks me inside. He doesn't know half of it.

"By the way…" I pop him in the stomach with a little force.

"What was that for?" he asks, rubbing his stomach.

"Why didn't you tell me about Declan's parents dying in a car crash a few years back? I feel like I should have known about this."

"I didn't need to add any extra stress to your life and have you worrying about him when you should be focusing on your book. I was just thinking of you. I'm sorry."

"It's alright. Just make sure you tell me important things like that, no matter who it is."

"Deal." He nods.

We walk to the front door, and he opens it, gesturing me inside.

Saige

"Surprise!"

I jump. "What is all of this?"

My family and friends are all standing in the living room, and I'm in complete shock. I look around the room for River and our eyes meet. I give him the death stare, and he smiles while shrugging his shoulders. Of course, he would be the one to think a girl needs a surprise party right after getting off a five-hour plane ride.

It was a complete surprise, though. While it's not an ideal time, I am thankful he did this because nothing cheers a person up more than staring into a room full of people who love you and are glad to have you home.

Gina, my best friend, runs up and tickles me. "Girl, if you stay away from Winter Springs anymore, I'll hurt you. Talking through Skype and Facetime has not been the same thing as seeing your beautiful face every day."

I look at her and notice she hasn't changed. Yes, she has

gotten more beautiful over time, but she is still the same girl that has been with me through all of life's adventures. She has kind green eyes with rings of gold around the irises. They are covered behind her large, black glasses. Her lips are thin and usually frowning, but when she smiles her eyes twinkle, and a dimple is uncovered on the left side. Her face is always done up in makeup because she thinks she needs to cover up what is underneath. She has red hair that is short and done up to look messy and unkempt. Not very many people can wear their hair like that, but she can. She has a booty that would grab anyone's attention. While it is a wonderful asset to have, I know she hates that it is probably the only thing people notice about her.

I pull away, put my hands on her shoulders and say, "I've missed you so much. No matter how much time passes without us seeing or talking to one another, I will always be there for you. No matter what." She starts tearing up, and we hug again.

"Bitch, this is supposed to be a party, not a sappy love fest," says Megan, and she swings one arm around me and hands me a drink with the other. Meet my other best friend.

While Gina is the calm nurturing one of our group, Megan is the one that you know will always have a plan up her sleeve that isn't always legal. She is the one who always builds you up when you are down by making you laugh or somehow distracting you by sneaking into Declan's room during a party and stealing his boxer briefs to hoist up the school flagpole for everyone to see.

Megan has straight, long, dark brown hair. She is also short and has beautiful, chocolate brown eyes. She is busty and has wide hips that give her an hourglass shape that all the boys like. She uses her sarcasm and smartass remarks as a coping mechanism and loves to break out in random songs on quotes from movies.

"Thanks, girl. You don't know how much I have needed this." I salute with my drink in the air and then gulp it down.

"Did you tell her the good news?" Megan says as she nudges Gina.

I turn to Gina. "What good news am I supposed to know about?"

Gina smiles brightly at me and says, "I'm pregnant."

"No way!" I throw my arms around her. "I'm so happy for you!"

She's blushing. "It's true! I'm three months along. Jeff and I are so excited!"

We all end up catching up and laughing so much that I'm having to cross my legs before I pee my pants and Megan has exchanged my first drink for, possibly, a fourth one.

I guess I had been chatting with them for too long because I see my mom out of the corner of my eye motioning at me with her finger. I excuse myself from them and make my way around the room to talk to everyone before I finally make it to her.

It's my party, so I let her wiggle in her pants a little more before I finally do as she says. By the time I make my way towards her, my brothers, Ginny, and my nieces have joined her.

"Hey guys." I turn to Riv and Ginny. The twins stand on each side of me, and they both reach for my hand. "Thank you both for hosting what looks like the entire town. It really was a wonderful surprise, and I'm eternally grateful."

"Sis, you know I would have stopped at nothing to get you here, but it was all my love that planned and hosted the party. I just had to deliver you to the house and make sure we had food." River looks at his wife with such a love that I wouldn't have known existed if I wasn't the one watching it firsthand. He leans in and kisses her temple.

Ginny smiles and stares back at him with equal love and admiration while rubbing her growing belly. She turns towards me. "It was the least I could do for you. We really miss you being home. The girls have talked about you coming nonstop." I squeeze their hands, and they look up and smile. "And this little guy will want his Auntie Saige to read to him and spoil him rotten."

"And I'm looking forward to doing just that. Jace and I will pull so many pranks on his daddy."

River glares at me. "Oh, it's payback, Bub, from when we were little."

"I want to pull pranks on Daddy," Paige yells.

"Don't you worry. We will." I look at River and smirk.

"I'm already regretting letting you stay with me," he says.

"No, you aren't. You love me."

"I take it back." We all laugh.

A look of shock comes across Ginny's face. "Oh my God! I forgot to mention that we read your book. It was wonderful. You have a gift, and I'm so glad you are sharing it with the world."

I blush. "Thanks, Gin! I tried to do something different, so I was afraid that the readers wouldn't like it."

Mom clears her throat. I watch her and wait to see what she has to say. She is overly dressed for the welcome home party, but that is her. She always dresses to impress, and today is no different. Her graying dark hair is in a fancy updo and she is wearing a green velvet dress. She is what society considers as in-between size, not skinny but not plus size. But since she is not plus size, she never understands my size and why I never lose weight.

What she doesn't know is that, over the years, I have tried to lose weight every which way. The weight has just wanted to stay. We butted heads in high school over it, which lead to me having hurt feelings. I was unhappy with my body because she was unhappy with it. I moved away from her lectures and got the confidence I needed until Philippe.

"I just wish that Saige would take a lesson out of the book she wrote and find a nice man to settle down with." She looks at me. "You aren't getting any younger, honey. Whatever happened with that Phillip guy you were dating? I thought you two would have been engaged by now."

I love my mom, I really do, but she is also always on my case about me not getting any younger and how I need to quit being so picky, mainly because I'm plus size, and find a man to settle down with. If we stay clear of talking about me being single and anything else pertaining to me, we get along well. But moments like this are why I love living in New York City.

Finn intervenes. "Mom, his name was Philippe, and they broke up six months ago because he was a cheating asshole who didn't know that being in a relationship meant being in a relationship with one person, not three." I tense up as all eyes are on me while I relive the wasted last year and a half in my head. Finn smiles at me apologetically as he comes over to me and drapes an arm around me. "And besides, I'm not settled down and I'm doing great. Smalls doesn't need a man to make her happy. Right, Sis?"

I nod my head yes. "Right."

Mom rolls her eyes. "I swear you two will drive me to an early grave. I just want to see you guys happy like your brother. My babies all deserve happiness and by God, you shall have it. Plus, I want more grandchildren." River and Ginny share the same lovey-dovey look as earlier. Finn and I just shrug.

~

After helping River clean up after the party, I sit down on the couch with an ice-cold sweet tea and pat myself on the back for a job well done. I think about how great the day has been so far. I've been back for six hours now, and I've loved every minute of it. It almost makes me forget the conversation I had with Declan hours ago. Almost.

There was so much I should have said to him, and instead I was snarky and defensive. But there is only one way to protect my heart, and this is the only way I know how.

Gina and Megan plop down on the couch next to me. I pat them on the legs. "So, what do we want to do ladies? We can go to dinner and the movies or stay in and rent something and order Chinese."

Megan puts on her 'I have a plan' smile. "Or we could go to the bar and catch up with everyone that's going to be there. It sounds like it might be one hell of a reunion."

I motion to Gina. "We can't go to the bar. Gina is pregnant." I wave my hands like a magician over her belly.

"I can still go to the bar, silly. I'll order a soda, and I'll be the DD."

Megan claps her hands together and giggles. "Hell yeah! Now that's what I'm talking about."

She turns to me. "Come on, Saige. It'll be fun." She tries to persuade me.

Sounds like hell. "Fun for you, maybe. You were the social butterfly, but I was a little nobody that everyone ignored. The girls only talked to me to get in with Finn or Declan, and the guys acted like I was never even there."

"I remember a guy who talked to you, and someone had a little crush on him," Gina says.

"Someone may still have a crush." Megan looks at me like she is studying me.

"Did you talk to River?" She shrugs her shoulders. "Ugh, I'll kill him! I do not still have a crush on Declan. Besides, he only talked to me back then because I was Finn's little sister. If I recall, he always called me Little Saige."

"So, what was his excuse today?" Megan asks.

"He was seeing if he could woo me with his Declan Wolfe charm. What did he think would happen? I'd fall at his feet like a lost, little puppy? I don't think so."

"Oh yeah girl. She still has it bad," Megan says to Gina.

"Yeah, she does," agrees Gina.

"What the hell!? After all I said, you think I have it bad?"

"Yep, because you're so defensive." Megan responds.

"Am not." I say sternly and they laugh.

I throw pillows at them both. "Shut up."

Megan looks at me and says, "You're going. You owe it to nobody but yourself to go. Prove to yourself that you are not enamored by him."

"It's not just him. It's everybody else that will be there. I'm afraid that everyone will take one look at me and just think I'm the same fat teenager and not even try to get to know me for who I am now."

Gina leans forward find holds my hands. "Where is this coming from? You were so confident in yourself after high school." I shrug. "You are not fat. You are a beautiful, plus size woman with a heart of gold. You were senior editor of the school newspaper and the yearbook editor and went on to be a bestselling author who lives in New York City. If they don't see that then they are not worth your time. You'll never know unless you go out there, Sweetie."

Megan grabs one of my hands. "We will be with you every step of the way. When you want to leave, we will leave. If you need me to beat the hell out of someone, I will do that too. Okay?"

I think about it and realize I really do need to build my confidence, and what better way than to show my face in front of old classmates and show them just how well I'm doing. "Okay. Let's do it."

"Do what?" I hear Finn yell as he is coming down the stairs into the living room.

Megan blushes, but it quickly disappears. I've never told her that I know she has a crush on my brother. For someone that is an open book, she has kept this hidden, and maybe she has a good reason. "We are all going to a bar tonight."

He smiles and throws himself down in between Megan and me. "This is going to be awesome. I promise, Smalls. Remember, the people in this room love you for you, so screw everyone else. You are a bad ass. We know it. Now prove it." He punches me in the arm.

I smile at him.

With these three, I can conquer the world. I stand up. "Well, I better start getting ready."

The girls go into my room chatting while I leave to take a shower. I turn the water on the hottest setting because we all know I need to relieve some muscle tension in my neck and shoulders. Tension from the city, tension from Declan, and tension from the anxiety of seeing everyone tonight.

I know Declan will be there at the bar tonight, but I can't

focus on that. I need to stop thinking about him along with everyone else and just enjoy spending time with the girls and my brother. I need to have a good time. I want to have a good time. It's time for me to be carefree again. I haven't felt that in over a year. The time I spent with Philippe cannot be taken back, but I can use it as a lesson to myself on what I do deserve.

I never let any of my friends or family into our relationship other than telling them that he cheated on me. He was controlling, but I never truly realized it until I found out he was a cheating asshole, and it was like this bubble I was living in burst, and I truly saw him for who he really was.

He didn't cheat once. He cheated multiple times and with two different girls. He was always telling me what I could or could not do or say. And somehow, my naïve little self just thought he was looking out for my well-being. Looking back now, I can see how big of an idiot I was.

How did I finally say good riddance? Well, let's start at the beginning. I met him at Sip, a cute coffee shop in Manhattan. I had just finished a meeting with my publisher, and I thought a nice coffee and a good book was exactly what I needed.

It was this perfect meet-cute. I was sitting there relaxing while reading with an occasional sip of coffee. I was so engrossed in the book that I almost didn't hear him say, "Can I join you? All the other tables are full."

I looked up and saw one of the most gorgeous men I had ever seen. Tall, shaggy, blond hair that swept to the side. It was long enough that the tips of his hair tickled his eyes. It was almost like the stereotypical surfer guy hair. Speaking of eyes, they were cobalt blue and shone brightly.

"Please," I motioned to the seat beside me. I reached my hand out. "Saige Wilson."

He extended his arm and shook my hand. "Philippe Cunningham. Nice to meet you."

"You as well." Suddenly, I felt very nervous.

"Business or pleasure?" he asked.

"Hmm?" I looked at him, confused.

"Manhattan. Are you here for business or pleasure?"

"Oh, well, business. I just came back from a meeting with my publisher for a book that didn't meet the deadline." I raised my coffee cup up and then took a sip. "So, I needed to relax a bit afterwards. I do live in the city though. What about you? Business or pleasure?" I was more interested than I let on.

"Business. The Goodwell Modeling Agency called for a meeting and flew me up here. They wanted to talk about me moving here and modeling for them." He looked me up and down. "I now have something to add to the positive side of moving here and staying."

I blushed.

That was it. I was gone. He moved to the city, and we started dating. At six months, we moved in together, and that was probably when the controlling started. When I was home and not touring with the book I finally finished, we would go to parties that Goodwell threw.

I was only allowed one drink because I didn't want to embarrass myself in front of the crowd since he knew I didn't like people laughing at me. When the plates of food came out, I didn't even make my own plate. Philippe would make it and it would only have fruits and veggies on it. Now, don't get me wrong, I love fruits and veggies, but I would have loved to be able to have some of the crab puffs or dessert too though. He said it was because he knew I was trying to keep my figure in check, and he didn't want to see my feelings hurt when I stepped on the scale, and possibly showing I gained five pounds instead of losing any.

He knew I was comfortable with my size, and he made it seem like he was okay with it too, but looking back, I remember him being frustrated for me more than I was when I would eat healthy, work out, and not gain or lose. He suggested I should make an appointment with the doctor to see if anything was medically wrong with me. When Dr. Toothman came back telling us that I was healthy and a-okay, he almost looked defeated.

I think when he knew he couldn't change me was when he decided to go out and find side chicks. I don't know why he didn't just break up with me. Maybe it was because he liked having someone to control or maybe it was because the bigwigs at Goodwell loved that he was breaking the norm with me, and it was bringing lots of good publicity to them.

Whatever the reason, he cheated, and he wasn't even trying to hide it. I think he did at the beginning, but by the time I found out, he couldn't have cared less.

The night of our one-year anniversary, he came home and went right to the shower. For the past two months he had started to do that. He even stopped giving me kisses as soon as he walked in the door. He always said it was because he felt dirty after work, so he wanted to shower first. I thought when he hopped in the shower, he was getting ready to celebrate our anniversary, so I went into the walk-in closet and brought out the gorgeous black number that I bought just for this occasion.

This was the night. I might have been coming home as an engaged woman. I put on my flats and makeup.

While I was waiting in the living room, Philippe's phone rang, and I didn't recognize the number, so I answered it. Before I could say anything, I heard in a whiney voice, "Philippe! You were supposed to be here at seven, darling, and it's already seven-thirty. I'm lonely. I need you. Please say you are on your way."

"Um, hello. This is Saige, Philippe's girlfriend. He's in the shower. Who is this?"

Silence.

"Hello? Who is this?"

"Hi. This is Grace. Philippe and I are models on the new J.L. brand together. He's supposed to be here for the shoot."

Why would she have said she was lonely, and she needed him if they were models together? Plus, they were waiting for him for a shoot? I remember thinking, please don't tell me Philippe is cheating on me and this is his mistress. No! There must be an explanation.

"Why did you say you are lonely and that you need him then?" I asked suspiciously.

"Well, because the shoot can't happen until he is here. That's it." She cleared her throat. "Just tell Philippe he needs to come."

It sounded fishy and I was super confused. I got the 'I need you' like 'I need you for this shoot', but why did she say she was lonely?

"A shoot isn't on the calendar and besides, we have a dinner date to celebrate our one-year anniversary in thirty minutes."

"Just tell him to call me." Her voice was shaking. Yep, this was exactly as it sounded.

"Wait! Please don't lie to me. You owe me this. Woman to woman, is Philippe cheating on me with you?"

Silence.

"Yes. We've been together for the past four months. I'm also not the only one."

Click. The dial tone of her hanging up rang in my ear.

I just sat there dumbfounded for five minutes until I heard, "Honey, have you seen my black tie?" He walked into the living room and stopped. I guess the look of utter shock on my face made him 'worried'. "What's wrong, Hon?"

"Hmm, let's see. What's wrong? What is wrong?" I said, tapping my finger on my chin multiple times. I jumped off the couch. "Maybe the fact that you are a two-timing whore!"

He came closer, trying to touch my arm. "What are you talking about, mi amor? You aren't making any sense."

"I'm not making any sense." I lifted his phone up and showed it to him. "Well, I just answered an interesting phone call. Grace." I saw the confusion waver in his eyes. "You know Grace, right? Well, she said she was waiting for you and that she was lonely and needed you. And another interesting tidbit. She said she isn't the only one you are cheating on me with either."

His charm dissolved and he turned into this different guy that I never knew. "So, I got caught, hmm? About time. Now I don't have to pretend to be with you anymore." He chuckled. "You know I never really loved you, don't you? I mean, look at you and then look at me. We are sugar and vinegar. I could never be with a fat woman forever. I just kept you around for the good publicity. So, thanks for that."

And that was that. I kicked his ass out but not after he ruined me from all the confidence I built from high school up to that point. I even spent the next six months alone in our apartment feeling horrible and fat and thinking I was a loser.

But that was then, and this is now. I'm going to let this hot water wash away all of Philippe and cover me in confidence, because I am beautiful, I am smart, and I am confident. Look out world!

Saige

I walk into my old childhood room and see that an outfit, my flats, and makeup have all been spread out across the bed. Not only that, but the girls have also hung up all of my clothes in the closet so the clothes don't get wrinkled.

I smile, look at the girls and thank them. While they chat, I get dressed and feel like I am a million miles away from them. I just don't know what to say to them, and that's not like me. I have always been a talker ever since I could speak. Just ask my mother, she will tell you the same thing. The twins take after me in that department.

I've missed out on so much with everyone and it's no one's fault but my own. I got wrapped into writing my book, touring, and then Philippe, that I couldn't be bothered to come home and see them all in person. It was easier to stay away when I was away, but being back makes the shame very real. I know I talked to them on the phone and facetimed, but you know it is never the same as seeing them in person. I look at my best friends through the mirror and catch them looking at me. I smile.

"Ready?" Megan asks as she stands up and walks towards me.

"Just about," I say while trying not to poke myself in the eye with the mascara.

She whistles. "They aren't going to know what hit them, girl."

"You think?" I twirl around.

"Oh yeah," Gina states as she comes to stand on the other side of me.

"I do feel beautiful in this outfit. I haven't worn it in years."

"Well, it fits in all the right places." Megan says before slapping me on the ass.

"Hey!" I yelp. "Come on. Let's go. I bet Finn is wondering if we are ever going to come downstairs."

Finn talks Gina out of driving her car, and promises to see that everyone gets home safe and sound. We all load into his jeep and listen to him talk about his photography business. He is a nature photographer, so he travels all over the world and takes the most beautiful shots.

It's a perfect job for him because he is an outdoor adventure guy, through and through. When he's not taking photos for magazines, he is rock climbing, skydiving, hiking mountains, bungee jumping, canyoning, parkouring and deep-water scuba diving. He is the ultimate extreme sports enthusiast and enjoys his life. His body is also built for those kinds of things. You know, the lean athletic type.

Megan starts squealing over pictures on Finn's phone. "It looks so scary but fun at the same time. I'm not sure if I'd have the guts to do it, but I'd like to try."

"I think you should try bungee jumping before skydiving, kid. Start small and work your way up," he says, taking his phone back.

She laughs. "If that's what you call small."

We pull up to Sherry's. It is a bar and grill in one and the food is so delicious. Sherry and her husband can also make you any drink you want. You name it, they will make it. They don't skimp on the alcohol either.

It's nine fifteen p.m., so by the time we make our way in, everyone's there and seating is scarce. I hear people calling Finn and Megan as soon as we make it into the middle of the main room, so they head towards those voices. Gina and I make our way to the bar. I need a lot of liquid courage, and she is always parched.

"Looks like Sherry and Bill hired new help, because I don't see them anywhere." I scan the bar, looking for them.

I find a woman who looks to be in her early thirties behind the bar. She has black hair thrown into a messy bun with a bandana wrapped in it. Her nose and lip are pierced and she is wearing ripped black jeans and a midriff ACDC shirt. It's a style that she pulls off flawlessly.

She catches me staring and walks over. "What do you want, Doll?"

"Can I get a Vodka Dew and a..." I look at Gina, "coke, right?"

She nods.

"You got it." She turns away to make the drinks.

"Put it on my tab, Becky," a deep, sexy voice comes from behind me.

I'd know that voice from anywhere. Only one voice has ever sent shivers down my spine and goosebumps on my arms.

"No, that's okay." I look back at him. "Thanks though."

Becky nods and starts making my drink. I turn towards Gina and ask her how she is feeling with the pregnancy. She eyes me and Declan, trying to figure out what's going on.

Then I hear a growl, and he says, "Alright then. Nice chatting with you, Little Saige." I hear his footsteps retreat.

Gina looks confused. "Alright. What was that about?" Gina asks with a hint of concern in her voice. "He just came over to buy you a drink. Why didn't you accept it and talk to him?"

"Who? Declan?" She nods. "G, he was just being nice about the drinks. He didn't want to chat with me."

She scoffs. "Are you really that naïve?"

"What?" I look at her questioningly.

Becky delivers our drinks, and I thank her.

Gina waits for her to leave before saying, "I love you, honey, but you really are an idiot sometimes."

"I'd expect Megan to call me out, but not you." I take a drink to mask the hurt.

"I'm just being honest. The man was over there sitting with all his friends and even all of those girls, but he saw you come into the bar and chose to come talk to you. He even looked a little hurt when you didn't talk to him. If he didn't want to chat, he could have just had one of the waitresses send you a drink if he was only being nice. I really think he likes you. What's going on with you?"

I sigh and run my hands through my hair, scratching my head. "I don't know." I blow out a puff of air and pull my hands out of my hair, rubbing them on my legs. "How did I not see any of that? Why is it when he's around that my defenses go up?"

She sighs. "Girl, I know how bad your heart broke when he didn't pay you any attention, like he did the other girls in high school. I also know all the guys you went on dates with after high school weren't even close to Prince Charming. And don't get me started on Phillippe. I know more happened than you let us know, because you are not the same Saige you were before you met him."

I try to cut in, but she silences me.

"Nope. I'm talking right now. It's like you started out as Saige in the relationship and he killed that girl. He turned you into this robot version of the Saige he wanted, and that's not right. It's okay if you don't want to tell us what happened, but don't pretend like nothing did, because we miss the girl we know and love, and she's not here right now. But if you close yourself off to all men then you'll become a bitter, old woman, and no aunt of this little one is going to be that crazy cat lady that lives all alone, angry at the world."

I lift my head and face her this time. "You're right. A lot happened. How can I trust a guy with my heart and life and know he won't rip it more than what it already is?"

She laughs, so I look up confused. "No one said anything about getting serious! You just have to talk to them and be nice. Don't close yourself off. Who knows, maybe something will come out of talking to one, but, if not, well then, you might just get a new friend out of it. We all need friends, right?"

"We do." I glance over and find Declan sitting at the table with girls surrounding him, but he isn't looking at any of them. He is staring right at me, and I see a mix of hurt and hunger swirling in his eyes. He takes a sip of his beer and looks away. "I'll apologize to Declan tonight when I get the chance. Let's go join everybody."

I give Gina my hand and she takes it. We hop off the bar stools and head towards the group. There are about ten to fifteen people sitting around tables pushed together. I see Finn, Declan, Megan, some old football players, and some cheerleaders. I don't see anyone else that I recognize, but now is my chance to get to know them all. Gina and I grab the only two seats that are empty and, unfortunately, they are not next to one another.

I'm seated beside Quinn and some guy that was on the school football team. He'd visit the house a few times when Finn had the entire team over for pizza and soda after a game, and Quinn was the head cheerleader.

She dated, and I use that term loosely, Declan for six months and was my worst enemy. I think she made it her life's mission to torment me every chance she had. But we are twenty-five now, and people change in seven years, right?

Declan is sitting on the other side of Quinn. I lean behind Quinn's seat and try to get Declan's attention.

"Hey, Declan. When you are free, can we talk please?"

He doesn't acknowledge me. So, he either is ignoring me or did not hear me.

When I lean back up in my seat, Quinn is looking at me with a scowl.

"Where are my manners? Hi, Quinn. How have you been?"

She looks me up and down, her green eyes scanning my body. A look of disgust is on her face. "Do I know you?" she says with the same snotty attitude I knew well in high school.

I clear my throat. "Well, um, I'm Saige Wilson. We were in the same grade together in school."

"Saige? Saige Wilson?" She pretends to think. Her face morphed into a sneer. "Nope. Doesn't ring a bell. Must have been no one."

As much as I am pretending on the outside that that didn't hurt, it did.

She flips her red hair to smack me in the face and quickly turns towards Declan. "How are you hotter every time I see you?" Her fingers walk across his bicep. He turns towards her. "Maybe we should grab a bite to eat somewhere sometime, or you can come over to my place and I'll cook us something."

"Sure," he says with no interest and takes a swig of his beer.

"Hi." I hear a voice and turn towards the guy sitting beside me.

"I'm Milo Toretto." He extends his hand to me.

I shake his hand. "Saige Wilson."

"We went to school together, right?" he asks.

"Yeah. You were one grade ahead of me. You were on the football team with my brother, Finn."

"Ah, yes. I thought that was you. How have you been and what have you been up to since we graduated?"

"I'm good. I moved to New York City right out of high school, got a writing degree at Columbia, and became an author. What about you?"

"That's impressive!"

"Thank you."

"You're welcome. I went to IU and got a business degree, came back here to run my family's bookstore, which I turned into a chain. Your book has definitely been sitting on our bestseller shelf. It was phenomenal!"

"I appreciate that. Turning one bookstore into a chain is equally as impressive. It seems like we have both done well." He agrees. "Do you enjoy running the bookstores?"

"I do. When I left for IU, I thought I would be going to school for computer programming. Somehow, it didn't sit well with me after two years into it, so I decided I needed to change degrees. I just couldn't throw away the bookstore that I spent many years working for. It was probably the most fun I had working there beside my dad."

I love listening to his story. "Sounds like your heart finally caught up with your head."

He smiles. "You're right. Would it be too forward of me to ask you out for dinner sometime this week? I know we've only chatted a little bit, but I'd love to get to know you better in a more formal setting and not one where I have to crane my neck to hear you above all the noise."

I remind myself of what Gina said to me at the bar. "You know what? That sounds great."

"Great! How is Wednesday night at seven? I can pick you up?"

"That should work. I'm staying with my brother in the house I grew up in. Do you remember where that is?"

"I sure do."

I can feel Declan's glare on the back of my head before I hear him say, "I've got to use the restroom, I'll be right back." It takes a minute before I hear a huff from Quinn, letting me know he has left.

Milo is still talking to me, but I tune him out to wonder why I felt Declan's glare on me. I contemplate walking to the restroom area to talk to him about what happened earlier at the bar. Quinn has staked her claim on him, and if she is around, I'm not going to be able to apologize unless I can get him alone.

I take a drink and look back at Milo. "Milo, will you excuse me for a minute?"

He stands up when I do. "Of course. Are you okay?"

"Yes. I just need to go to the bathroom for a second."

He moves out of the way for me, and I walk through the bar to the back where the game room and restrooms are. I stop in the doorway and find Declan leaning against the pool table with his arms crossed at his chest. He's looking down, his face in a frown.

"Hi, Declan."

He looks up in surprise. "Saige. What are you doing here?"

I point behind him. "I need to use the restroom." He looks at the restroom doors and then back at me. "Same. I just needed a breather first."

I walk towards him and lean against the pool table beside him. "It is a little stuffy in there, isn't it?"

"You can say that." He glances back at the bar.

There is silence wrapping around us, and it makes me nervous.

"Well, I'll let you get your breather in." I straighten up and walk towards the bathroom but stop myself from walking too far.

Actually," I turn around. Before talking myself out of it, I walk back and stop in front of him, "I saw you leaving and thought I should talk to you."

"Me? Why?" he asks in confusion. "Don't you have better people to talk to?" There was hurt in his tone.

"No. I need to talk to you. I wanted to apologize for the way I behaved earlier. It has nothing to do with you and everything to do with me."

He stares at me and tries to get a read on me. "No need to apologize."

"Yes, there is." I touch his bicep with my fingertips and immediately feel electricity. I pull my hand away in shock.

I lock eyes with him, and it looks like he feels it too, but he closes his eyes, and the look is gone when he opens them.

"Okay. Let me ask you a question. Why did you just ignore me?"

I think for a few minutes and reply, "Well, I have just gotten out of a bad one-year relationship, and it did a number on me. But that was no reason to act the way I did, and I'm sorry."

"Really? It must not have done that bad of a number if you are already making dates," he pushes.

Understanding fills my body. "Oh, you heard that?"

He nods.

"Well, Gina and Megan have been trying to get me out of this funk. Philippe, the other half in this bad relationship I'm trying to get over, made me lose all confidence in myself. I worked hard on getting it after high school, feeling beautiful and empowered, that kind of thing. So, after you left the bar, Gina told me I was stupid and that if I closed myself off, I'd be old and bitter and alone. I kind of lost the old me and I'm pretty sure I need to find her."

My eyes go wide. "Shit I did not mean to say all of that." My eyes scan the room. "Please ignore that."

I start to walk away when he grasps my hand. "I'm glad you did."

He runs his thumb over the back of my hand. Our eyes connect, and it sends an electrifying pulse through me. He comes closer, and his cologne is intoxicating. I press my thighs together, and I feel weak in the knees. The power this man has over me by just standing here next to me is scary and exhilarating all at the same time.

He moves a strand of hair behind my ear and uses his thumb to brush up and down the side of my jaw. I hold my breath. "I don't think you lost her. She's in there somewhere. She just needs someone to believe in her. She also needs to look in the mirror and really see her in the eyes of others. Because then, she wouldn't doubt if she is powerful or beautiful. She would see a feisty, gorgeous, smart, talented woman, and she would hold her head up every day. Philippe was an idiot not to see that. He was an idiot not to see that you are an endgame for someone."

"You think so?" I whisper out.

"I do."

After rubbing his thumb on the back of my hand again, he lets go and walks back towards the bar.

I lean forward and rest my arms on the side of the pool table where he was just sitting. "What just happened?" I say to myself.

I blow out a puff of air and walk into the restroom. I gather some water into my palms and splash the cool water on my face. I glance up at myself in the mirror and listen to my mind whirl. I lean across the counter to grab a paper towel out of its holder and blot my face with it.

After what feels like a lifetime, I compose myself enough to head back out to everyone. People have moved seats, so the only ones available are across or next to Declan. And after what just happened back there with Declan, I can't sit beside him without losing my mind.

I walk to the empty seat across from him and try to catch his eye as I sit down. He never looks up to meet it. However, that doesn't stop Quinn from catching me trying to get his attention. She gets out of her seat and sits in the empty one beside him. She runs her fingers down his chest. "Baby, would you be a dear and buy me another drink? My Cosmo is empty."

He snaps out of his trance and nods. He looks at me and my half full drink and asks, "Little Saige, would you like another one?"

"I'm good. Thank you." He nods and leaves the table.

Quinn's smile drops as soon as he is out of earshot, and she leans forward across the table.

"Listen bitch, I don't know what you and Declan were talking about back there, and quite frankly, I don't care. But he is mine. Do you understand? Mine! No one will take him from me and definitely not someone who looks like you."

I lean forward across the table to match her. "Well, I don't know how you know that we were talking back there, but Declan is his own person, and if he wants to talk to me, he can."

"Just know that when he calls you Little Saige, he is making fun of you. Who in their right mind would call you little? Fat Saige is more like it." Insert bitchy laugh. "It was a running joke all throughout high school."

My mind is running a mile a minute, but I try to contain a cool composure outside. "Whatever you say, Quinn. If it was a joke, I would have known about it."

She tilts her head. "Are you sure about that?"

"Yeah, I'm pretty sure. My brother would have told me if he had heard it. He probably would have knocked some teeth out."

"Or he and Dec came up with the nickname together and secretly laugh anytime Dec says it."

My eyes go super wide as I'm now weighing whether my brother and his buddy could really do that to me. Quinn smiles, and I know that she knows she has won.

Rationally, I know my brother would never. But it was high school and people are stupid enough to do anything to fit in.

"So, I hear you have a date with Milo." Finn drops into the seat next to me and slings his arm across my seat.

"What?" I jerk my head up to face him.

"Hi, Finn. You are looking good. Those extreme sports are doing wonderfully for your body." This girl is unbelievable. First, she flirts with Declan and tells me to back off, and now that Declan is gone, she is flirting with my brother.

"Hi, Quinn." He never takes his eyes off mine and leans into whisper, "Anyway. Milo?" A smirk plays on his face.

I shrug.

"Well, I heard he is fantastic in bed," he whispers in my ear.

I just look at him and chug the last of my drink. I slam it down on the table a little too roughly and leave the table.

Finn follows me and grabs my arm, spinning me to face him. "Smalls, what's going on?"

I look him in his eyes, zoning in on his tell when I ask him, "Was there a joke about me?"

"What are you talking about?"

"In high school? Was there a joke about me? My nickname that Declan gives me, Little Saige. Was it a joke because I was fat, so it really meant Fat Saige?"

"Of course not! Why would you think that?"

I eye Quinn at the table but stay quiet.

He looks over at her too and rolls his eyes. "Saige, you can't listen to anything that bitch says. I don't know what her vendetta is with you but there was no joke. Declan just called you that because you were my little sister. End of story."

I walk to the bar and order another vodka dew and sling it back in one gulp. Finn is right on my heels.

"Saige?" I'm silently thinking. "Saige?" I look at him. "Declan never once made fun of you. He thought you were actually cool."

I laugh at that.

Finn grabs my shoulders and says, "Seriously. He always told me I could invite you to anything we did when we were younger. I promise he would never have done such a thing. One, I would have killed him, and two, he really did think you were cool. You should have known Quinn was lying the moment she said I was in on it. You know that would be the furthest thing from my mind."

I take a long sip and enjoy the silence. "You're right! I believe you. I should have known anything coming out of her mouth was a lie. I'm sorry."

"Okay, good. But don't forget what I said about Declan. Besides, I saw you two back there in the game room." He wiggles his eyebrows. "You can't tell me that that was him thinking you were Fat Saige."

I sigh. "What exactly did you see?"

He clears his throat. "Well, I could practically feel the electricity while you two were talking. And don't even get me started on that touch."

I cough into my drink. "Touch?" I ask innocently.

"Yes, touch! Don't play dumb, Saige. You know the touch and I saw the touch. I could feel the sexual tension a mile away."

"That was nothing," I whisper.

"Nothing my ass." He laughs. "But if that's what you think, then okay."

"You know I had a crush on him in school."

"Yeah."

"I haven't seen him since graduation, though. Nothing will come from what just happened back there because he doesn't see me that way."

"How do you know?"

I scoff. "Doesn't this bother you knowing your sister likes your best friend and that there is a slim, very slim, chance that he likes her back?"

"Smalls, you are my person. I want nothing but your

happiness, and you deserve all the happiness you can get. And if you find that in Declan then I'm ecstatic. Declan is a great guy. He might have been sort of a douche in high school, but he had a lot of personal things going on in his life too. You ever wonder why he was over at the house any chance he got?"

I nod.

"His home life was not really the greatest."

"I didn't know the exact details, but I figured some things were going on."

"Nobody knew the details but me. But I think you both deserve happiness and I know you both could give each other what you need and want."

"I wouldn't go that far."

"Okay. Then what about this date with Milo?"

"I don't know. He seems nice."

He sighs in frustration. "Well, maybe this date with Milo will help you figure out your 'I don't know'. You sure got a lot of them. Milo was cool in high school and like I said earlier, I heard he is a fantastic lay."

I spit my drink out. "SERIOUSLY?!

He looks confused. "What?"

"I never thought I'd hear my brother tell me some other dude is a good lay, let alone basically say it as if you think it would be something I need."

"Maybe a good lay is what you need. You are wound like a freaking top."

"Really?! I just need to think."

He sighs. "No, you don't. Just go on your date with Milo. Keep it casual and whatever happens, happens. Maybe things will start to clear up for you. You will know what to do with everything because you are Saige freaking Wilson. Alright?"

"Okay." I pause for a moment. "How fantastic of a lay is Milo?" I raise my eyebrows and smile at him. Finn laughs.

I see movement out of the corner of my eye, and Finn and I turn to look at the same time. Declan Wolfe is walking away from where we were standing.

"Declan!" I yell, but he doesn't turn around. He just storms off.

If I didn't know any better, I'd say he probably just heard us talking about sex with Milo.

"Do you think he heard us?" Finn asks.

"Uh, yeah. I'd put that as a hard yes. I wonder how much he heard, though? Hopefully it wasn't a lot."

He puts his hand on my shoulder. "He heard that we were talking about Milo being a fantastic lay and now he has hightailed it out of here." He laughs. "I think you got your answer about whether Declan likes you or not."

"Maybe he just didn't want to hear about another guy getting busy. I'm still quite weirded out that you are telling me you heard he is great in bed." I look out towards the empty space that once had Declan standing in it. "What am I supposed to do now?"

"Well, what are your options?"

What was I supposed to do? Some people in my position might say it would be an easy choice for them.

"The younger Saige in me wants to go back to the table and talk to people so they can see me for who I am now and not the girl they knew. The romantic in me wants to run to Declan and see if he really does like me and have that happily ever after that only happens in Hallmark movies. But the rational part of me is telling me that I should just go to the table, confirm my date with Milo and then excuse myself for the rest of the night. I can talk to everyone another time and Declan lives across the street, so I can try talking to him in the morning."

"Well, what does your heart say?"

Instinctively, my heart knows, and my feet answer for me before my head can tell them not to. I run out the front door of the bar and look around everywhere, but I can't find him. His truck is still here, but he doesn't answer when I yell his name out multiple times. I wait a few more minutes in hopes that he will come back or answer, but he doesn't.

Sighing in defeat, I head back in towards everyone. I tell Finn that I couldn't find him but that his truck is still here. I let him know that I'm going to walk home and that I'll see him later. Finn offers to drive me home and then come back to make sure Megan and Gina get back safely, but I tell him he should just stay because I need a walk to clear my head.

I walk to Milo last and make sure we are set for Wednesday at seven and then I tell all the people as a collective that I'll talk to them later. Most say bye, but the select few that I knew wouldn't care don't. I make sure my keys, ID, and bank card are still in my pocket, and I walk out the door.

Saige

When I walk outside, I breathe in the fresh air of Winter Springs. I smile to myself and look around the square. I love how small this town is. It only takes roughly thirty minutes to walk the entirety of it, but that was my favorite thing to do at night when I lived at home. And tonight, it looks like the perfect night to do it again.

I head to the center where the town hall is and lay down on the lawn. It's in the low seventies, according to the town sign above me, no breeze, and the sky is so clear that I can easily point out Orion's belt and the dippers. My mind jumps to the past, and I remember checking out astronomy books at the library and reading about all the constellations.

I would learn what stars connect to make the constellation, the origin of the constellation's name and even the position of the stars during each time of the year. I know, nerd alert. But it was a wonderful pastime.

I would then lay down on this lawn and spend hours trying to find them. Time would always get away from me. It was always the perfect way to forget all about the troubles in my life.

After some time of getting lost again, I stand up and continue my journey around the town, because I'm not ready to go home to my brother's house just yet. I listen to the crickets rubbing their wings together and the sound of thunder far away. A storm may be blowing in soon, but I can't leave just yet.

Almost every piece of this town is covered in memories. Good or bad, they are memories that I cherish. I walk by the park and sit on the swings. This playground is where I sliced my hand open when I fell off the monkey bars trying to do what Finn was doing. I swear Mom was going to blow a coronary when she took me to the ER to get stitches. It took her almost two months before she let me go back and play.

After twenty minutes I hop off the swing and walk next door to the library. As I sit on the steps, I remember this is where my first kiss happened. Neither one of us knew what we were doing because we both leaned in a little too hard and smacked our heads together. Once the laughing subsided, we tried it again, and it was perfect. Well, perfect for any thirteen-year-old. I chuckle to myself.

Across from the library is the community center. The community center was where my brothers and I would go after school while Mom had to work. We loved going there and it's where I learned to be good at dodgeball. I was once nicknamed 'killer' at only seven because I showed no mercy to the other team.

I wander my way to the corner of the square and stare into the bakery. It was where we all had an ice cream when Mom told us that Dad had left and took everything but the house. I remember crying into River's shoulder the entire time. He was already planning to move in and change his life to help all of us, and Finn didn't say one word that day until Riv showed up late that night with luggage and boxes.

I continued to walk and peer into the rest of the shops, restaurants, and the bookstore, but I stop in my tracks when I find myself at the last shop on the square, the local apothecary. In high school I worked here after school and on weekends helping Mrs. Winters.

At first, Mom wasn't sure that working at an apothecary was really an ideal place for a teen girl to work. I begged and begged, but she wouldn't budge, until she met Mrs. Winters. She may have been in her early seventies, but she was fit as a fiddle and full of sass. She wooed my mother with so much class. It was hard after that for my mom to say no. My initial reason for starting this job was because I knew how much Mom was struggling financially, and I wanted to help. But it didn't take long for the job to become so much more than that.

Mrs. Winters became family to me. It wasn't even a week in that I started calling her Grams, and she would introduce me to anyone that would come into the shop as her granddaughter Saige. We would both beam from ear to ear.

She would always have some cookies and sweet tea to welcome me to my shift, and then when the shift was done, we would chat for hours about everything. Some of my best childhood moments were here with her.

Unfortunately, two months before my high school graduation, she suffered from a stroke and passed away. I would say she was also a big reason why I needed to get away from Winter Springs. She was always in my head telling me to get out and explore the world and show it the wonder of Saige Wilson.

I can almost see her walking through the store sweeping up

and turning around to smile and wave at me. The tears start streaming down my face as I remember her fragile tiny hands grabbing my face and her saying, "You're a storyteller, Saige. Show the world your words and write as many books as you can." Then she would kiss my forehead.

I sit down on the bench right in front of the shop and just allow the tears to flow. This has probably been the first time I have cried in a really long time. It was one of those cries that you didn't know your body, mind, and soul needed until it happened. One where you just have to let it all go until there are no more tears to shed. When I can't shed one more tear, I stand up and head to my destination.

As I'm walking home from Pine Street, it starts raining.

A fog has set inside the woods on the right side of the road from the drop in temperature. I shiver and pull off the long-sleeved shirt that has been wrapped around my waist and stop long enough to put it on. Good thing I'm only five minutes from home, because this shirt won't keep me warm for very long.

I hear a noise somewhere off to my right and stop in my tracks.

"Hello." I spin in the direction the noise came from, trying to pinpoint where it is.

"Hello," I say louder this time. The rain starts coming down harder, and I'm about to give up.

After a few seconds, I hear a howl and a yelp.

I repeat myself. "Hello."

I hear another rustling, followed by a thud and then a whimper that sounds like an animal is hurt.

Right as I turn on my phone flashlight and start to go into the woods, I see the headlights and noise of a vehicle driving in the direction I am going in. If only I didn't hear what I am guessing is a dog, I could have gotten a ride the rest of the way back home out of the rain.

I shrug and keep walking, knowing that there is no turning back now, but if the dog doesn't make a noise soon, I may have to go back and bring reinforcements. Who knows if I'm even going the right way. Thankfully, as if it can hear me, the dog starts rustling around and making a lot of noise, and I'm able to find it.

Laying in front of me is what used to be a white Golden Retriever. This poor thing, however, is muddy and looks like it got its entire body wrapped in something. I lean closer to see what it is caught on and find out that it got tangled in some vines growing on a tree.

As I'm trying to get the vines unwrapped, I notice that it is really she. She is laying still, so I can quickly get her untangled. I try to get her to follow me, but I realize that she has hurt her foot either before, during, or after getting trapped in the vines. So, I do the next best thing. I lift her up and carry her.

I'm so glad that she isn't a fully grown Golden because there would be no way I'd be able to carry her. Even as a puppy she is still a heavy thing, and with us both being wet and now muddy, it's hard to keep a grip on her. I have to stop every few seconds to readjust her in my arms.

After the fiftieth adjustment, I've almost given up hope because of fatigue, along with being cold and wet, which is just the tip of the iceberg. I sit down in the wet grass on the side of the road and just hold the puppy close, trying to get my bearings back in order.

A vehicle pulls over to the side of the road in front of us. Its headlights shine in my face so I can't see who is driving or what vehicle it is.

I hear a door open and close.

"Saige? Is that you?" I recognize the voice.

I stand up and use my hand to shield the light so I can see his face.

"Declan!" I'm relieved as he draws near, and I throw my arms around him. "I'm so happy to see you. What are you doing here?"

He holds me and then pulls back to wipe the sticky hair from my face. "Hey there. Why were you sitting on the side of the road?"

"Well, this girl and I got tired." I look down at my arms. "Poor thing was in the woods all tangled in some vines. It took some time, but I got her untangled."

"Luna girl! Is that you?" The puppy wags her tail and tries to jump out of my arms into his.

"Be careful with her back foot; she hurt it." I hand her over.

"Come on. Get in the truck. We need to get out of this rain before either one of us gets sick." He leads me back to the truck with one arm holding Luna and one hand on the small of my back. A shiver runs down my back, and it's not because of the rain.

After buckling up, I warm my hands in front of the vents. "I'm sorry for getting your seat wet and muddy."

Luna is between us on the bench seat, and she is happy as a lark with her owner scratching the top of her head. "No apology necessary. I took a walk after the bar, and when I got home, I noticed the back door was wide open and she was gone. I looked for her everywhere, and I was afraid she would have to spend the night in the pouring rain if she didn't find her way back. You rescued her for me. I am forever in your debt."

"It was just fate that I found her. I was on my way home, and it started raining, so I stopped to put on this shirt, and I heard her and had to help."

"You really are amazing, you know that?"

"I just did what any decent human being would do."

"I'm not so sure that's true." Our eyes meet and an unspoken word is said.

The rest of the drive is in silence. The rain ends up stopping before we make it back.

When he pulls into the garage, I unbuckle the seatbelt and climb out. I turn to walk next door to the house.

"Saige! Hold on." He puts Luna in the utility sink in the garage and stands in front of me. "Would you like a cup of coffee or something else to drink?"

I point towards my clothes. "I probably should go shower and get out of these."

He looks disappointed in my comment.

"Of course. Right." He nods. "Again, thank you for finding Luna for me. I was worried sick for her."

"That's the last time you thank me. It really is no big deal."

"Okay." He laughs. "Let me walk you to the door at least."

"No. That's okay. I think Luna is waiting to be a clean puppy and receive some love after the night she had."

"Fine. Then wait here for just a minute."

I nod.

Not even a minute later he comes back to the garage with a sweatshirt and hands it to me. "Please put this on to keep yourself a little warm while you walk back home."

"Thank you." I can already tell it smells like him before I put it up to my nose and inhale his aroma.

By the time I make my way into the house, it is already after midnight, so I know everyone is asleep. The only one missing is Finn, and I'm sure he is still catching up at the bar or sleeping on Mom's couch. I send him a quick text to make sure he is alright and head upstairs to take a shower.

I laugh at myself when I look in the bathroom mirror. I somehow have mud caked in my ears and nose, along with both of my entire arms being covered. I probably looked like the swamp monster in front of Declan.

My phone goes off when I'm showering, and I check it as soon as I get out. It's a message from Finn saying that he took the girls home and is going to walk back to the bar for a few drinks and then pass out on Mom's couch so that he can nurse a hangover in peace without hearing the nieces screaming in the morning. I don't blame him one bit. I look out the window and see that it has stopped raining completely, so I tell him to be safe and text when he gets to the house.

I throw on the closest pajamas I can find, get in bed and try to doze off. I can't even turn my mind off because I'm not even remotely tired, and I toss and turn for thirty minutes before laying on my back and staring up at the ceiling.

My mind first jumps to Declan and how I really wish I was able to take him up on that drink offer. That man invades my thoughts and stirs something in me that I haven't felt in a very long time. And we still need to talk about what he overheard Finn and me talking about.

Scary thing is I really want to go over there. I know it's late and all, but he still has to give Luna her bath, so chances are that he is still up, right? Before talking myself out of it, I hop out of bed and take my pajamas off. I throw on some sweats and his hoodie, thankful I didn't put it on over my dirty clothes. I grab my phone and house key and head out.

Declan

I just step out of the shower when I hear pounding on the front door. I check the time on my phone, and it says twelve forty-three a.m. The pounding continues, so I throw on a towel and walk to the door.

I crack the door a smidge and see Saige standing on my porch. I take in her sweats and my hoodie and think to myself that she couldn't look more gorgeous. The towel no longer covers up what I was intending it to. You know, with the hard on of the century and all. My body wants her, I want her, and I'm pretty sure she wants me too, but she's holding me at arm's length. If I knew she didn't have a reason for reigning in her feelings, it would just take one slip of the towel, and I'd ravage her body.

My dirty thoughts quickly turn into worrisome ones knowing she is here at my house at this hour.

I throw open the door to get a good look at her. "Saige? What are you doing here? Are you okay?"

"Yeah. I'm okay. I just couldn't sleep, so I thought I'd take you up on your offer for a drink. Plus, I think I need to talk to you." She looks nervous as she runs her hands through her hair.

I wonder if she's talking about what I heard her and Finn talking about. I start to feel anger burning inside me. Milo is a good enough guy, I suppose, but he is horrible with relationships. He is possessive and clingy and is not the man Saige deserves. She deserves someone that will think about her needs before their own and will worship her body every night. One that will be in her corner forever and help her see the person she truly is.

Milo doesn't know she runs her hands through her hair when she is nervous or that she has five different smiles that mean something different. He wasn't in school secretly watching her every chance that he could, knowing that every guy was stupid not to notice her.

He didn't hear her talking to Gina and Megan about how self-conscious she was of her body. How badly I wanted to wrap my arms around her and tell her she was beautiful no matter what. I would have been honored to date her and show the world how lucky I was to have her, but with my family life gone to hell, I couldn't drag her through it. She deserved so much more than that.

"I'm sorry, I shouldn't have come. It's after midnight, so of course you are busy." Her voice pulls me out of my thoughts, and I focus. I see her start to walk off my porch.

"No. I'm not busy and I'm not ready for bed. I just got out of the shower after giving Luna a bath. Please come in." I gesture for her to walk inside. Her eyes leave my face, and she stops in her tracks after taking one long look at me. Her eyes widen, and I hear her breath hitch. I look down and remember that I'm just wearing a towel.

I look back at her, and she can't take her eyes off the towel.

The look on her face makes me know she is picturing what is underneath. It gets my blood racing, and my need for her increases. My dick twitches at the thought of dropping the towel and enjoying the pleasure it could give to her. She inhales quickly and looks back at my face.

She finally blinks and her eyes focus. Crimson paints her cheeks, and she turns around shyly. "Are you sure? I don't want to intrude."

"You won't be. I just need to put some clothes on." I gesture for her to come in again. "Please. Come in."

I hear her walk inside and close the door as I walk down the hall to my bedroom. I put on my favorite pair of gray sweatpants because there is no way I'll be able to hide this bulge inside my jeans. Hell, I wouldn't be able to even fit it in my jeans right now.

I count to ten and try to think of things that would make my dick soft, but all that comes to mind is her. Saige and her face, combined with heavy breathing, are the only things that invade my mind. I adjust myself and walk back down the hall towards the front door. The door is closed, so I turn around and see that she is curled up on my couch with one of the blankets thrown over her legs. Luna is lying in her lap and soaking up all the affection Saige is giving her. What a lucky pup.

She looks over at me and smiles.

"I think she loves you," I say and sit down on the sofa beside her.

"I think the love is reciprocated." Luna kisses her face.

"About that drink. I have red or white wine, beer, tea and coffee."

"I'll take a beer if you have it." My kind of girl.

"One Bud coming up." As I make my way into the kitchen, I

think about her and me sitting on the porch drinking a beer with her feet in my lap, watching the sunset after work.

I stop in confusion for a moment because I have never been able to picture a life with any woman I've been with. The only person I have thought about a life with is her. In high school I pictured us running away together when life was tough because she felt like a savior to me. And when I came home from college to watch her graduate from high school, it took everything in me not to run up to her and ask her to do it. Because after not seeing her for two years, my feelings never wavered. If anything, seeing her always makes my feelings intensify.

After high school I dated a lot and even had a few serious relationships, but none of them could stop me from thinking about what Saige was doing at that point in her life. She was why people always told me I'd be a bachelor forever because no one could hold a torch to her.

Saige

Declan is in the kitchen grabbing us both a drink, and I cannot get the image of him in those sweatpants out of my head or the fact that the man answered the door in only a towel. His body is the definition of perfection. I swallow hard and tell myself mentally that I can't think like that.

I tell myself to reign it in, but my body does not want to listen. The hard on I saw tells me he wants me, but my head keeps telling me he doesn't.

Saige, do not give your heart to a man that doesn't want you as the woman you are, flaws and all.

"One Bud Light for the lady." He sits down on the other side of Luna and breaks me out of my daze.

We drink for a few minutes in silence. It is a good kind of silence.

"So…" we say simultaneously.

We stare at each other and laugh, that hearty laughter that is felt deep within the body. It warms your extremities, and you feel a rush of elation surrounding you. Luna stands up and starts running back and forth from my lap to his with a wagging tail.

"Her leg looks like it healed."

"Yeah. I gave her a bath and a doggy massage that the vet told me on the phone to do, and she is good as new. I'm still going to take her in in the morning to make sure, but I think she will be fine." He clears his throat. "What are you doing this weekend?"

"I think I'm going to spend time with my family, pulling pranks on River with the twins, hanging out with Gina and Megan, and whatever comes to be. Not a whole lot, but I just want to be with my family. What about you?"

"I'm going to go hang out with a bunch of guys from high school. A lot of them are in for the Bicentennial, so we all decided to have a football match tomorrow afternoon. You should come if you are free."

"I remember Finn mentioning the game to me in passing. I should be able to be there."

"Great!" He clears his throat. "I mean, good. I'm sure Finn would like that."

I look at my hands in my lap and swallow. "I'm sure he will." I pay attention to Luna as silence engulfs us again.

I watch him take a long swig of his beer out of the corner of my eye, so I do the same thing.

He sighs. "Actually. I'd be really happy to see you out there also." I look up at him quickly. He's smiling brightly.

My smile returns. "You will?" I ask him.

"Of course. I'm glad you have come back for the Bicentennial. It's been a long time since we have all seen you."

"I am too. It's honestly been an adventure thus far. I'm looking forward to the rest of my time here and what will be thrown my way. Unfortunately, I have to get back to New York soon. I was only able to get so much vacation time off."

His face drops slightly. Not so much for many to pick up on, but I see it. "Right." He clears his throat, and the smile has returned. "Of course."

"I have to try and get another book out there or else I'll have to add another job on top of the three I already have."

He looks shocked. "Wait a minute! You have two other jobs on top of being an author?"

I nod my head. "Oh, yes! I only made maybe $10,000 on my book, and I got lucky to even get that. Many first time authors hardly make anything. But that bit I got is not enough to live on. Especially in New York. So, I'm a barista full time and then I work at the women's shelter on the days that I am off."

"I see." He stares off for a few seconds and then he adds, "I had no idea. So, why do you do it if you don't make enough to live on? It seems like it would have just been easier had you found something that allowed you to live with just one job." His eyes go wide, and he slaps his hand to his forehead. He looks so embarrassed. "Shit! You do not have to answer that. I'm sorry."

"No. I'll answer because it's a very good question and the answer is simple: my love for reading. I loved reading growing up and then that eventually led me to writing for fun just because, why not? Then, I found out that I loved writing. So, I set my mind on wanting to write a book, and I would have been okay with just selling one. I didn't do it for the money. I did it for the love of something. I knew I would need an actual job to live on while I enjoyed writing. The only reason why I said I might need another job is because I'm going to have to pay for my apartment alone now, and I'm not sure I'll be able to afford it on my own. I used the last of my savings to pay for it for the last six months."

"That makes sense. I am so sorry for opening my mouth about something I had no business asking."

"No, you are fine. Please don't be embarrassed. I would be curious too if I was in your place." He eyes me suspiciously. "Honestly." I place my hand on his leg.

"You have got to be one of the most amazing people I know. You do what you love plus work two extra jobs, one of which is helping people that need it, and you somehow find time to eat and sleep. Most people would have given up easily or just taken the easy way out."

"Well, sleep and food are optional." I chuckle. "But I could never stop writing or volunteering at a shelter. I even plan on heading to the women's shelter in Huntington and seeing if they need donations or need help while I am here."

I feel something on my hand and don't have to look down to know that Declan has put his on top of mine. My body feels hot, and a blush has grown on my face.

"You are a breath of fresh air, Saige Wilson."

I look into his eyes. "I'm really not but thank you for saying so."

With his other hand, he reaches forward and tucks a stray hair behind my ear and rests his hand on my jawline. He slowly rubs his thumb up and down my cheek, and I lock eyes with him.

"Yes. You are."

My breathing speeds up, and I'm pretty sure the house has become ten degrees hotter. Declan inches forward a little, and I'm frozen on the spot. He waits a few more seconds and inches forward again, never breaking eye contact. I let go of my restraint and meet him halfway.

Our lips crash together, and I can feel the same electricity that I felt at the bar earlier. Our tongues entwine as his hand moves to my hair. I find myself gripping his shirt, trying to pull him closer than he already is. Our hands start doing a dance, exploring each other's bodies like they have a mind of their own. He grabs my butt and pulls me onto his lap, our kiss deepening. It's quite euphoric.

In the haze, it dawns on me that I'm kissing Declan Wolfe. I'm not supposed to be kissing him, but my body and mind enjoy it. This is the reach for the moon, can't eat and can't sleep type of kissing. I'm supposed to be casually seeing people with no strings attached but damn, does his kiss not taste spectacular.

I pull away for a second and place my forehead on his. Our breaths are erratic. It's intoxicating. But in the back of my mind my inner self is screaming at me, telling me if I continue this dance then it will lead to something. So, if I don't want it, I need to stop.

"I'm sorry. I can't do this." I whisper. I climb off his lap into the spot I was originally sitting in on the couch. I place the throw blanket back over me to cover my body like a shield. I stare at the empty bottle of beer sitting on the coffee table, too afraid to look at him.

After a dreadful minute or two, I repeat what has been playing in my mind. "I'm sorry."

"No. I'm sorry." He takes a deep breath. "Would you like me to walk you back home, or do you want another beer?"

"I'll have another beer please." He leaves and heads towards the kitchen.

In true woman fashion, my mind is running a mile a minute. Does he know what my sorry meant? Does he know how badly I wanted him but how afraid I am that I'd just be another notch on his bedpost? And if I wasn't another notch, does he know that I'm sorry that he gets a ruined Saige and not the Saige I worked hard for? Does he know I'm sorry that I don't feel worthy to even get a kiss from him? I'm sorry for knowing I'm returning to New York and that this can't happen?

Of course, he doesn't know what my sorry was for because even I don't know. All I know is that I enjoy spending time with him and that he makes my heart flutter anytime he is in the same room as me. And that is something I never had. Declan is the only one who has made me feel this way, and the feeling is even stronger years later. I've only been back a day and I'm as lost as ever.

Fear is a strong emotion. It can consume you if you let it. I can leave his house and avoid him the rest of the trip, or I can be a strong woman who knows there is something between Declan and me. Something stronger than maybe either of us have ever experienced.

Declan

My heart is beating rapidly, and if it doesn't stop, it's going to hop out of my chest. I place the empty beer bottles in the trash and lean on the counter.

I run my hand across my face and through my hair, frustrated. We were kissing and it was fantastic and then she pulled away suddenly. Did I do something wrong? Does she not feel this connection that I feel? Did I read the room wrong? Was it because I asked personal questions?

No. It can't be because of any of those. She had to have felt what I felt to kiss me back with as much passion as I kissed her. She also told me that I asked a good, honest question that even she would ask if she was in my place.

Finn told me that she was in a horrible relationship, and it didn't end well. Maybe that was it. I don't know the particulars of what happened in said relationship, but it has to be too soon if it didn't end well. And, of course, I let my dick do all the thinking and now I might have ruined any chance I could have had. I wouldn't blame her for sneaking out as soon as I came in here.

I hear something and stop in my tracks to listen. If I'm not mistaken, there is music playing softly in the living room. Music that wasn't there when I left. I smile and grab two new beers out of the fridge, thanking my lucky stars that she didn't run out of here when she had a chance.

When I make it to the living room, she is standing in front of the fireplace and staring deep into the fire. The light from the fire makes her body glow like an angel that swooped down to save me yet again. The same angel that saved me so many years ago. She turns around and smiles. I get a jolt of electricity. Something I've never felt before, but something I fear to lose.

"Would you like to dance?" She holds out her hand.

If I was a cartoon, my jaw would be lying on the floor. That is the farthest thing I thought she was going to say to me. But here she is, looking like a goddess with a smile on her face that would light up any room.

I smile back. "Yes. I would love to."

I walk up to her and slide my left hand around her waist, and I feel her body tense up. When I take hold of her right hand, I catch her eye and smile at her. She smiles back, and I feel her body slowly relax into my hold. We start to move to the song, and she places her head on my shoulder.

It fits perfectly. Her body fits perfectly. She fits perfectly.

I smell her lavender scented shampoo and feel her soft curves press perfectly with my hard body like we belong like this forever. She smells like heaven and feels like home. And with that thought, I smile the biggest smile I have ever smiled into her hair.

Home.

I have never, not once, felt at home anywhere or with anyone. I tried with Mom and Dad, but they never wanted me. I was a mistake to them. I was also never good enough and was used as a punching bag by my dad. When I went to college for Law, I met some incredible people, but I still never felt like I was at home.

Moving back here to open my own practice and having Finn as my best friend and brother has been the closest thing I have ever felt to a home. But something has always been missing. And now I know what it is.

A girl that was always within reach, but never taken. A girl that takes no shit from me and would easily give it back if need be. A girl that ran away from home years ago, and even though I haven't seen her since then, the pictures of her, the sound of her laugh, have been the things I see right before I go to bed.

And I know what you are thinking. I am thinking the same thing. I've never dated her. I never told her I liked her. I still dated other women and I'm still hung up on her. Why?

Well, it's easy. When my dad would come home drunk, I'd run off to Finn's house to spend the night. No announcement, I just showed up. Finn and his mom would welcome me with open arms and no questions asked, even though they both knew what my home life was like. Saige never knew though. Maybe she had an idea, but I never told her.

After coming over about the second time in a week because my dad was drinking himself to death, she asked her mom to run her to the store. They came back home while Finn and I were munching on pizza and watching TV.

I turned around to see her with bags of stuff for me. Inside these simple plastic bags were things filled with love. She had bought me a towel, toothbrush, toothpaste, deodorant, cologne, comb, shower items, some clothes, and some of my favorite snacks. I looked up and thanked both her and her mom. Her mom corrected me and told me that all she did was drive and that Saige got it all and bought it with her own money.

When I looked at Saige and asked her why, she shrugged, smiled, and said, "I did it because no one should ever not feel at home. I got you things to keep here at the house so that whenever you feel like running from your life to our home, you will have things that are just yours. I hope that you know our home will always be your home." And she walked away.

That night I came downstairs to get a glass of water and found their mom sitting on one of the barstools. I scared her and made her jump when she saw me in the kitchen.

"Sorry to startle you. I'm just getting a glass of water." I walked to the sink and filled a glass up.

With my back to her, she cleared her throat. "Declan, you know Saige has a crush on you," she said matter-of-factly like I had known that.

My back stiffened and I stilled in place. How did I not know this?

When I turned back around, her mom was gone.

After that night when Saige would see me in their house at night, she'd know I was staying over. She would make one of my favorite meals for supper, and she designated a cabinet space full of snack items that I liked. When it was time to go to sleep, I'd go upstairs to Finn's room and find a bed pallet on the floor and my items that she bought me laying on top of it.

She never took credit for the dinners, snacks, or the made-up bed, but I knew it was her. Because that was and is the kind of person she is. A simple gesture to her, but it meant the world to me.

"You are beautiful." I whisper into her hair.

"What?" She lifts her head and looks at me. A cross between shock, fear, and something else is on her face.

"What did you say?" She asks quietly.

"I said the moon is beautiful." I lie out my ass. I point through the sliding glass door at the moon.

Stupid, stupid, stupid. I am stupid. I should have just admitted what I said.

Her body tenses up, and she pulls away to hug herself. She looks out the window. "Oh, yeah! It is." She looks back and gives me a fake smile. Her eyes dart to the front door, looking like she wants to flee.

"Well, I appreciate you coming over, but it's getting late, and If you want to get any sleep before River and the family wakes up, I should probably see you home," I tell her. Not that I want her to leave, but I'm giving her a way out without having to make an excuse to flee.

"That's probably best." She walks to the couch to fold the throw blanket.

"I can do that. You don't have to."

"Um. Yeah. Okay." She hands me the blanket and still doesn't make eye contact.

"Do you need me to walk you to the house?" I know she will turn me down since it's just across the street, but I'm trying to get her to look at me so I can get a read on her.

She doesn't turn around as she opens the door. "No. I think I can handle it." She walks onto the porch, and before she takes off across the yard, she stops, and I hear her quietly say, "Thank you."

I watch her run to her brother's house. She unlocks the door, but before she runs in, she turns towards me and smiles. Another jolt hits me, and I realize what it is. I'm in love with the girl next door, and I don't know what I am supposed to do about it.

Saige

Saturday

I could lie and say I slept great, but, with the little sleep I could get, I'm too tired to do that. I tossed and turned, reliving the kiss, the dance, and everything we said to each other. Declan called me beautiful! I know I should have handled it differently when I heard him call me that. I was scared and confused when he said it at first, but my whole being wanted to hear him say it again, pick me up and carry me to his bedroom and dominate the hell out of me. It was at that moment that I knew Declan Wolfe had gotten under my skin more so than what I thought. But we know that was just a fantasy I made up in my mind; one that will not come true. Because I repeated the question, and his answer was not what I expected.

When he lied and said, 'The moon is beautiful,' it killed me, and I just wanted to run away. I felt moisture start to form in my eyes, and I am thankful he made up an excuse to end the night. I walked to the couch and tried to rein in my tears as I started folding the blanket I was using. Imagine what would have happened had he seen me cry in front of him? He'd probably freak and never want to see me again.

So, I left, and by the time I made it to the house, my eyes were blurry from the tears. I turned around and glanced towards his house. He was still standing there, and the glow from the moon made him look even more wonderful. I managed a smile and went inside.

I groan and throw the blankets off me. I reach for my phone and my ear buds and listen to a few songs to clear my mind. When Bruno Mars 'Count on Me' is over I pick up my phone and google Huntington Women's Shelter. It only takes a few rings before a lady named Emma answers. I ask her for any volunteer openings she has, and she is happy to say that they need help on Monday. I give her my info, so she can run a background check, and we set a time to meet at ten a.m. that day. When I hang up, I am in a better mood, and I head to the shower.

When I get out of the shower, I remember that I still have a date with Milo on Wednesday. I'm not even sure that I want to go on the date since I admitted that Declan is getting under my skin. Is it even right to go on a date when you are hung up on someone else? I'm not sure about the proper etiquette for this kind of thing, and I let out a frustrated growl. I grab my phone and stare at it like I'm willing it to tell me what to do.

I'm not able to make up my mind because Paige and Phoebe, my twin nieces, barge into my room and tackle me on the bed.

"Auntie Saige, are we going to pull any pranks on Daddy today?" Phoebe asks.

"Yeah, I want to do some of the pranks that you, Uncle Finn, and Daddy used to pull on each other!" yells Paige.

"Shhh," I say as I put my finger up to my lips. "You can't be loud or else your daddy will hear, and he won't fall for the prank because he will know it's coming."

"Oh, right," Paige quietly says and starts giggling. Phoebe joins in.

There is a knock on the bedroom door, and River peaks his head in.

"What's going on here?"

"Nothing, Daddy. We are just hanging out with Auntie Saige," says Paige.

"Yeah, Daddy. We are just talking. No boys allowed." Phoebe agrees.

"Right! No boys allowed." I nod, and Phoebe and Paige try to close the door on their dad.

"Okay. Okay. I got the hint," he says as he gets pushed out of the way. "I just wanted to let you know that I'm going to take a shower, but breakfast is made so you can go down and have some."

When we know he has left, we start thinking of things to do. The girls decide that they are going to go grab all their dad's pants and shirts in his closet and hide them in their closet. I go with them, and we rush into his room.

"What are you doing?" Ginny asks as she meets us in the hallway.

"We are pulling pranks on Daddy. Want to help Mama?" Phoebe asks.

"Okay, I'll help. What are we doing?"

The girls run into the bedroom and run to River's closet. Ginny and I follow them, and she sees what they are doing. They start grabbing everything out and running with it to their room, giggling.

"The girls want to hide all of Riv's clothes so when he gets out of the shower, he won't have anything to wear."

"I should probably sneak in there then and tell River to put his pjs back on and pretend he doesn't have his clothes hanging in the bathroom to wear."

We laugh. "Oh, yes. I would. Speaking from experience in trying to keep up with the brother's pranks, it's not fun when your prank doesn't go right."

"Right." She nods.

"I'm sorry if the clothes get wrinkled. I'll pay to have them all dry cleaned afterwards."

"You'll do no such thing." She touches my arm. "We can steam them and iron what needs to be done right here." I forgot they have one of those fancy washers and dryers that practically do everything.

The girls come running back in and grab the rest of the clothes. They are beaming at us and so proud of themselves.

Ginny turns back to me once they leave, "I better get on it then."

"Oh, Ginny?"

She turns around. "Yes."

"Do you drink coffee or orange juice?"

"Orange juice, why?" She eyes me suspiciously.

"Once you tell River, come down and have breakfast with us. Only drink the orange juice we pour into your cup. Do not get more from the fridge."

She raises her eyebrow at me. "Okay." She heads to the bathroom at the same time the twins' motion for me to come into their room to see what they did with River's clothes. I'm so glad they own that fancy dryer because all the clothes will definitely be wrinkled by the time he gets them put back up into the closet.

I hi-five them. "Good job girls. Okay, let's go downstairs to the kitchen. I have a few pranks we can pull down there."

"Yes!" they both yell. I shush them, and they pretend to lock their lips and throw away the key. They turn around and tiptoe down the stairs.

By the time I make it to the kitchen, the girls are already bouncing with anticipation. If only we all had as much energy as little kids.

"Okay girls. Give me the sugar your daddy uses for his coffee and the salt."

They hand them over. River uses regular sugar that he puts into a small dish with a lid. I have Phoebe pour that sugar into their big sugar container and Paige pour enough salt into the coffee sugar dish to fill it up as much as it was with sugar. I grin. The girls don't quite understand why salt in coffee is so bad, but they will get a kick out of it later when River takes a drink.

I then have Paige get the pitcher of orange juice and four glasses and have Phoebe get me two boxes of mac and cheese. They look at me weird, but they do as I say. I pour the leftover orange juice into four glasses and have the girls set those at the table where their mom, them and I will be sitting. They run back over and watch me pour the two packets of mac and cheese flavoring into the pitcher. I have Phoebe get me a container for the leftover macaroni shells, and Paige throws our evidence away. We fill the pitcher up with water and mix the cheese with it to make it look like orange juice. They giggle some more, and this time I join in. Once all the evidence is put away, we sit at the table and giggle together.

I clear my throat. "Now, girls. Once we hear your daddy, you have to keep a straight face. If you keep laughing, then he will know something is up."

"Okay, Auntie Saige," Paige says.

We start eating our breakfast and drinking our orange juice when we hear Ginny coming down. She looks at the orange juice in front of her.

"You're good. Enjoy the show."

"Oh. I intend to. He should be coming down in a few minutes."

A few minutes later, right on cue, we hear River walking down the hall towards the kitchen, and I motion for the girls to be quiet and keep a straight face. "That's what I like to see. My girls are all in one place having a great time." He walks into the kitchen wearing only basketball shorts and stands behind Paige.

Phoebe laughs. "Daddy? Where are your clothes?"

He bends down to tickle Paige. "Some little gremlins came in and stole my clothes when I was taking a shower."

He walks over to Phoebe and tickles her too. "I wonder where they are?" He stands with his finger tapping his chin and looks around.

He looks at the girls. "Do you know?"

"They are on our bed, Daddy. Wasn't that a funny prank?" Paige asks. She and Phoebe start giggling again.

River laughs with them. "The funniest, Little Duck." He kisses the top of both of their heads before walking towards the coffee pot.

"Sis, would you like a cup?" He motions to his mug.

"No. Thank you. I was craving some orange juice this

morning."

We watch as he puts the 'sugar' into his coffee and comes to sit down. He takes a bite of eggs and bacon and then finally takes a sip of his coffee. Salted coffee sprays everywhere. Ginny, the girls, and I are rolling in laughter. We wipe tears from our eyes, not caring that coffee is sprayed all over us, the table, and the floor.

"What the hell was that?" Riv asks while wiping his mouth and the table. He keeps smacking his mouth open and closed like he's trying to get rid of the taste.

I get up to get a rag to clean the mess on the floor. "Whatever do you mean?" I try to act innocent.

"Saige, what did you do?" he asks in a stern voice. I shrug when I get up off the floor to clean the table.

"I did nothing, Bub. I just came down with the girls to enjoy a delicious breakfast. I did not know that you would spray us with coffee."

"Little Ducks, what did Auntie Saige do?"

Phoebe blurts out, "We replaced your sugar with salt, Daddy."

She turns to me, "You were right, that was very funny."

"Sure. Very funny," he says sarcastically. He looks over at me and shakes his head. I can't help but chuckle a little more.

"We helped Auntie Saige," says Paige. "It was so much fun!"

"Oh, this had your Auntie written all over it." I smile at him.

He looks over at his wife. "And you, my dear beautiful woman. Why would you not tell me?" He pretends to be wounded.

"Oh, suck it up, Dear. Are you getting a little salty?" We all start laughing.

He shakes his head again. "Is the orange juice good at least?" he asks no one in particular.

Ginny takes a sip and smiles. "It's delicious. Do you want

some?"

He looks at his coffee again. "I think I will since the coffee is no good."

When River is at the fridge, she looks at me and gives me a look that asks, 'did you do something to the orange juice?'. I nod. She smiles and shakes her head. River comes back to the table with a glass of freshly made 'orange juice' that the girls and I made with love.

He takes a sip and runs to the sink to spit it out. We are all laughing harder this time. Ginny and I have tears running down our faces and River is rinsing his mouth out with the water sprayer.

When he's done trying to get rid of the taste in his mouth, he asks, "Do I even want to know what that was made out of?"

"Think really hard, Bub."

He looks at me curiously and then his eyes get big. "Mac and cheese water?"

I nod. "Payback, big brother."

"Oh, dear. This is going to be a long two weeks."

We all continue eating breakfast and just enjoying each other's company, but quickly my mind runs back to Declan again. When I'm finished with my food, I start cleaning up the kitchen and realize this is the perfect time to call one of the girls to talk about what is going on in my head. I would call Gina, but I don't need to be mothered right now. I need someone to get straight to the point and slap me when I'm an idiot. So, I dial.

"Hello?" Megan asks.

"Hey, girl."

"What's going on?" she asks.

"Well, that's the reason why I called."

"Tell me whose ass I have to beat! I need to know if I should take my earrings out." She is worked up.

"Keep them in your ears, crazy. I just need some advice."

"Love, finance, life, etcetera? I have a lifetime of knowledge."

"Well…"

"Love. Got it. Now tell me who before I have a coronary." She knows me too well.

"Declan."

"Declan? Oh my God! Hell to the yes, Sis!" I can tell she's doing the happy dance right now.

I let out an exasperated breath. "Will you listen to me?!"

"Right. Yeah. Sorry. So, Declan?"

I tell her everything that has happened with Declan since I've been back. I don't spare any detail. I tell her about not being able to read him. I also mention how attentive he is, how flirty and hot he can be and what it does to me. I know he called me beautiful twice, but the first time he said it discreetly with the words 'looking at myself in the eyes of others in how they see me', and the second time he said something else when I asked what he said. He hasn't flat out told me I'm beautiful. I also tell her that Milo and I connected at the bar and that we have a date on Wednesday night and give her the details about our conversation.

"So, yeah. That's pretty much it. Advice?"

She lets out a breath. "Wow. Okay. Um. You currently have two men. One who you connected with at a bar. He went to our school and was on the football team with Declan and Finn, but you have no prior history with him. He is good looking and a family-oriented man. And now you have a date scheduled with him this week?"

"Correct."

"Then you have Declan. Your lives have intertwined since you were in school. You most definitely have history. You have also crushed over him for years and obviously still do."

"Hey!"

"Just stating facts. He is drop dead gorgeous and is a great guy. You both obviously feel something or that kiss wouldn't have happened. But he is still a man of mystery because you don't know if he just wants to have sex with you and leave, if he is lying, or if his feelings are genuine."

"Yeah. Pretty much. Plus, I'm leaving in thirteen days to go back to New York. What's the point of any of this?"

"The point is that you can have fun while you are home. Or you could move back home. You can be an author anywhere, even a barista, and the women's shelter here isn't very far away."

"We talked about this. I built my life there. I got away from Mom's constant nagging, and I love the nightlife of New York."

"We could also talk about the cons of living there. Congestion, Philippe lives there, you are paying triple the rent for a one-bedroom apartment compared to the cost of one here. You are even paying more for living than you would if you moved back. Plus, Gina, your family, and I are here, and we all miss you so much."

"I miss you all too. But I do like living in New York City. I can't explain it. It's something that only people who live there will understand."

"I know you do. But another pro of living here is that you got a McHottie who lives across the street from River and another potential boyfriend, too. And before you say it, I know. I know that a man will not be the reason you move anywhere. But look at this. Girl, your love life is far better than mine, and you've only been home for one full day. My love life is as dry as the Sahara Desert. I don't even remember the warmth of a man."

"I know someone who would be perfect for you."

"Do tell." Her tone is layered with anticipation.

"Finn."

She scoffs. "You're kidding, right? Your brother Finn?"

"No, I'm not kidding and, yes, my brother."

Once she is done laughing she says, "Yeah. Okay."

"I'm serious."

"So am I. So will I see you at the game?" she asks.

I chuckle at her. "Good job changing the subject."

"I aim to please."

"That's what she said." I reply

We both laugh. "I'll see you at the game." I tell her.

Her tone gets serious. "Saige?"

"Yes."

"Is it that obvious?"

She hangs up before I can answer. Yes, it is obvious, but I need to find out how Finn feels about her. I may be doing a little matchmaking of my own.

Saige

River and I load up in his car and head to Moms to pick her up for the football game. Finn already left to go get ready to play, and Ginny stayed back with the girls since she is about ready to pop, and she didn't feel like sitting on hard bleachers for over an hour. If I was in her position, I would stay home too. Even while not being pregnant my butt goes numb after thirty minutes. Then I have to do that little wiggle to try to bring the feeling back.

I'm honestly nervous to pick up Mom and be alone with her for a while. I love her, please don't get me wrong, but the constant need to tell me what I need to do or say and hearing her say she knows best, even though I am a grown adult, grinds my gears. At the end of the day, she is my mom, and we love each other, but I always feel like I can't be who I am in front of her. I'm constantly walking on eggshells, but it's partially my fault. I should grow a pair and stand up to her, but I don't. That's why I love having one or both of my brothers here.

We pull up to her drive and wait a few minutes. She doesn't

come out, so River starts taking off his seatbelt to go get her. I stop him and tell him that I will do it. I walk up to the door and ring the doorbell. No answer. I knock a few more times. No answer. I'm starting to get concerned, so I start beating on the door.

She finally opens it up and immediately out of her mouth is, "Why are you banging on my door like you are the police?"

She looks outside to the left and then to the right and then back at me. "Do you want the neighbors to come out of their homes and gawk at you and realize it's not the police but my daughter who is supposed to be a lady?"

Deep breath. In and out. "Mom, I had to bang on the door because you didn't answer the doorbell or the knocking that I did before. I was concerned that you were hurt or that you fell or something."

"Well, as you can see, I am perfectly fine. I had to touch up my makeup."

She looks me up and down. Please don't do it. Please don't. "Are you seriously wearing that? Saige! Really?"

I have on my favorite New York City tee with the jeans that hug my curves in all the right places. My hair is thrown into a messy bun, and I accessorized with my slip-on sneakers, mascara, and lip gloss. "What is wrong with what I'm wearing? I'm wearing comfy clothes because we are going to be outside watching a football game."

"Saige. You should always look your best, no matter what. Your potential husband could be at this game, and you want him to see how pretty you look." She gestures with her hand at me in a head-to-toe motion. "Not some plain Jane. You're not skinny honey; you have to work harder at it."

See what I mean. This is another reason why I had to get the hell out of here. She's either passive aggressive or upfront, and she makes it seem like she is doing me a favor by giving me all of her 'advice'. She hasn't always been this way; it started when Dad left. As she tried to hide the inner hell she was going through, she somehow decided that she was above everyone, and that the world needed to know it. She tried to push that onto all of us.

That's why River is her favorite. Finn and I don't blame him. We love him and love how successful he has become and know the love he has for his family. He is a state trooper and the chief of police in Winter Springs. He busted his butt to get where he is right now, on top of taking care of Finn and me when he was just starting out. I know that couldn't have been easy.

Even though he is Mom's favorite, it did take a lot of convincing to get Mom to be okay with him doing this job. She wanted him to be a doctor or lawyer or even a veterinarian. But this was in his heart, and as she saw how much good he was doing, it didn't take long for her to brag to everyone she knew that her son was a state trooper and police officer. Then she yelled even louder to the people in the back when he progressed up the ranks and became chief of police.

We were outranked once him and Ginny had kids because that meant that Mom had grandbabies. Not only does she have one grandbaby, but she has twin grandbabies. She is in love with those girls, and they can do no wrong in her eyes. They have her wrapped around their fingers. This is the mom I love to remember. When she is with them, she reminds me of her being that way with me before Dad left us.

"I'm a beautiful, healthy, plus size woman, Mom. I know I'm not skinny, but I am not a plain Jane either. The fact that you said that hurts deeply. Can we just go?"

She didn't say anything but just nodded and grabbed her purse. I think I saw her wipe her eye as she looked away, but I'm not entirely sure. She locks up the house, and we walk to the car.

"You can sit up front." I open the front door for her.

"Thank you."

When I get into the back seat behind River, he looks at me through the rearview mirror and mouths, "Are you okay?" I shrug.

Riv and Mom talk all the way to the field, and I put in my earphones and listen to some music. I lay my head back and close my eyes. Music has always been an anxiety and stress reliever for me. I have just finished listening to 'Unwell' by Five Finger Death Punch when River pulls out my earphones and tells me we have arrived. I sit up and look around. Wow. I really did get lost in the music.

~

I'm on a mission to find Gina and Megan when I run right into what feels like a boulder.

"Oh my God! I am so sorry." I back up from the hard body that I am pressed into to stare into the same eyes that haunt my every thought. Declan is with Quinn, and she is wrapped around his arm. "Declan. Quinn."

"Can you watch where you are going?" Quinn says as she fixes her hair and makeup while looking into a compact mirror.

"I was looking for Megan and Gina, and I wasn't paying attention. I apologize."

She rolls her eyes and throws as much attitude into her tiny body as she can. "Well, how about you start paying attention? You could have seriously hurt me."

"Quinn!" Declan says sternly.

She turns towards him. "What? I swear her ugly, fat ass broke my arm."

"She didn't even hit you! You would be lucky to be half as beautiful as she is." He tells her angrily, and she looks shocked that he didn't agree with her. She turns around and storms off.

"Thank you. You didn't have to do that. I've been dealing with her and her hurtful remarks since high school."

"Doesn't mean you should have ever had to deal with it. She is supposed to be a grown ass woman who is a respectful member of society. She doesn't realize how her attitude makes her look."

"For some people it just takes longer to hit. She'll get there one of these days. At least I hope so."

"Would you want to join me at my house tonight for another beer and dancing?" he blurts out. "You know, to celebrate winning the game."

"But you haven't played yet. What makes you think you will win?"

"You'll be in the stands. You are going to be my good luck charm." He winks at me and gives me a side smirk.

"So, if you win, I come over tonight for a drink and dancing?" I ask, looking up at him.

The ref blows the whistle to let everyone know the game is about to start. "Yes," he says before running onto the field.

I hear my name and turn around. Sure enough, the girls are sitting at the top of the bleachers. Which means they witnessed the whole thing. I take a deep breath and walk up to meet them. I slide in beside Gina and see Megan giving me a knowing look.

"What?" I ask.

"Oh, I'm just waiting to hear what made your cheeks that crimson color," Megan jokes.

"You were right here. I'm sure you were watching everything."

She smiles at me and winks. "Yes, I was, and the physical tension was on fire, but I could not hear anything. Give me the details."

"He stood up to Quinn for me, basically called me beautiful again, and then he asked me to come to his house tonight after the game for another beer and dancing."

"Oh my Go—"

"Hold up. Wait a minute. What do you mean basically called you beautiful again? What have I missed?" Gina cuts in.

I fill her in on what happened, every minute detail.

"You've been holding out on me. So, are you going to go tonight?" Gina asks me.

I blush. "I think I will if they win the game."

"You know that Declan's team is going to win. It's him and Finn on one team," Megan says.

"Who is on the other team?" I ask.

"Jess, Tyler and I believe Mi—oh hi, Milo." Gina says.

I whip my head to the right and see Milo standing beside me on the bleacher steps. He is dressed in jeans, boots, and a polo shirt. His hair has been slicked back with some product. Milo has light brown hair and beautiful blue eyes that are matched with a smile. "Milo! I thought you were playing in the game today."

"Nope. I decided to just watch instead. I haven't kept up my physique since high school, and I figured I'd get a chance to sit with you and chat some more instead of embarrassing myself in front of the whole town. Is it okay if I sit?"

"Of course." Gina blurts out, and she scoots over for me to follow suit.

Milo sits so close to me that our thighs and knees are touching. He looks over and smiles, and I smile back. It's like Megan says, I have two guys who I could have a chance with right in my hands. Just knowing that they both are in the same place with me makes me nervous though. I hope Declan doesn't take this the wrong way since he told me I was his good luck charm and now Milo is right beside me.

As soon as I think of him, I see him along with Finn and the rest of their team running onto the field from the school. Declan looks up, waves, and smiles in my direction, but he looks left and sees who is sitting beside me. His smile drops.

Of course, Milo has impeccable timing because as soon as Declan's face turns serious, Milo grabs my hand and squeezes it. I look down to see his hand on mine and look up at him to figure out what he is doing. He isn't looking at me. Instead, his face is hard and looking right at Declan, a smug look on his face. Is this seriously the 'I got the girl' macho throw down? I pull my hand from Milo's and get angry because I am no one's pawn.

I look at Declan as he pulls his eyes away from Milo and meets mine. Hurt is on his face, and I know he thinks something is going on that I didn't intentionally mean to happen. He put himself out there with me yesterday and now he thinks I came with Milo on some sort of date. I completely understand where the hurt is coming from.

I promise to make sure he knows that it wasn't planned, and I never meant to hurt him. But before I can even try to explain through hand gestures to him that it's not a date, he puts his helmet on, glares one more time and heads out on the field.

"Saige?" Milo's voice fills my ear.

"Hmm?" I say, following Declan with my eyes.

"I asked if you wanted to change our date from Wednesday to Monday night at seven. I have a thing that came up with work on Wednesday and I'm not sure I'd be done in time for the date."

"Oh. Uh. Yeah. I think that should work out." I answer without thinking because I'm still upset with the whole thing.

"Good. I'm really looking forward to it."

I snap out of the cloud my head was in and ask him, "Looking forward to what?"

"Our date on Monday." He throws his arm over my shoulder.

I shrug out of his hold. "Monday? I thought it was Wednesday."

He gets frustrated. "You need to pay attention to me when I'm talking to you. I asked if we could change it to Monday because I have a thing at work."

I tense up at his tone and feel uncomfortable until he adds, "Sorry to get frustrated. Unfortunately, it's one of my pet peeves when people don't listen. Honestly, I didn't mean for it to come out that way."

I look at his face, and I think I see sincerity. "Okay."

The rest of the first half we make small talk, with Gina and Megan chiming in occasionally. Once halftime hits, I announce that I need to use the restroom and grab a bite to eat. Milo tries to accompany me, but I decline. There is just something about him that makes me uncomfortable.

After using the restroom and grabbing a hot dog, chips, and a Gatorade, I see Finn by the football team's water jug.

"Hey, you guys are great! It's like being back in high school all over again and watching you all win."

"Except my body will feel this tomorrow morning instead of bouncing back like I did back then." He takes a big swig of water.

"Well, you better win so that it will be worth it."

"That's the plan." He takes another drink of water. "Smalls?"

He catches me mid bite. "Yes." I manage to say while chewing my food.

"So, Milo, huh?"

"Huh?"

"You know, Milo. The one you were sitting with in the stands. The one who made Declan so angry that he has been wiping the floor with these guys. The same who is standing behind you at the concessions pretending to look at the food while secretly stealing side eye glances at you."

I glance over to where Milo is, and he gives me a small wave and a smile. Shock and anger fill me. I turn away from him without acknowledging him. Who does he think he is?! I told him I wanted to go alone to the concessions. Either he can't take a hint, or he is really hungry, and this is just a coincidence.

"Oh yeah. We talked at the bar, and he asked me on a casual date for Wednesday, but now it's going to be Monday night. He's kind of been making me feel weird in the stands and now here after I told him I wanted to go get food alone."

Finn eyes him again with a glare. "Hmm. Just be careful, okay?"

"Why?"

"I just heard that he is very possessive and clingy with his girlfriends."

"I can deal with him being a little clingy and territorial. Now, cheating dirtbags who lead me on is a different story."

"Just be careful with him. What about Declan, though?"

"What about him?"

"Well, the bar, and then I hear from a little birdie that you snuck out of the house really late last night and didn't get home until even later. This little birdie also saw you running home from his house."

I groan. "River! I'm going to kill him."

He laughs. "Well, at least you aren't denying it. The only problem I have is that I had to find out from him when we are supposed to be best friends."

"If it makes you feel better, Gina and Megan just found it all out today also."

"It does. So, I have Declan and Milo wanting to shack up with my smalls? Hmm."

"No one said anything about having sex, Finn."

"Not yet anyways." He playfully pops me on the shoulder.

I give him a playful push. "Oh, shut up."

"You didn't truly answer my earlier question. What about Declan?" he asks.

"I really like him, and I think he likes me too, but I'm trying to keep things casual since I'll be leaving soon. That night I ran over to his house, we had a very passionate kiss that almost led to something, but I stopped it. Then we danced together afterwards."

"Well, that's something more than casual. Have you guys talked about what this is?"

"Well, no. We keep beating around the bush instead of figuring things out, and I'm also trying to just be relaxed with figuring myself out again. I'm afraid to rush into something again and it turns out I find another tool."

"I think you have grown since kicking Philippe out. You knew your worth then because you didn't just keep him around. You realized you deserved so much more. Plus, look at what you are wearing today and what you wore to the bar last night."

"What does what I'm wearing or what I wore have to do with it?"

"Anytime we facetimed when you were with Philippe, you wore loose clothing like you were trying to hide the body that you have. Last night and today you are wearing clothes that flatter your figure. You also walk with a lot of confidence while wearing them."

"You know what? I never thought about it, but you are right. Last night I felt beautiful in the outfit the girls laid out for me. Also, I can't remember the last time I looked at myself in the mirror and smiled, but I did last night and I did this morning too. I smiled at myself and felt beautiful."

Maybe being home has been doing me good. Rediscovering my roots has helped heal me in some way. It also doesn't hurt that I have two guys that like me, but they aren't the sole reason for this. I'm surrounded by people that love me for me. Having that support heals you in ways that you don't know until your eyes are open to it.

It's kind of like a wilting flower. A little love from friends and family can start to perk those leaves up, but when you tell yourself and believe that you are great, amazing, beautiful, whatever you are having trouble seeing, the flower gets its color back and turns its petals to the sun. It shines brightly, saying 'look at me'. We all need that in our life. Some of us just need a little bit more to shine as brightly as all the others.

I throw my arms around my brother. My rock, my strength, my inner voice that needs to speak up, my life coach.

I plant a kiss on his cheek. "What was that for?"

"You have opened my eyes, and I appreciate it. Now, I have to find Declan." I look around the field for him.

"Why?" He raises one eyebrow and gives me a smirk.

"I think I pissed him off when Milo showed up and asked to sit down beside me. At the exact moment Declan looked over, Milo grabbed my hand. And the worst part is that Declan told me I would be his good luck charm today when I got here."

"Well, I can see why he'd be mad if he thought you were coming here for him. He probably thinks you invited Milo here and it's like a date."

"That's why I need to talk to him, but I can't necessarily do that when he is nowhere to be found."

"I thought I saw him heading off to the school to grab his drink that he left there. Maybe you can catch him in that location."

"I'll do that. Thanks!"

"Hey, Smalls. It's just a misunderstanding, and I'm sure once you explain he'll understand. But what about him?" He points behind me to Milo, who is still at the concession stand.

"I don't know. I don't want to put all my eggs in one basket if I'm not sure that the basket doesn't have holes."

"I get it. Just date around but remember that you need to also follow your heart. Date both and see where it leads you. And before you say it, I know you are leaving for New York, but it never hurts to open your heart. Long distance has worked out for many people."

"I could say the same for you."

"What do you mean?" He looks at me questioningly.

"When's the last time you opened your heart?"

"I travel all over the world for my job. I don't have the time to give to someone."

"How do you know? Long distance has worked out for many people."

"Hey! You can't use my own words against me!"

"Sure I can. I know someone who might be perfect for you. Someone who loves adventure, is funny, smart, and beautiful."

"And who is this dream girl?"

I motion my head and eyes towards Megan, smile at Finn, and then turn to walk away.

"Good luck big brother." I call over my shoulder.

As I'm walking away, I feel a presence behind me, and I turn around. Milo almost runs into me.

When I ask him what he's doing, he tells me he wants to just hang out before the game starts. That's why he waited until I was done talking to Finn. There was a hint on anger in his tone, like he was mad that I spent time talking to my own brother.

Everything is awkward since I told him I was going to the concession stands and bathroom alone and he still thought he should come down. If he had sat in the bleachers, he would have seen me talking to Finn and then came to join me afterwards.

We get stopped by Mom and some of her friends on the way back to our seats. We say our pleasantries and I try to get away, but Milo is being his charming self, so I just stand there, and half listen while scanning the surrounding area for any sight of Declan. The ref blows his whistle, and I look at the field. The game is about to start again in two minutes.

As Milo and I say our goodbyes, we head to the bleachers. His hand is on my lower back leading me. He points out where our seats are, like I didn't know. I meet the eyes of the girls and I start to climb the steps.

I feel eyes on the back of my head as I'm walking up. I let it go, thinking it is Milo since he is one step below me with his hand still on my lower back. We slide into our seats once we make it to the top.

I look at the field and meet Declan's eye. I smile at him. He is standing in the middle of the field, helmet in hand and disappointment on his face. He shakes his head and runs off to get into position. Oh boy! I have really got to talk to him.

Saige

Finn and Declan's team won, of course. However, I swear the second half of the game Milo played fifty questions with me. At this rate I'm not sure what we can possibly talk about on our date on Monday. I'm also bummed that because of these questions, I missed a lot of the game that I was trying to watch. I look over at Megan and Gina and motion for them to help me.

"Milo, if you don't mind, Saige promised she'd go maternity shopping with me after the game, and so we must be off," Gina, my savior, says.

"Oh, of course. Let me walk you ladies to the car." He stands up.

"No. That's okay. Megan is walking with us, and we have some things to discuss that are just for our ears only," Gina says. She rolls her eyes when she looks at Megan and gives her the 'it's your turn' nod.

"Yeah. I'm having some girl problems, and I didn't get to talk about them while we watched the game. So, we need to talk about it now," Megan replies.

"Gotcha. Just remember our date Monday." He squeezes my hand and runs down the bleachers.

"OH. MY. GOD! Saige. You cannot go on a date with that bore. He gives me creepy stalker vibes." Megan loops her arms in mine as we descend the bleachers.

Once on the ground, Gina loops her hand around my other arm. "As much as I'm all about giving someone a chance, I think you should steer clear from Milo. He was clearly stalking you the entire time you were at the concessions and talking to Finn," she says.

"I get what you guys are saying, but maybe he is just awkward around girls," I reply back.

The girls exchange a look. "I don't know," Gina says.

"Although, he said some things that gave me red flag vibes. When the game first started, he purposely grabbed my hand and egged Declan on when he saw us together," I add.

We get stopped by Dustin, River's best friend and a fellow police officer, in the parking lot. He wants to know if River is here because he has a question for him, so I send him off in the direction where I saw Riv last. We watch him go, and then the girls and I walk between a row of cars towards Gina's car.

As we are making our way between another row of vehicles to get to her car, Milo jumps out from one of the cars we are approaching. We all jump out of our skin and scream.

"Milo! What the hell are you doing? You scared the shit out of us!" I yell at him.

"Sorry, that wasn't my intention." He stands in front of me, blocking my path to the car. "I just needed to ask you something. That's it."

"Okay. Shoot." I rub my hands up and down my jeans nervously.

"Alone?"

I glance around and see the girls waiting at the car. They start to walk towards us, but I shake my head to let them know to stay back for now. "The girls can't hear you and you were told we had somewhere to be. Can this wait?"

"Yeah, I guess it can." He turns to walk away but stops and comes back towards me, even closer than he was last time. I back up, but he moves closer again. "On second thought, it can't. Who was that you were talking to earlier?"

"What?" I look at him in confusion. "Do you mean Dustin? The one in the police uniform?"

Milo nods. "Did you two date?"

"Not that it's any of your business, but no. He is my brother's best friend."

"Are you sure?" He gets a little closer and grabs my arm.

I pull his arm off mine and see the girls walking back towards us. "Yes."

"Okay. See you Monday." He kisses my cheek and runs off.

I turn towards the girls with my mouth wide open. Their eyes are big as they come to stand on both sides of me. We wait until Milo is long gone.

Megan turns abruptly towards me. "You are not going on that date Monday!" she says, and Gina agrees.

I grab their hands. "You're right."

"Not to mention he was definitely spying on us if he saw you talking to Dustin," Gina says.

"You need to talk to Finn and River, especially River. Open an informal report with him just in case something happens," Megan adds.

~

On the way to Special Delivery, the maternity shop, I give Finn and River a call and replay what happened with Milo at the game. They both agree I shouldn't go on the date and that I need to be extra cautious around him, just in case. We set up a plan, and I feel much better. I still have to cancel my date with him, and they told me to do that over the phone tonight where they can hear everything that is said.

We spend two hours inside Special Delivery, and Gina comes out with a full maternity wardrobe and a few gender-neutral baby items. While Gina was trying on clothes, Megan and I even ordered the crib that she fell in love with, and it should be delivered to them on Monday. We can't wait to see her face when it shows up. I'm so thankful we had this planned because I needed to take my mind off Declan and the hurt on his face and now Milo and his craziness. But it is time to get to my brother's house and call Milo to cancel the date.

When I walk in the door, Finn and River are sitting on the couch drinking a beer.

"I hope that you didn't cancel your evening plans to be here for me?" They both look up when I start talking.

"Even if we did, you are more important. How do you feel?" Finn asks.

"I get over Philippe, come back home, and today I felt a sudden change for the best. Things were looking good. Then, Declan looks like a wounded animal because he thinks I betrayed him somehow by being with Milo, and Milo makes me very uneasy. How would you feel if that happened to you?"

"Touché."

River interjects. "Well, it's better to stop it now before it gets any worse. When you do it and he asks for a reason, you do need to point out why it didn't work. Talk about him stalking you and making you feel uneasy because he is very territorial anytime you talk to a guy around him. Maybe he will go get the help he needs. Tell him you need to just stop it all and that you wish him well in life. If he starts bothering you after this call, then we will do something about it at the station. Okay?"

I nod.

I dial his number and put him on speakerphone.

Milo answers. "Saige!"

"Hi."

"It's so good to hear your voice. I miss you."

River motions for me to go ahead and do it.

"Milo, the reason I'm calling is because I think we should cancel the date."

He sounds panicked. "What? Why?"

"I just don't think this is going to work. I didn't appreciate being followed at halftime or into the parking lot with Megan and Gina when we told you we had somewhere to be."

"What do you mean? I was attentive to you. I asked you all about your life. Yeah, I followed you, but I just wanted to make sure you were safe."

"You were. And I appreciate you being interested, but you still followed me when I left at halftime, even though I told you I wanted to go alone. You then stayed around the concession stand and watched Finn and I talk the entire time. And you were mad about me talking to him, don't even deny it. You left before the girls and me, but then you reappeared when you saw me talking to Dustin. It bothered you enough that you had to ask me about him.

We aren't dating, and it is none of your business who I talk to."

"I don't know what to say. I thought we had something. I was just looking out for you. I didn't mean any harm."

"I'm sure you didn't. I just don't think this is going to work out. That's all."

"Saige, please. I really like you, and I know you like me."

"Milo, I like you as a friend. Like I said, we haven't even been on a date to prove how much we like each other."

"We had great chemistry. I know you felt it." His voice gets louder.

"I'm sorry, Milo, but I didn't feel anything."

"It's okay if you are feeling nervous about what we have. I'll wait for you to come to your senses and realize we are perfect for each other."

"Please, don't do that. Find someone who likes you as much as you like them. I need to go. Bye Milo."

I hang up before he can respond.

"How did I do?"

River smiles but says, "You did great, but it seems like this Milo is a little delusional. Don't take any of his calls and try to avoid him. Okay?"

I nod.

"Okay." I rub my hands together. "Well, now that that is over, I need a beer."

Finn holds out a beer to me, and I shake my head. "No. A beer next door. Declan asked me to join him tonight for a beer if you guys won the game."

I throw on my jacket and open the door. "Finn?"

"Yeah?"

"Can you watch me walk across the street? You can close the

door when he opens his."

"I was going to watch you whether you wanted me to or not," he says as he makes his way to the door.

As I walk next door, I must admit that I'm on high alert. Do I think Milo will try anything knowing my brother is chief of police? No. But I still know that River and Finn won't always be there, and I'd be stupid if I didn't take precautions. I make sure to listen to any noises and look all around me as I walk towards Declan's door. I even glance over my shoulder a few times and make sure Finn is still watching.

He gives me a thumbs up when I get to Declan's porch. I knock a few times, but Declan doesn't answer the door. I knock a few more times and just wait, but he never comes to the door.

I dial his number on my phone and can hear the muffled noise of a cell phone ringing in the house, but he doesn't pick up. I try to look inside his window through the space between his curtains.

"Declan! It's me! Open up!" I yell.

Feeling defeated, I step off the porch, turn to look at his front door once more and then run back to the house.

Finn is there to welcome me back inside. He wraps me in a bear hug and hands me his beer.

"What happened? He wasn't there?" He asks me this as he joins me on the couch.

"He's there. I heard his phone. He just isn't opening the door for me. Why won't he talk to me?" My voice comes out as a whine in the end.

"Leave it up to me." He walks back to the couch.

I looked up at him "What are you going to do?"

"I'm going to call his ass and see what's up. I would go over there, but if he didn't answer your knocks before you announced it was you, I doubt he would open up for me."

"And how will that help?" I ask.

"Because he is my best friend. I know his ways, and I know that he likes you and you like him. So, if I have to slap his ass in gear to understand what happened, I will. That way he can act like a man that opens the door for a woman and talks about what he is upset or mad about."

I kiss his cheek. "You're the best."

"Don't I know it." I push his arm, and he laughs. "Why don't you go ahead and take a shower while I call him? I know you have a shift at the shelter tomorrow, so you'll want to go to bed soon."

"That sounds wonderful. Thanks." I take the last sip of beer and run upstairs.

Declan

My phone rings on the couch arm, and I reach for it. Finn's number appears this time. I grab the remote and silence the TV so we can hear each other better.

"Finn. We saw each other all day today. Do you miss me already?" I joke.

"Well, your phone isn't broken." His tone is furious.

I sit up. "What do you mean? What's going on?"

"I'm at River's house," he grits out.

"Oh shit." I shift in my seat.

He sighs. "What gives?"

"What do you mean?" I ask even though I know exactly what and who he is talking about.

"You know what I mean. Why didn't you answer the door for Saige?"

I sigh. "I don't deserve her, man."

"Okay. So, you thought ghosting her and coming off as a jackass was the way to send that message?"

"Look. I saw the way she looked when she was with Milo at the game, and she looked so happy after halftime. I just don't want to screw up her happiness."

"Man, you are an idiot. We need to talk. I'm coming over so unlock the door for me." Then he hangs up.

A minute later he comes barging into the house and heads to the fridge. He grabs two beers and the bag of chips laying on the counter, sits down, and just stares at me.

"What do you need to talk about that couldn't be said on the phone?"

He throws a chip into his mouth. "I shouldn't be saying anything because this is between you and Saige and what she wants to tell you. But I have to tell you so that you realize something."

"Okay. Shoot."

"Saige wasn't happy at the game. She was pissed."

"That's not what it looked like to me."

He gets angry. "Yeah? Well, looks can be deceiving."

"What do you mean?"

Finn explains that Saige was shocked to see Milo there because she wanted to be there for us. She was looking for me at halftime to tell me that she didn't invite Milo so that I wouldn't be upset with her. He downs his beer and starts to get red in the face. I know this isn't the red-faced, drunk Finn but the seething, mad Finn. He continues to tell me about everything that happened with Milo. The attachment, stalking, and jealousy when they hadn't even had a date yet. By the end of it, I'm fuming.

Finn stares at me to try and read where I am at on the matter.

"What are you thinking?" he asks.

"Three things. One, I'm pissed that Milo is acting this way. Two, I'm scared for Saige. She comes home after all these years to have to deal with this. We don't know if he will back off or if he will try to stalk her some more."

"River knows what happened, and we have talked to her about not being alone for the time being, just to be sure. He said he will have extra patrol cars out to keep an eye on the neighborhood."

I nod. "Smart move."

Finn asks, "What is number three?"

"Number three isn't as important as the other two, but I'm angry at myself. I jumped to conclusions when I shouldn't have. I should have seen that something was up with Milo and jumped in. I, also, shouldn't have ignored Saige when she came by tonight."

"Why did you ignore her?"

I shrug. "Like I said, I don't deserve her."

"Shouldn't she be the one to say who she does and does not deserve?"

"You're right. I just don't want her to think she has to choose me. Plus, I know about her relationship with Philippe and just don't want her to rush into anything when she isn't ready."

"Dude. How long have you known my sister? You know she never does anything she doesn't want to do. She has her own mind, and she will let you know about it."

"That's very true. I also know that Philippe stole from her. He stole her happiness and confidence, and I don't want to do the same thing."

"Do you like my sister?"

My heart flutters just thinking about her. "More than you'll ever know."

"Why?" he asks.

"Well, for starters she's beautiful inside and out. She's giving, loving, and doesn't have a mean bone in her body unless you make her angry. She always puts others first and saves the lost."

"Saves the lost?"

"Luna was lost Friday night and she rescued her on her way home. And she rescued me." I whisper the last part.

"I thought I was the one that rescued you?"

"Oh, you did. You rescued me many times from my home life, but I'm talking about actually saving my life."

He looked at me shocked. "What do you mean 'saved your life'?!"

"Do you remember Warren Brady?"

"The convict at our school who was always getting in fights or selling drugs?"

"That's the one. A teen can only take so much from an abusive home. Being physically, verbally, and mentally abused does a lot to an impressionable teen's psyche."

"What did you do?" I don't say anything. "Declan?"

"At one of Jason's house parties, our senior year, I found Warren." Finn looked pissed, but I continued. "After taking one of the worst beatings of my life because we lost the football game, my chemistry grade slipping from an A to a C, and I was just there in his way, Dad said that I should just do them all a favor and kill myself. 'It's not like anyone will miss you in this world'."

"So, I headed to Jason's in search of Warren. But before I could find him, I got super smashed on vodka and Fireball. After stumbling around and almost giving up, I found Warren in the back yard behind the pool house."

"I told him I wanted some pills. He asked me which ones, but I had no clue, so I just said I wanted enough to end it all. He apparently knew what I was talking about because the next thing I knew he was handing me a bottle of pills and asking for $200. I told him that I didn't have that much money, and he laughed and tried to take them away."

"In my drunken stupor, I told him I'd do anything for those pills, and this pleased him. He made me an offer, and I took it. Halfway through doing what Warren wanted, I must have sobered up enough because I tried backing out. He was furious and called me every name in the book to get me to keep going, but I wouldn't. I wouldn't steal the car for him."

"We were already in a back alley, and so he thought this was as good of a time as any to beat the shit out of me. I laid there and took it. I was already bruised up, and I thought maybe this was my way to go."

"Next thing I know, I hear a thwack and Warren goes down. I looked up and saw your sister standing there with a tree branch in her hand. She didn't take her eyes off Warren as she yelled at me to get the hell up so we could go."

"Warren was too stunned to do anything. Knowing a girl got the best of him, he kept his mouth shut and laid there as we backed away. After that he never came near me again."

He blows out a puff of air. "So, that's how she saved your life?"

"Part of it."

His eyes go wide. "I'm afraid to ask, but what's the other part?"

"We walked down the road to our houses in complete silence. She pulled me towards your house and upstairs to the bathroom. She got out the first aid kit and started mending my injuries. It wasn't until she got to my hands did the silence end. She saw the pill bottle in my grip and knew what I was going to do."

"She grabbed them out of my hand and flushed them down the toilet. She turned towards me seething. 'Look at me.', she said. 'Look at me.' I couldn't bear to look at her knowing that even after keeping her at arm's length, she was pulled into my muddy life."

"Then she smacked the shit out of me. 'I said look at me!' She grabbed my chin and forced me to look into her eyes. 'What the hell were you thinking Declan?' she asked. I broke down with my face in my hands. I told her I wanted to make it all go away and that it wasn't like anyone in the world would miss me."

"She crouched down between my legs and held my hands. She made me keep looking into her watery eyes as she said, 'I will miss you. Anytime you feel like no one loves you and that no one will miss you, think of me. Because I will miss the shit out of you Declan Alexander Wolfe'."

"Shit," is all Finn can say.

"Yep."

He looks me in the eyes. "You fucking love my sister, don't you?"

I jump off the couch and pause for a few seconds, but not because I need to think about his question, because I know my answer straight away. I even knew my answer the first moment I laid my eyes on her in her brother's driveway after all these years. Hell, if I am being honest, I knew my answer back in high school. It scared me back then, but not now. We were given a second chance at a life together, and I'm not going to screw it up. I would give her all the time in the world for her to realize the same thing.

I turn towards Finn and say, "I think I have always loved your sister. I just didn't want to bring her into my horrible life back then. I know this is my second chance with her."

He stands up and pushes his finger up against my chest. "You need to make it up to her then. Don't screw this up."

"I know, and I won't. I promise."

Finn nods and walks out of the house.

Once Finn leaves, I get to business figuring out how to apologize to Saige.

I immediately call her, but it goes straight to voicemail.

"Saige. Its Declan. Look, I'm so sorry for not answering the door when you came by and I'm so sorry for not answering your phone call. I was wrong. I have to work tomorrow, and I won't get home until late, but my phone will stay on if you want to call or text me. Can we get together on Monday? Please."

Then I hang up.

Declan

Monday

I wake up in a good mood, even though Saige never called or texted me yesterday, or the night before when I left a voicemail. Today is the day that I will apologize for being an ass in person, and I can only hope that she will accept it.

I take a shower, have a big breakfast, and then take Luna on a walk. I rehearse what I am going to say to Saige and decide that ten is the perfect time to head over to River's and talk with her.

When Luna and I get to my street, I look up at a noise. Saige is walking out of the house with a bag slung over her shoulder, heading to Finn's jeep.

"Saige!" I yell when I'm four houses down.

I make her jump, and she wheels around to see who is yelling at her. There is fear in her eyes that turns into recognition after she sees Luna, and then me. She turns away quickly and tries to get into the jeep.

I run up to her. "I was hoping to talk to you."

She puts her bag in the jeep and her hand on her hip. "Oh, so now you want to talk?"

I deserve that. "Yes, I do. I tried to call you Saturday night."

"Save it." She throws her hand up.

"What do you mean?"

"I made a fool of myself, Declan. I knocked and even banged on your door. I thought maybe you just weren't home, but then I called you. I heard your phone ringing in your house, so I knew you were just ignoring me. Then Finn came back from your house telling me you had a nice chat. I didn't want my brother to be the reason why I received a phone call that night."

"It was a misunderstanding, and I was lost in my head thinking I was doing you a favor. Finn and I did talk, and he made me realize what an ass I was for just ignoring you. But I had to work all day yesterday, and I didn't take a lunch break or come home until midnight. I planned on coming over this morning to talk to you, but I wanted to give you enough time to wake up. Please, just listen to me."

"Fine," she sighs. "Let's hear it."

"I thought I was doing you a favor by leaving you alone."

"You've said that already."

"Just listen, please. I thought stepping out of the picture was what you wanted. I thought you had chosen Milo, so I wanted to back off and give you time to explore that relationship without me in the way."

"You could have asked me what I wanted, Declan. I would have told you. I never once told you to stay away. And I didn't invite Milo to the game. I was there for you and Finn. And now he—."

"—And now Milo is stalking you."

Her eyes get big and round. "Finn told you?" she asks quietly.

I nod. "He did. I'm here for you in whatever way you'll have me." I step closer to her.

She puts her hand up again to stop me. "I'm not going to be worried unless I need to be. He probably got the picture Saturday night when I called him to tell him we wouldn't be going on that date and that we should just part ways. At least I hope so."

I'm not so sure of that. If I know Milo and believe what I've heard about him, he won't be leaving her alone just yet. He doesn't like to hear a woman say no. He likes to leave them, not the other way around.

"You may be right, but I know I would feel better if you weren't alone when you are out and about."

"Well, I'm not going to stop living my life, especially because of a guy that just doesn't know boundaries. Yeah, he gave me the creeps, which is why I ended it before it started. But that doesn't necessarily mean he's a stalker." She looks at her phone. "I have somewhere to be."

"Where are you going?"

She starts to get into her car. "The women's shelter to volunteer."

She studies my face. I'm not sure what she sees in my expression or eyes, but it causes her to add, "Would you like to meet up with me afterwards?"

"Yes. Of course. Thank you for giving me another chance."

She nods. "I'll call you when I'm done."

The last thing I see is her heading west in her brother's yellow jeep. I know she is still hurt by me and that I'm on thin ice, so when we get together, I need to prove to her that I'm sincere.

Saige

On the way to Huntington, I think about Declan and my situation. Yeah, he messed up by ignoring me, but I can see why he thought he was doing what was best for me. I just really wish he would have asked me.

When I get to the shelter, it doesn't take long for Emma, the woman who runs the shelter, to put me to work right away. I wash clothes, clean, and do all the little things that get pushed to the back burner, because the workers are so busy helping the women and kids with their needs. They make sure they get their undivided attention because it is the least these women deserve.

This place and these people who work here are the closest place to a real home where these women don't have to fear for their lives. They come here knowing they are safe and will be given the help they need to walk away from the situation they left.

Let's not forget the women who are living here. Some are alone and some have children they left with. They woke up one day knowing they couldn't live the way they were anymore, and that this place was the safest place for them. Now, not everyone just wakes up and leaves. Others are rescued by a friend or family member or maybe even the police.

Hopefully, with time, these women will be able to live on their own and walk down the street without fearing for their lives. They will be able to find a job that makes them happy, see a smile on their kids' face and maybe find a person that helps them heal the wounds and loves them the way a woman should be loved. One day they will find their worth, find their power, and they will love without fear.

After my three-hour shift, Emma and I exchange numbers. I let her know about the Bicentennial in our town and we discuss me doing a clothing and item drive booth in the square to help get them the items that they desperately need. I, of course, need to talk to the mayor about it first, but I'm sure there will be no problem at all, seeing as the mayor is Anne Carter, my mother's best friend.

When I get into my car, I pull up Declan's number and call him. He suggests that we meet up at City Lake in town and tells me to bring my appetite because he's going to bring food. My stomach growls at his words.

~

After a long drive and my butt going numb, I pull up to City Lake. City Lake is just what it sounds like, a lake in our city. It has a nice walking trail and wildlife, and it's the perfect fishing hole for all the locals. It is perfect to get out and just relax in the fresh air.

When I pull up, I see that Declan is sitting with a guy on the dock who is fishing. I sit in my car for a few minutes because I still can't believe that Declan and I are about to hang out. This is something I dreamed of in high school.

I get out of the car, take a deep breath, and walk towards the dock.

As soon as my boots hit the old wood, Declan glances in my direction. He grins widely and waves. When I get to him, he gestures for me to join him and the gentleman he is sitting beside. The man introduces himself as Leo. He is a skinny, old man with snow white hair.

We spend thirty minutes talking to him. He gives us advice, tells us jokes and talks about how fishing is a thing he and his wife used to do together. So, when he gets lonely and misses her, he comes to their favorite spot on the dock and fishes. It's a way to think about all the memories they had shared together.

"How long have you two been together?" he asks.

"Oh, we aren't together. We're just friends," Declan responds.

Leo looks at us both with squinted eyes for a few minutes and responds, "Uh-huh. Sure."

"It's true, we aren't and haven't ever been together," I answer.

He stares for a few more minutes, stands up, and then grabs his tackle and pole. He looks at us both and says, "Well, you both are damn fools then. I know soulmates when I see them." He tips his fishing hat and nods a goodbye to us.

Silence engulfs us, and I know we are both thinking about what Leo just said. I know we have feelings for each other, but I'm not sure one could call us soulmates. I'll admit there is just something about Declan that makes keeping my emotions in control so hard. I felt so strongly about him back then in high school, but a different feeling is taking over now. I always felt like we were kindred spirits. I always knew when he needed me growing up. It was just a feeling, and I acted on my emotions, and these few days have made me feel like he knows when I need him also.

I think this date will be perfect because it will let me get to know him a little more. Trust me, I know a lot about the boy I went to school with, but I do not know the man I am sitting with. Maybe after getting to know him more, I will then know if my feelings are real.

"Anyway. Want to have some lunch? I have a basket and blanket laid out under the willow tree over there." Declan points to a gorgeous old willow that makes a little hidden cave under its graceful arching branches.

"Yes, please. I'm famished."

Declan wasn't lying when he said to bring an appetite. There is turkey, ham, and bologna sandwiches with American and pepper jack cheese. He brought ranch, mustard, ketchup, and mayo as condiments. Potato salad, macaroni salad, and a baggie of a variety of veggies, chips, and coleslaw are also inside the basket. Then he packed water and beer as drinks. We definitely won't be hungry after this.

I pick up a bologna sandwich, pull off the cheese and add mustard and some Lay's chips over the bologna, before putting the second slice of bread on top.

"What did you just do?" Declan asks, looking mortified.

"What are you talking about?"

"What did you just put on your sandwich?" He looks disgusted.

"Mustard and chips."

"Chips on a sandwich?"

"You cannot tell me you have never gotten out of a pool in 90-degree weather and had this sandwich!"

He shakes his head. "Nope. Never."

I offer the sandwich to him. "Here, try it."

"No. Thank you."

"You can't knock it until you try it."

"Fine." He grabs the sandwich and takes a bigger bite than most people would do while trying something. "It's okay."

"Just okay? This was a go to pool side sandwich for me growing up, and it sounded like the perfect thing to eat in this heat." I try to take the sandwich back.

He jerks the sandwich away from my reach. "Just playing. I used to have these all the time, and I love them."

"You jerk!" I playfully push his arm.

"Here, you can either have this one back or I can make you one since my bite practically took off half of the sandwich." He offers the sandwich to me.

"That's what I thought when I saw you take a bite to try. I knew I'd never seen anyone take that big of a bite when trying something new." We laugh. "You can make me one, please."

"As you wish."

I watch Declan making my sandwich and realize how lucky I am to be here with him. Even if we become nothing more than friends, he is a great listener, and we just flow together so easily.

He hands me the sandwich, and I smile.

"That potato salad looks amazing. I think I'll have some of that with this sandwich." I look in the basket for plates. "Uh, Dec?"

"Hmm?" he mumbles while chewing a big bite.

"Where are the plates?"

"Damnit! I knew I was forgetting something. I'm sorry, Saige. I wanted this to be perfect."

He looks so distraught. I can tell he really put in time and effort to pack all of this for us, and I hate that he feels this way. I look back into the basket and find a spork.

"Don't apologize. This spork is perfect enough. I'll just eat it out of the bowl. Are you okay with sharing cooties with me?" I ask before taking a bite of the potato salad.

He laughs. "Cooties? I haven't heard that since elementary school." He draws circles and pokes his bicep in random places. "There, I got my cootie shot. I think I'll take my chances with you." He grabs the spork from my hand and dips it into the potato salad for a big bite.

"How was the women's shelter? I bet they were thrilled to have you."

"It was great. I tried to get as much done as I could on my shift. I told Emma, the woman who runs the shelter, that I was going to ask Anne Carter if I could set up a booth at the Bicentennial to raise money and take donations for them."

"That's a wonderful idea! Let me know if you need any help running the booth. I'll volunteer to help anyway."

"Thanks. I'll take you up on the offer."

He clears his throat. "What are you doing tonight?"

"Tonight? Wait, is the date over?" I joke with him.

"Hardly. I'm just wondering if you want to have drinks tonight?"

"Well, Finn, Megan and I were going to head to Sherry's tonight for karaoke and drinks. Do you want to come?"

"Gina isn't coming?"

"She's got a hot date with her husband. Dinner and a movie at home. Growing a baby has been stealing all her energy, so that's all she is up for. I'm sure she will be in pj's and in bed by nine tonight."

"Dinner and movies at home with the one you love sounds perfect to me."

His eyes twinkle when they meet mine.

"Yes, it sure does." I blush. "So, Sherry's at nine?"

"Sounds fun. Want me to give you a ride?"

"Yes. Thank you."

We finish eating our meal and talk about everything that has happened to us since we graduated high school. We laugh and cry with each other. We even pump each other up about our accomplishments. We aren't the same people we were in high school, and that's okay. We live and grow and even learn along the way.

By the end of us catching up, we are lying down on the blanket, and our fingers keep brushing up against each other. The birds are singing inside the willow's branches, and a beautiful silence fills us. It is a peaceful moment brought to us by nature's wonder.

I roll over to my side and face him. "Declan?" I ask, ending the silence.

"Yeah," he says, still looking up into the branches.

"Did you know I had a crush on you in high school?" I am nervous waiting for his response.

He takes a minute before responding. He then rolls over to face me. "I didn't until your mom told me."

"My mom told you?"

"Yes."

"When?"

He brushes the hair from my face, and I hold my breath. The tips of his fingers send shivers down my back. "That night that you came home from the store with bags full of items for me to use when I would escape to your house. I came downstairs that night to get a glass of water, and she told me and then disappeared."

"Oh. I didn't even know she knew."

"Did Finn know?"

I scoot closer to him. "Yes. I made him swear he wouldn't say anything, though."

He nods, "He's a good brother."

He stares at me for a moment, and I lick my lips. It doesn't go unnoticed as his eyes drop to my lips, making me think he might kiss me again.

He sits up quickly. "If you are done, do you want to walk the nature trail with me? I have something cool to show you, and I think you will love it."

Not exactly the response I was hoping for, but he has been patient with me, and I will be with him also. "Let's go."

We pack up the picnic basket and blanket and load them into his car. He grabs us both a bottle of water to take with us, and we head down the trail. The nature walk is about a mile long and at the end is a wide open field full of weeds. But before you get there, you get to connect to nature by witnessing the blessings of Mother Earth. Whether it be wildlife or just nature, you always leave the trail feeling grounded. At least I do.

We walk the first six minutes in silence just enjoying the view and the sounds of nature. I had forgotten how peaceful the walking trail is. When we can't take the silence any longer, we make a game of guessing the owner of sounds we hear.

Halfway through, we come across a log that had fallen in the middle of the trail during a storm. Declan grabs my hand to help me over it.

"I wonder why this log hasn't been moved?"

"They moved it out of the way a little so that those who couldn't climb over it could go around because by the time they got to it, wildlife and organisms had claimed it as their own."

I walk around the log to observe what is living in and around it, and Declan follows suit. Sure enough, we find a bunny nest. It is lodged up beside it, using it as shelter from predators and the elements. We can see a lot of movement underneath the grass that covers the hole and know that this nest has baby bunnies in it. We know that the mommy bunny will be back soon, so Declan grabs my hand to pull me away.

He doesn't let go of my hand when we walk away, and I smile. He stops a few feet away, and instead of letting go of my hand, he holds on tighter and points to a doe off to the right. I smile at him to let him know I see her. For the rest of the walk, we point out things we see and hear.

Declan stops again and turns around to me. He lets go of my hand. "Okay, I need you to close your eyes."

"Okay?" I am apprehensive, but I close my eyes anyway.

I feel the heat from his hands on my shoulders as he guides me forward, until I stumble over a twig and fall in the muddy dirt. I start laughing. Of course, I would be the one to fall.

Declan is very nurturing and squats down to make sure I am okay. I tell him I am and realize that he has given me the perfect opportunity to pull him down into the mud with me. Unfortunately, I pull a little too hard, and he falls face first smack dab into the mud.

He lifts his face up, and all I can see are the whites of his eyes. I laugh. I'm laugh so hard that I snort.

In between laughing, I manage to get out, "Oh my god! I'm so sorry. Are you okay?"

He is quiet, and for a minute I think he is furious with me.

He lifts himself up onto his knees. "Oh, you are going to get it now."

I look down at his hands and see mud dripping from his fists. I squeal and try to get away, but he grabs my waist and yanks me in front of him. He rubs mud all over my face. I roll away from him onto my knees and try to wipe the mud off from around my eyes.

"You are so dead!" I yell.

I throw mud at him, and it hits his shirt. We launch into a mud fight.

Declan comes up behind me when I'm trying to gather some more mud, and he picks me up and lays me on my back. "Declan! You are cheating."

"This is not cheating. It's called being a good thinker. I've got you in my grasp. Now, what will I do with you?"

Our eyes lock, and he smirks. I think he is going to throw mud on my face, so I try to cover it. He pulls my hands away and pins them above my head with one of his. Declan crashes his lips to mine, and we lose control. It tastes like mud, but I would taste mud everyday if I knew the lips that were touching mine were his. His kiss sends shockwaves all over my body, and I know he feels it too because he shivers and then deepens the kiss. His tongue asks my lips for permission to enter, and I grant him access. The kiss is intoxicating, and when we stop, our lips are perfectly swollen.

"So…You said you had a surprise?" I ask while still blushing.

He looks like he is about to say something but then clears his throat and nods. He helps me up and says, "Close your eyes…again, and try not to fall…again."

I playfully punch his arm and close my eyes. "Hey now, I would trip on air if I could. I blame you. You are my navigator."

"I apologize, Ma'am. I'll try to be better this time," he whispers in my ear close enough that I feel his breath on my neck.

He leads me ahead and then stops. "Open your eyes, Saige."

I cannot fully describe what I am seeing. We are in the clearing that was once full of weeds. Today, I see stones set up in the shape of a large labyrinth with wildflowers surrounding it on all sides and weaving throughout. There are stone benches all over the perimeter of the clearing for people to sit and enjoy the scenery.

I walk to the stones with him following me. I see wild violets, daisies, sunflowers, milkweeds, coneflowers, lavender, poppies, and honeysuckle. There are a lot of other kinds, but you get the picture. They are all gorgeous and in full bloom, and not only the flowers but all the butterflies surrounding them. If I died and went to heaven, this is what I think it would look like.

I do a one-eighty and throw my arms around Declan, laughing. He hesitates for a moment, realizing what is happening, and then gathers me in his arms and spins me.

"Thank you for showing me this. It's just breathtaking!" I spin to look at the entire clearing.

"You are welcome. I love seeing a smile on your face."

I press a kiss to his lips and smile up at him. "You say I am a breath of fresh air, but so are you, Declan Wolfe."

I know something has shifted because all I feel is warmth.

The walk back is filled with flirty banter and just goofing off with one another. Declan runs to his car to get me a towel, so I don't get the seats muddy. I walk to the jeep and see a white piece of paper under my windshield wipers. I unfold it, and I'm struck with a little bit of fear.

My, you've been a busy girl
A picnic under the willow
A kiss covered in mud
Don't be fooled by him.
He doesn't really like you.
You are just a plaything to him.

My eyes search City Lake for signs of anyone who could have left it. Nobody looks out of the ordinary. I fold the paper up and put it in my pocket. I don't want Declan to see it and jump into protective mode. I'm not about to make it into something it may or may not be. It could just be a harmless prank.

"Here you go." I spin around fast and see that it's Declan behind me. "Are you okay?"

I nod. "Mm-hmm."

"Ready to go and get this mud washed off?"

"Yes, please. I have mud in my ears."

Declan follows me home, and I watch him pull into his garage through my rearview mirror. He runs across the street towards me and opens the door of the car. I take his hand in mine and climb out.

"Still want me to come with you guys tonight?" Declan asks.

"Of course. Want to pick me up here at eight-forty-five?"

"Sounds like a plan. Have a great shower, Saige." He winks.

Saige

After my shower, I look for something cute to wear now that Declan is coming with us. I tear through my closet, finding mostly my comfortable clothes. Luckily, I find a few selections in the back of the closet that are okay, but I'm going to have to go shopping if I want to embrace the new Saige that Finn so gratefully pointed out. I need some new clothes that shout 'I am back, and I will embrace my body and won't cover up for anyone'.

You know how a lot of people say that sometimes you just need a change of scenery to give you a new perspective? Well, I thought it was hogwash until I came back home.

I start typing into the note section of my iPhone.

1. Buy more clothes.

2. Embrace yourself!!

3. Look for a new place to live.

My eyes pause on number three. I do need to look for an apartment that is more in my budget and style when I get back. I only moved into the one I'm in now because Philippe liked it. It's an industrial modern apartment, and the décor is the same. My style is considered more eclectic and bohemian. Total opposites.

I suddenly become overwhelmed with emotion. I hated that apartment and I still do. I need a place that is home. Thinking about finding a new apartment in New York fills me with dread because it means having to leave here.

That thought takes me by surprise, because I've stayed away from this place for years but being back again has made me real homesick. I suppose I could just make time to come home and visit more, but I still have this nagging feeling that that isn't what I want.

3. Look for a new place to live HERE.

One word. I add one word just to see what it looks like on paper, and suddenly it dawns on me. I don't want to move back to New York. I want to move back here permanently. I want to be with my brothers, my sister-in-law, my nieces, and my best friends. And if I'm honest, with Declan.

After today, there is no denying our feelings for one another. I am in love with Declan Wolfe.

4. Call publisher, call renter, call women's shelter, and Just A Sip.

I continue to type on my phone. I'm not going to take any drastic measures just yet. I need to sleep on it some more because this is a very big step. But if the shaking is any indication, I'm anxiously excited about it.

I start rummaging through my pockets for my Chapstick and my fingers brush across paper. It's the note on my windshield.

I know I should probably say something to River, Finn, Gina, Megan or even Declan, but I don't want it to be nothing and then I have everyone all worried about me for no reason. I promise myself that if anything else happens out of the ordinary, I will let them know.

I pull it out of the pocket and put it into the book I have on the bedside table.

"Yo, Smalls. Are you in there?"

"Yeah. Come in." I close the book.

Finn comes strolling inside and plops down on my bed. He hands me a Subway melt, and my stomach thanks him greatly. We cheer the subs, and he watches me take a bite.

"Yes?" I ask.

"So, how was the date?" He wiggles his eyebrows.

I pull the pillow from under his leg. "None of your business."

"Oh, c'mon! You have to tell me. This is my best friend and my sister. You have to let me know!"

"It was a perfect first date. We talked to an old man fishing on the dock who called us soulmates. He had a picnic for us under the willow tree. Then we went hiking and had a mud fight, and it ended with him taking me to the wildflower clearing."

"It does sound like a perfect date for you, but I have to ask, where did you have a mud fight?"

I start giggling thinking about the fight and the kiss afterwards.

"Earth to Saige. Want to let me in on what you're giggling about?"

I try to be as straight faced as I can. "I wasn't giggling."

"Oh, you totally were. You are even blushing! Look at you!"

I turn around and look in the floor length mirror. He was right, I am blushing.

"Well, he blindfolded me." I brush my finger on the side of my eyes, picturing the blindfold on.

"Sounds kinky."

"We were in the woods!"

"And your point?" He waves his sub around.

I hit him in the head with the pillow. "Do you want to hear this or not?"

"Alright! Alright. I do."

I recap the mud fight and the kiss with Declan. I don't even have to look in the mirror to know my cheeks are bright red, because I feel heat in my core just thinking of him.

"Like I said. It was perfect."

"I'm happy for you, Smalls. Truly."

"But?" I am nervous about what his response will be.

"Just make sure you are going at the pace that you want. I don't want to see either of you hurt. And before you go further, make sure you know that he will be here, and you will be in New York. Are you ready and prepared for a long-distance relationship?"

"About that… I might be moving from New York to back here." I mumble quietly.

"What did you just say?" He's shocked.

"I said that I might be moving away from—"

"New York. Yeah, I heard." He pauses for a moment. "Is this because of Declan? Because if so, this is really soon to just up and move for a guy that you've only been on one date with."

"What do you take me for? No! I'm not moving for a guy. I've done enough for a guy before, and we both know what happened with that. I only thought about moving back just thirty minutes or so ago. Nothing is set in stone, and honestly, I never used Declan as a reason to move."

"Declan is great, and our chemistry is amazing, but neither he nor I are in the stage of changing our lives completely for each other. I just thought about moving apartments there and the next thing I know I'm sad about it and the thought of moving back here made me happy."

"You know how much I love my family and Gina and Megan. I want to watch the twins and Jace grow up. I want to be a hands-on aunt to them and to Gina's baby, whether it's a boy or girl."

"And you just thought all of this thirty minutes ago?" He lifts one eyebrow.

"No. I guess I've been thinking about missing everyone for a while now. But it's different thinking it when you are away versus when you are surrounded by those people. It's been slowly building since I've arrived."

"Well, whatever your decision is, I have your back. You know I love you and how much I miss you."

"I know. I've missed you too."

He kisses my forehead. "On a lighter note, are you ready for some karaoke tonight? I've been wetting my whistle ready to blow you out of the water."

"And how many drinks has that been to make you think you are going to win?"

"Only two. Enough to relax me, but not enough to be too intoxicated to drive or lose to you." He points to my chest.

"As if. You know everyone prefers my actual singing to your cat screeching."

"I guess we will see tonight, won't we?" He pokes me on the nose.

"By the way, I invited Declan to join us. Are you okay with that?"

"Of course. Now I won't have to be the third wheel."

"You wouldn't have been anyway. You and Megan go on those tirades that last hours and I become the third wheel."

"Hey! Sometimes that woman grinds my gears! She hardly agrees with me, except for lately she's been quite friendly."

"You've been the same way."

"No! I have not."

"Whatever you say. You two are seriously cut from the same mold. We shall see how tonight goes. Declan is going to pick me up at eight-forty-five." I look at my phone and see that it's eight-thirty. "Crap. I've got to get dressed. What should I wear?"

He looks at the few outfits I have pulled out of the closet and spends forever looking at them. I sit in front of the vanity and apply my makeup.

He turns to me, "You need to update your wardrobe. Most of these are very unflattering for you."

"I know. I'm going shopping tomorrow. Just pick something, please. Something that is the least unflattering."

"Shouldn't Megan or Gina be doing this for you? Or Ginny? She's just down the hall."

"Finn. You are one of the most stylish guys I know when you aren't in the wilderness. Just look at what you are wearing now. You have always helped me with my outfits, and you're not going to stop now. So, pick! Declan will be here in like eight minutes."

"Geez. Fine. So bossy."

He turns to grab an outfit and flings it at me. It is my black leggings, a white tank top, and a floral, floor-length kimono. He then pairs it with my flats. He walks out so I can get dressed, and when I come downstairs, he tells me to tuck in the tank into my leggings. I was nervous about it, but it actually accentuates my curves in the right places.

The doorbell rings, and Finn opens the door. My heart stops in its tracks. Declan is standing in the doorway, and he looks perfect. He is normally a plain tee and jeans or jogger guy, and they fit him so well, but tonight he is in a black button-down shirt and gray slacks. I suddenly feel so underdressed.

"Wow, Declan! You look fantastic," I manage to get out.

"And you look beautiful." He walks towards me and plants a kiss on my cheek.

He whispers in my ear, "I know what you are thinking, but you look perfect, so don't you dare tear yourself down and try to change."

When did he become so observant of my body language?

I blush and smile up at him, "If you say so."

"I do." He grabs my hand. "Ma'am, your chariot awaits."

"Let me grab my purse really quick."

He squeezes my hand and let's go. I walk into the kitchen and find it sitting on top of the island. Before I walk out, I hear Finn ask Declan what his intentions are with me, and I pull myself against the wall and eavesdrop.

"Finn, you have nothing to worry about. You know I would love nothing more than to be with Saige. I'm just taking everything at her pace. I promise."

Declan likes me? My heart does that fluttering thing.

"What if she just wants to be friends?" Finn asks him.

Yeah. There is no way that I could just be friends with Declan. My feelings are too deep to do that and see him happy with anyone else.

"Well, I will have to accept that and just be her friend then. I'm not going to lie; I will be hurt. But I still haven't got the guts to tell her how I feel yet, because I'm still not sure where she is with all of this. I know she is still healing from the last guy, and I know that this has only been day three of her being back home. If we didn't have any history then even I would call me crazy. But after our date today, I can't deny the chemistry we have and the way I feel when she is around."

I'm going to change that tonight. Tonight, he will know how I feel, and I will know the same. We are done not being honest with our feelings. Of course, we both know there is some physical attraction or else we wouldn't have kissed a few times already, but I want him to know that I like him more than just physically.

"Found it," I say, while walking out of the kitchen holding my purse up. "What are you boys talking about?"

"Oh, I'm just letting him know about our karaoke bet and that he wouldn't be a best friend if he didn't vote for me," Finn answers.

"No cheating, Finn. If you want to win then you better be a male Beyoncé. Besides, Declan will vote for whoever is the best singer, despite who we are, right?"

"Right." He loops his arm for me. "Shall we?"

I wrap my hand around his bicep. "We shall."

Declan looks back at Finn. "Are you going to ride with us Finn?"

"If you both are alright with it."

"Come on, Biggie. I call dibs on shotgun, though."

~

We pull up to Sherry's less than five minutes later, and I spot Megan seated at a table in front near the stage. Someone is already on the mic, and they are way too intoxicated to be up there. No lie, even I need a little liquid courage to get up there, but when you can't even read the lyrics, and you are just slurring random words, you've had enough. When he is done, his wife pulls him off the stage laughing. He asks if she recorded it and she laughs harder.

"Yes, dear. It's recorded. Your colleagues are going to appreciate hearing your amazing voice on Tuesday."

"Told you. I got beauty, brains, and a singing voice like an angel. Maybe I should go on American Idol."

"Why don't you watch it in the morning and then decide if you are American Idol material? If you want to go, I'll be there, dear."

The gentleman tries to turn to the crowd and says, "See, men. This is what you need. A beautiful woman on your arm and your biggest fan in your corner. Love her, men. She deserves to have you place that crown on her head and for you to treat her like the queen she is."

They then stumble out the door towards their truck.

"Stew and Fran Jones. They've been married thirty years. Moved here two years ago and they support the community in everything. They will give you the shirts off their backs if you need it. Every Sunday they come here to let off steam, and every Sunday Stew has a little too much and graces us with that beautiful American Idol voice of his," Megan says as I sit down.

"Well, I'm going to need a few of whatever he had to get up there and sing again. What do y'all want?" I ask.

They give me their orders, and I walk up to the bar to find Becky working again. This girl sure knows how to rock her hair and outfits.

"Blue! I love it." I motioned to her hair.

"Thanks. You were here Friday night, right? You wouldn't let that guy buy you a drink?" She points at me.

"Yes, I was. Well, tonight I'm buying him a drink." I point to our table where Declan is sitting.

She leans across the bar to get a good look at the table. "Thank God! I could read you both so easily that night and I knew you two wanted each other. Are you guys together yet?"

"No, but we may be by the end of tonight. I hope at least."

"You go girl! What can I get you all?"

"I need two Buds, one Jack and coke and one vodka and Mountain Dew, please."

"You got it. You can go sit down and I'll bring them to you. I need an excuse to read everyone at the table anyway."

I freeze. "You read people? Like actually read people?" She nods. "Do you do tarot and other stuff too?"

"Sure do. Are you scared?"

"No way! I'm actually the opposite. I'd love for you to read the table."

"Well then, I'll bring these out to you."

I walk back over to the table, and on the way, I swear I see someone at the bar watching me, but when I turn to look no one is there. I do a double take, still feeling the hair on my arms standing at attention.

"I put everyone's name on the list for karaoke," Finn says, making his way to the table at the same time I do.

"Now, why the hell would you do that, Finn? I can't sing! I make Stew sound like Frank Sinatra. I'm just here for you and Saige. Take my name off the list," Megan yells at Finn.

"I'm with Megan. No way will you get me up on that stage," Declan says while fist bumping Megan.

"Sorry. No can do. Once it's on the list, it stays on the list."

"Like hell it is!" Megan storms off to the man in charge of the karaoke table.

She comes back with a smile on her face. "Declan, I got our names off the list. I only had to show one of my boobs."

"You did what?" Finn asks.

Megan and I both start cracking up at the look on their faces. The shock leaves their faces once they realize that Megan really didn't do that, and it was just a joke.

"Good one," Declan says, laughing.

"Ha-ha," Finn says sarcastically.

"Oh, lighten up, Finn. It was funny, and you deserved it for putting my name on that list," Megan says seriously.

Becky shows up at the table just in time and delivers the drinks. She makes small talk with everyone and then excuses herself only five minutes later. I excuse myself and follow her back to the bar.

"So?" I ask.

"You're an eager one. Are you sure you really want to know?"

I nod. "I do."

"Well, take this at face value, alright? Many do not believe those of us have gifts to read others. They call us quacks."

"Well, I know there are some people who are fake and use their 'gift' as a way to steal money, but I didn't pay you and you offered to read everyone, so let's hear."

"Well, your brother loves the outdoors. He feels connected with nature. He also is funny and loves to make others laugh. The one person he is really trying to get to is the girl sitting next to him."

"Megan?"

"Yes. He likes her and she likes him, but they have been in the continuous cycle of making each other angry to deflect the feelings they truly have. If they don't stop this cycle, it will never be anything more.

"Megan is a loyal person. She will always be there through everything. She has an old soul and loves fiercely. She is also not afraid to stand up for what is right."

"So far, you are spot on. I'm trying to get them to realize they like each other."

"Well, this may be something they have to figure out themselves. There might have to be a big event that sets things in motion. Now, on to you and Declan. Let's start with you first. Every time I have talked to you, even if it is just to order a drink, I have read you. You have changed quickly in a few days. Friday when you were here, you were pissed at the world, had a huge chip on your shoulder, and you were afraid to let anyone in. Probably from someone who really did you wrong?"

I nod.

"But today your aura is bright. You are happy and looking towards the future and not back at the past. You are an old soul as well, which is probably why you and Megan get along well. And you are in love with him." She points to Declan.

"Are you sure you read that I'm in love with him?"

She nods. "Yeah, that's super clear to me. You guys have a past, am I correct?"

"Yes."

"While it wasn't a romantic past you had, both of you had feelings for each other, and you being back has only intensified those feelings. He loves you too, you know?"

"He does?"

"Yep. His feelings are super clear, too. He's been in love with you longer than you have. I feel like you really liked him when you were younger, but he fell in love with you back then and hasn't been able to get you off his mind."

"What did I do to make him fall in love with me back then?"

"I can't tell you that. You'll have to ask him when your relationship comes to fruition. I have kept you away, so I'll let you get back, but Saige? Declan is a good guy. His aura is bright and aligns with yours. He wouldn't hurt anyone unless it was necessary. He is genuine. He looks for the best in others, and while he has some past things he holds on to, he strives to make the best out of the future."

"Thanks Becky. I really appreciate this."

"No problem. Here is my number." She hands me a card with her name and number on it. "Call me whenever, alright?"

"Thank you."

I walk back to the table and apologize for leaving. They ask what Becky and I were talking about, so I tell them the truth but not all of it. I'm not about to tell Megan and Finn that they like each other or tell Declan that she said we are in love. Generally, Megan and Finn know I would be one to meet a life reader, and they are stoked about hearing how she read them so well. Declan is quiet though, and I am afraid I just freaked him out.

"Hey. I'm sorry if I freaked you out by telling you that stuff. I understand if you don't believe it, or you are skeptical or creeped out," I whisper.

"No. It's not any of that. I've just never had someone read me and actually know me that well. She is right about me always being there for others and still holding on to some things of the past. But that's not something to discuss here," he whispers back.

"Whenever you are ready." I rub his arm.

The conversation with everyone flows so naturally. We all get along so well, and I can see us doing this all the time. We laugh hard and just enjoy our time so much that I don't want to see the night end. Along with chatting, we listen to many good singers and some that just went up there as a dare. Before I know it, it's one hour later.

"Our next singer is Finn Wilson," the DJ announces.

"This seems like a perfect time to put these babies in." Megan says as she pulls out some earplugs and puts them in her ears.

Declan and I burst out laughing, but Finn isn't amused.

"I'm not that bad, kid!" Finn tries to tell her, knowing she hates that nickname as much as I hate 'Little Saige'.

"What? I can't hear you." She pretends not to hear him even though her ear plugs aren't all the way in for them to actually work.

Finn rolls his eyes and walks onto the stage. He grabs the mic and chooses the song 'Don't Stop Believin' by Journey. He only chose it because he knows it gets the crowd pumping, whether the singer is good or not, because everyone sings along. He winks at me when the song starts. That fool really thinks he will win, even with this song.

During the song the crowd is pumped, and I have to admit that Finn has been working on his singing voice, because it doesn't sound like cats scratching their nails on a chalkboard anymore. Even Finn looks surprised by his voice.

Megan nudges me, and I look at her. "I had the DJ add autotune to his mic."

"You didn't," I chuckle, looking back at Finn. "He is going to kill you."

"No. He'll thank me and so will everyone else in this bar."

"You are bad!"

Finn's song ends, and he bows and tries to wink at all the single ladies. He's just looking for wins. What a turd burglar.

Sherry's has everyone vote on their favorite singer at the end of the night. Even though Finn and I have never won, we still look to see who has the most tallies out of the both of us and the loser has to buy dinner one night. We've been doing this since high school when we would sneak in here with our fake IDs. Of course, we were smart enough to remember it's a small town and everyone knows exactly how old we were. Sherry and her husband still let us come but let everyone know we were not to be served alcohol at all, or they would be fired.

"I didn't do half bad." Finn says. "Especially with that autotune." He turns towards Megan.

She just shrugs and pulls out the ear plugs.

"Our next singer is Saige Wilson. Looks like the brother and sister are at it again. Come on up Saige and show Finn how it's done," the DJ announces.

"Hey!" Finn yells.

Declan

"You'll be blown away by Saige's voice." Megan leans over to tell me.

"Even I have to admit she is a fantastic singer. I've never won our bet, ever." Finn joins in the conversation.

"Then why do you have a bet with her?" I ask curiously.

"Because she wouldn't do it if he didn't bet her, and the world deserves to hear her," Megan responds.

The music to the song starts, and we all just stare at her. She starts to sing, and it sounds like I'm in the presence of an angel. I'm not big on karaoke, and I only came here because she invited me, but I would come a thousand times if I could listen to her over and over again.

Then it hits me what she is singing. My breath hitches and my heart beats faster listening to the lyrics. She is singing Adele's 'One and Only'.

I whisper to Megan, "Does she usually sing this song?"

"No. This is definitely different from her go to songs. You better listen, dude, because I think she is singing this to you." She looks at me with a 'don't you hurt my girl' face.

I continue to listen to Saige, and I light up. This girl has made me the happiest man if she is really telling me she loves me. We need to talk together tonight, because I am ready to give her my all if she is willing to take me. I fell in love with the girl next door, and I will continue to always love her.

I look away when she finishes, and both Finn and Megan are staring at me and smiling. I swear they both are daring me to do something now.

"Megan, can Finn get a ride with you? I think I need some alone time with Saige?" I ask.

"If I have to," she says, smiling.

"Hey, buddy?" Finn pulls me down to his level and whispers in my ear. "Make sure you wrap it."

"Oh, geez. Is this shit not awkward enough for you?"

"She's a grown adult and so are you. I love you both and wish you the best, but I know neither of you want a baby right now with your relationship so new and all."

"I'm not going to have sex with your sister. We've only went on one date, and we don't even know what we are. I respect her too much for anything like that to happen right now. I told you I will go at her pace."

I meet her at the bottom of the stairs. "Would you like to get out of here?"

"Sure!"

I help Saige into the truck and close the door. I take a few deep breaths before hopping into the driver's seat. Her hand is sitting palm up on the center console, so I take it in mine. I squeeze it, and she smiles brightly at me.

"Why didn't I know you could sing like that?" I ask.

"I don't normally sing for anyone, but when Finn makes a bet with me, I can't back down from it. And besides, Sherry and her husband are family, so I have always felt at home there and never judged."

"Well, will I ever hear you sing again?" I ask hoping to hear the right answer.

"Depends on how the night goes, maybe." Her beautiful face lights up in a smirk.

"Well, I better not screw up then. Is there anywhere you would like to go?"

"We could just go back to your place and hang out. If you don't mind?" She's blushing.

"Not at all. Do you want to go home and change first or are you comfortable with that?" I want her to feel safe and at home when she is in my place. Plus, we have a lot to cover.

"Would you mind terribly if I go home and change first? I'm glad I am starting to find myself again and wear clothes that feel more like me, but when I'm just relaxing at home or at someone's house, I enjoy wearing joggers or sweats and tanks."

"If that makes you feel comfortable, please go change."

Saige

Declan drops me off in River's driveway. He offers to wait for me, but I tell him he is being silly and that I'll run over to his house when I am done.

I run into Ginny on the way up the stairs. Sadly, even though we live under the same roof, we haven't seen each other since Saturday morning. With her having all of these doctor's appointments and me running around, our schedules just haven't aligned. She follows me to my room, and we chat while I change into my favorite sweats and red tank top that give my girls the perfect lift.

"Well, I'll let you get to your Casanova. But before I go, would you go with me to my ultrasound appointment tomorrow? River has to work, and I normally go alone, but I miss you and I need some girl time alone with you. We could get pedicures and lunch afterwards? My appointment is at nine."

"I'd be honored to go with you, Gin."

Ginny leaves, and I head downstairs. I close the front door

behind me and start to turn around to take off to Declan's when something white catches my eye. There, with its corner tucked under the porch rug, is an envelope addressed to me. I pick it up, but it feels like hours pass by before I open it.

Now listen to me carefully.

You need to break it off with him.

No more dates and no more singing.

Or I will kill him.

That's a promise.

Saige

Tuesday

I couldn't sleep last night thinking about both of the letters. Rays of light peek through the curtains in the room and my pillows are crumpled up in a ball on the edge of the bed. My head is currently lying flat on the mattress. At one point in time, I kicked the sheet and covers onto the floor. I remember being hot all night but getting chills. My mind went back and forth between finding out who is leaving the letters and booking the first flight out of town back to NYC.

Every time I try to book a flight on my phone, I chicken out. I don't want to leave my friends and family early. I haven't spent enough time with them, and I've only gotten two notes. Granted, one was left on the porch of my brother's house, so this person knows where I am staying.

When I walked back into the house after reading the note, I contemplated telling Finn and River. River would put us all on police protection if I told him about the letters, but I still wanted to know if this was a prank before getting the police involved. Instead, I walked up the stairs, and around the corner to my room.

Once in my room I thought about telling Declan, but instead I texted him an excuse as to why I couldn't come over. He tried calling and texting me, and I silenced my phone and sat it on the bedside table. I sat down on the side of the bed and threw myself backwards with a frustrated groan.

I laid there for a few minutes going back and forth. My mind was whirling, and I couldn't decide if I was making the right move or not. I told myself I was being an idiot one minute and went to sit up and yell for River. Then, I'd say I was not being an idiot and threw myself back on the bed.

I looked over at my phone on the table and groaned. I reached for it, staring at the screen showing me all the missed calls and texts from Declan. I placed the phone beside me on the bed, missing the man with the piercing green eyes.

This was the time I needed Megan and Gina. They would be blatantly honest with me. I picked my phone back up and sent a message asking if they wanted to grab dinner.

"Dinner with my best friends? Hell yeah," Megan replies.

"Sounds perfect. I need a girl's night. Just don't kill me if I fall asleep at the dinner table," Gina responds.

~

I hear Phoebe, Paige, River, and Ginny walk past my bedroom to go downstairs. They snap me out of my thoughts.

"I want eggs and bacon!"

"I want biscuits and gravy!"

"Shh! You need to keep quiet. Aunt Saige and Uncle Finn are sleeping, and there is no reason to make them endure a six-thirty a.m. fight over what we are having for breakfast," River says while yawning.

"How about I make biscuits, gravy, eggs, and bacon? Now, hurry up. We don't want to wake them."

I hear footsteps running down the stairs. I can already taste Ginny's cooking, and my mouth starts to water. But it is going to take me at least thirty minutes to even crawl out of this bed after not sleeping.

I grab my earbuds out of the bedside drawer and connect them to my phone's Bluetooth and listen to Bastille's 'Pompeii'. I close my eyes and allow my mind to absorb the music only.

A knock brings me out of my trance.

I crack my eyes. "Come in."

Finn walks in with a wild case of bedhead. "Hey."

"Hey yourself. What are you doing up at six-thirty?"

"It's not six-thirty. It's eight," Finn says.

"No, it's not. I just heard River and the girls walk by loudly and he said it was six-thirty."

"Yeah. I did too. One and a half hours ago. If you don't believe me, look at your phone."

I grab my phone off the bedside table, and sure enough, it is eight a.m. It suddenly dawns on me that my earbuds aren't playing music anymore. I feel for them in my ears, and they are gone. I throw back the covers and look in the bed, but they aren't there.

"Uh, Saige. What are you doing?"

"After they all went downstairs, I put my earbuds in to listen to music to wake up. They are missing."

"Did you look under your pillow?" he asks, looking around the room.

I move all of the pillows. "They aren't there."

Finn gets down on all fours and looks under the bed. "They aren't under the bed or on the floor either."

I pull open the bedside table, and there inside the charging case are my buds. I hold them up to show Finn. "I swear I was wearing them." I freeze and look back on the bed. The pillows are not bunched on the side of the bed anymore and the blankets are off the floor. "Now, I know I'm not crazy. The blankets were on the floor and the pillows were over there when I woke up," I say, pointing to the right side of the bed.

"How much sleep did you get?"

"None."

"Well, there's your answer. Maybe you really did sleep and you dreamed you woke up with the pillows and blankets off you, and after hearing the fam in your dream sequence, you put your buds in."

I sigh. "I don't know. Maybe."

Something still doesn't feel right.

"Are you feeling okay?" Finn asks with concern.

"Yeah. Why?"

"Weren't you and Declan supposed to have a date last night? And now you are here looking exhausted." He peps up. "Did Declan keep you up all night?" He winks at me.

"No, I came home and told him I wasn't feeling good, so I didn't go over there. And before you ask, no. I do not want to talk about it."

Finn is searching for something in my body language or facial expressions to tell him the truth in what I said. "Sure."

I hop out of bed. "Want to go see if there is any breakfast leftover? I've got to leave at eight-thirty to take Ginny to her doctor's appointment."

Finn stops me with his arm. "Smalls. You'd tell me if there was anything going on, wouldn't you?"

"Sure."

He eyes me suspiciously. "Is there something going on?"

"Finn, I'm hungry. Let's just go get some food, please."

He runs his hand through his hair, "Fine."

We go downstairs, and Ginny is in the kitchen tidying up.

"Oh good! You're up. River is going to take the girls to your moms before his shift. We need to leave in half an hour."

"That's fine. I only need ten minutes to eat and the rest to get ready. We will be out the door by eight-thirty, promise." I reassure her.

I can't imagine being nine months pregnant, raising twin girls and having a household to run, so anything I can do to help her relax is my mission today. She deserves it.

"I'm not too hungry, I'm going to go see if River needs any help with the girls," Finn says and turns quickly out of the room.

"What's up with him?" Ginny asks me.

I shrug, shoveling food into my mouth. I finish eating in six minutes flat. Correction: I inhale the food in six minutes flat.

"Let me just wash my plate and then I'll go get ready."

"Don't you dare! Give it to me and go get up there." She reaches her hand out to take my plate.

I hop off the barstool and walk through the hallway.

"Riv, I'm serious. Something is up with her," I hear from the bottom of the stairs.

"But you know her. If something was really up with her, she wouldn't be able to hide it from us. It would eat away at her until she couldn't help but tell us. So, if she says it's nothing then we just have to believe her for now. She's going with Ginny to her doctor's appointment and then they are doing lunch and other things."

"I don't know. She blew off Declan last night and it looked like, to me, that they would be tangled up in bed this morning with the way it was going. And she wakes up and freaks out because she swears she laid down with her earbuds in her ears and they were still in the charging case."

"First off, I don't need to know about my sister's sex life. Two, maybe she had a legit reason to stay home and not see him. It is all so new still. Three, maybe she is stressed or dreamed of being awake. Happens to the best of us. Four, I need to get the girls out the door."

River calls for the girls, and they run into me on the stairs as I make my way up. I smile and give them each a hug. When I reach the top of the stairs, Finn is standing there with his arms crossed like I am a kid about to be punished by my dad.

"Finn, whatever it is, it will have to wait. I have to get dressed so I can take Ginny to her doctor's appointment."

I wave him off and walk into my room. I close the door in his face and search for something decent to wear.

"Okay. We will talk about this when you get home. I know something is up, and you are going to talk to me. You can't hide anything from me," Finn says through the closed bedroom door.

"Ginny and I will be gone awhile and then I'll only have time to come home and get changed before meeting the girls for dinner. I probably won't be home until late," I say as I'm throwing on some leggings.

"I'll wait up," he says and then I hear him walk downstairs and out the front door.

I wonder, where is he going? I finish getting dressed and run down the stairs. Ginny is in the foyer struggling to put on her shoes.

"Here. Let me help you." I squat down and tie her shoelaces for her. "You know you could just wear flats or some other slip-on shoes."

"I would if I could fit these fat feet into them. I never swelled with the girls, but I have swelled everywhere with Jace."

"Well, you still look beautiful. I only hope to look as beautiful as you when I'm pregnant."

"You will, and I cannot wait to see that."

"Let's get you up so we can go see the little man." I grab her hands and pull her up.

~

We arrive at the appointment on time and wait for Ginny's turn. She is guzzling an orange juice that I ran into the gas station to get her. She told me it helps get the baby moving so we can see better on the ultrasound. I look around the waiting room at all the pregnant women and I smile to myself.

I daydream of being pregnant myself and having that mother's glow that everyone has. A hand wraps around my belly, and I look down at the hand with the white gold band on the ring finger. I turn around and look at my…

"Earth to Saige!"

I blink and look up at Ginny who is standing at the office door with the ultrasound tech.

"Sorry. I'm coming."

Ginny hops on the table and lifts her shirt. I'm in awe of her. I mean, how can you not be? It's miraculous what a woman's body goes through to grow a human and then what it can go through to deliver that baby.

"This will be a little cold," the tech says as she squirts clear fluid on her belly.

I watch as the tech uses the probe to rub the gel across her belly. Jace's face appears on the screen. She measures his body and the fluid around him. The tech and Ginny are talking about what everything looks like, and I can't take my focus off the screen. A little tear escapes my eye, and I quickly swipe it away.

When Ginny is done, we head to the examination room and wait for Dr. Walker to come in. There is a knock at the door, and he walks in. We exchange pleasantries and then he and Ginny discuss Jace and her. He is concerned about her swelling and says that if Jace doesn't come in the next week that he might have to go ahead and medically induce her. He isn't worried that it will be too soon since she is already thirty-eight weeks along.

After the appointment we decide on pedicures and then lunch. The pedicure was fantastic for my stress, and I know Ginny had a great time because she kept moaning when they were massaging her legs and feet. I couldn't hold it in and laughed a few times. She tried to swat at me, but of course, she missed.

Ginny chooses to have a sandwich at the mom and pop shop that's located on the square. She tells me she has eaten here after every doctor's appointment for all of the kids, and she couldn't ruin the tradition. I don't argue because my turkey club wrap is probably the best I have ever had. I try to ask the owner how they make it, but they say the secret ingredient is love.

I ask Gin if she is up for a little shopping around the square, but she says she is tired. I start walking back to the van, but she tells me to still go shop and she will park her butt on a bench and people watch.

"I love people watching, and it is gorgeous out. I'm going to bask in this quiet moment because they are about to be few and far between." She lays her head back and closes her eyes. Her arms are resting on top of her belly.

"I won't be long. Call me if you need me."

"Take as much time as you need." She waves me off without opening her eyes.

I shop for forty minutes and finish paying for the clothes at the last store. My arms are covered in bags. I'm not sure how I'll fit everything into my suitcase if I leave to go back to NYC. I'm either going to have to buy a new suitcase for the plane or just get rid of some of my baggy clothes. I decide on the latter right away.

When I exit the store, I try juggling the bags and opening the door at the same time. The door swings open and I almost fall, but I bump into someone instead.

"I'm so sorry. Thank you." I say this while looking up.

This is not someone I expected to run into in this town, let alone this store.

"No worries, Saige," Milo replies while smiling. He smells strongly of a campfire.

"What are you doing here?" I look around for Ginny or anyone I recognize.

"Can't a guy shop in a town other than Winter Springs?" He sounds amused.

"Sure, they can. But what are you doing here though? In the doorway of this store?" I point into the lingerie store.

"Can't a guy just buy some lingerie for the girl he's seeing?"

I immediately relax hearing that he is seeing someone. So, he can't be the one leaving the notes if he is seeing someone.

"Oh. Who is the lucky lady?" I ask him curiously.

"It's new so we aren't telling people yet. Is there anything in there you recommend?"

"If it's new, are you sure that lingerie is the way to go?"

He looks pissed at me for asking for a minute, but then he smiles again, "It's not that new, if you know what I'm saying?"

I nod, but I don't know what he is saying. It was only three days ago that he met me at the football game, and we had a date planned for this week. But if finding something for him to buy for his new girl gets him the hell away from me, then I'll definitely find a few pieces for him.

"Of course. Come this way. There are a few sets that I saw that were really cute." I pull a garnet-colored set and an eggplant-colored set off the rack and show him.

"Which do you like? Did you get any of these sets?"

No way am I telling him what lingerie sets I bought because that's just awkward. I answer and avoid the second question altogether. "I think you can't go wrong with either. What size is she?"

"She is a 2xl. Are there sets in her size in here?"

Interesting that she is the same size as me but not so much if plus size is his type. "Yes. They have every style in every size. It's an exclusive store. That's why I love it."

I grab both of the sets in her size off the rack and hand them to him. "Here you go."

He smiles brightly at me, but it's a smile that makes me nervous. "Thanks. I'm going to buy them both. I bet she will love them!"

"I'm sure she will. Well, see ya. My sister-in-law is waiting for me."

"She's inside the van napping."

I look at him strangely. "Okay."

I walk quickly to the van and startle Ginny when I slam the door.

"I'm sorry," I say, trying to calm down.

"Are you okay? What's wrong?" She is concerned, and I don't need to stress her out.

I put on my best fake smile. "Oh, I'm fine. I'm just out of shape. I got winded just carrying these bags everywhere."

"Oh shoot. You scared me for a minute." She relaxes.

"All good."

We sing to the radio all the way home, but my body doesn't relax. I know Milo said he has a new girl, but I find it so odd that she is the same size as me and he just so happens to be in the same town and shop as me. Winter Springs is a small town, so bumping into him there I could understand, but here?

When we make it back, Ginny tries to help me with the bags. I shoo her away because I know she is tired, and the twins will be home soon.

"Go take a nap. If you aren't up yet before Mom drops the girls off, then I will start on their schoolwork if you want. I don't have to shower and leave to meet Megan and Gina until four."

"Thank you." She hugs me and heads to the front door.

I grab the bags and lock up the van. When I make it to the front door, I feel like someone is watching me. I spin around and see Declan on the phone with someone on his front porch. We make eye contact. I break it after a minute and walk inside the house and lock the door.

Oy, this is going to be hard.

Saige

Ginny ends up coming down the stairs as soon as the girls hop out of Mom's car. I head into the kitchen and grab the cookies I made off the counter. Mom sees me and turns to hop in the car to leave just as I make it to the door. I ignore the fact that Mom left to probably avoid me.

Ginny gives me a look that says 'sorry' and squeezes my shoulder before turning to the girls. "Hey, you two. Daddy said he is coming home a little earlier and wants to take us out for dinner. How does that sound?"

"Yes!"

"I want to go to Jesse's pizzeria!"

"Sounds great." She massages her lower back. "Why don't you all go play for thirty minutes and then we will start on your schoolwork so you will be done when he gets home."

The girls groan about only having thirty minutes to play but quickly run to their play set in the backyard, because Gin gives them the mom look.

"When I have kids, you have got to tell me how that mommy look works," I tell her.

"When you have kids, I'll give you all the trade secrets. Promise."

When four rolls around, I head upstairs to get ready. I throw on one of my new outfits and smile at myself in the mirror, looking at the teal V-neck shirt and black high waisted jeans.

Even though Finn's mad at me for not telling him what's going on, he still let me borrow the keys to his jeep. I head upstairs to his room to get them, and I hear a knock behind me.

"I'll get it. You go get the keys," Finn says as he makes his way to the front door.

I hear Megan and Finn chatting at the bottom of the steps when I walk out of the room. I walk down the steps and stand there awkwardly, watching and listening to their conversation, since neither one has noticed that I have come down the stairs.

"I figured I'd pick Saige up so she wouldn't have to borrow anyone's vehicle."

"I was going to let her borrow my jeep if you didn't come, but I was hoping you would."

Megan blushes and looks up at him. "You did?"

Finn rubs the back of his neck "Yeah. I had a great time with you last night."

"I did too. We should do it again."

"Sure. You're paying next time, though." Finn says this with a mischievous smile.

"No way! If it's a date then you, my good man, are paying." She pats him on the chest.

"Then I'd like to retract my statement about doing it again." He smiles.

"You're an ass!"

"But at least I'm a beautiful ass." Their eyes connect and neither one pulls away.

I clear my throat and they both turn abruptly to look at me standing right in front of them.

"How long have you been standing there?" Finn's voice is laced with nerves.

"Since borrowing the jeep or her picking me up, to you being a beautiful ass." I bat my eyelashes and link my hands under my chin.

"Looks like being an ass is hereditary," Finn says and rolls his eyes.

"Maybe so." I smile my biggest smile.

I turn to Megan. "Ready to go?"

"Yes."

As I leave, Finn grabs my arm just under the bicep and spins me around to face him. "We will talk tonight."

"Yes, we will. I want to know what happened last night between you two." I place his keys back into his hand and walk out the door.

~

The restaurant is packed for it being five on a Tuesday night. Gina is sitting at a booth in the back corner near the wide wall of windows that overlook Main Street. Megan slides into the booth next to Gina, and I sit across from them.

"Have you been sitting here long?" I ask Gina.

"Not that long. Why?"

"Because you have eaten the entire basket of breadsticks and your tea is empty," I say in observation.

"Girl, you have crumbs all over your boobs," Megan says while trying to wipe them off.

"I can wipe the crumbs off myself, Meg. No need to fondle me." Gina is mortified that Megan just did that in public.

"I know. Whew wee. That was the most action I've gotten in a long time."

"Meg, do you need to fondle my boobs too so you can feel better?" I say, chuckling, knowing Gina is so embarrassed.

Megan leans over the table like she is about to grab my boobs. "Will you two quit it!" Gina squeals out. "My god! I can't take either of you anywhere."

"Relax, G. We were only playing. You need to take something for that tense mood of yours because you are wound up like a freaking top," Megan says to Gina.

The waiter comes over in time to ask for our order. Once he leaves to give us a few minutes to look at the menu, I look up and out of the windows, sensing someone watching me again. But, yet again, no one is there.

"What are you looking at?" Gina asks me, turning around to look outside.

I shake my head. "Nothing. I just felt like someone was watching us but there was no one. I swear I'm losing my mind."

Megan and Gina exchange glances.

"So, how has everything been since Milo stalked you at the game?" asks Gina.

"Fine. I volunteered at the women's shelter and had a date with Declan afterwards, and then last night Finn, Declan, Megan, and I did karaoke."

"That's not all Saige did with Declan last night." Megan winks at me.

Gina looks at me and smiles. "Oh yeah? What did you do Saige?"

"Nothing. He dropped me off at home and I went to bed."

"Uh-huh. I'm sure that's what happened. We are your best friends. You can't fool us and tell us you didn't roll in the sheets with that beautiful Adonis," Megan says, not believing anything I say.

"I'm serious. He dropped me off and then I texted him I was sick, so I stayed home."

"Oh. You were sick? Do you feel better?" Gina asks with sincerity.

Before I could respond to Gina, Megan blurts out, "I call bullshit. You were not sick. You and him were practically undressing each other with your eyes at the bar last night. What really happened?"

I rub my hands on my jeans and look at both of them. I tell them everything from the beginning, from the date with Declan and receiving my first note, to the earbuds and blanket fiasco, and then to finding the other note as I was heading out the door to go to Declan and confess my feelings to him. I pull out the notes from my purse and hand them to the girls. It takes both of them a few minutes to comprehend everything I am telling them.

"Was it Milo? Do Finn and River know?" Gina and Megan ask at the same time.

"I don't know if it was Milo. The notes are still vague, but it is weird that after I broke it off with Milo these started showing up. River and Finn do not know any of this, except for the earbuds and blanket thing, and they think I just dreamed it all up. Finn does want to talk when I get home tonight because he knows something is up."

"If you don't tell him, I will." Megan is pissed that I haven't told anyone.

"And Declan deserves to know also. You and him like each other, and you can't have this secret between you two, especially if you are both serious," Gina adds.

"Which is precisely why I told him we need to just stay friends and that I need some space. I'm not going to drag him into this."

"Saige," Megan grits out.

"Megan. I love you, but please stop. I don't know what to do any more than anyone else. I'm not going to drag anyone, and I mean anyone, into this. That's why I haven't told anyone until now."

Gina grabs my hand across the table. "But you have to tell people and allow us to help you in any way we can. You can't push us away. That goes for all of the guys in your life, too."

I nod. Tears start falling out of my eyes. "I know. I feel like I'm a magnet for trouble. I go to New York and start a life there and then Philippe enters my life. Then I come here and all of this shit starts happening."

"Here you go, ladies."

The waiter puts our plates of food in front of us, and I turn away to wipe my eyes with the napkin. I turn towards the waiter and smile in thanks.

We eat in silence, as all of this is a huge cloud in between us and none of us know how to break through it. But I can't let this be caused by me either.

After finishing my drink in one gulp, I muster enough courage to try and break the silence. It seems like the other girls manage to do the same because we all talk at once. I'm so thankful for it because then we all break out in laughter.

"Megan. I have a question for you?" I ask.

"Okay, shoot."

"What's going on with you and my brother?"

"I figured this question was going to come sometime tonight. I'm just surprised it took you so long." She looks down at her hands in her lap.

"Brother? Finn? What is going on?" Gina leans in to hear the juicy details.

"Nothing is going on. We just had a good time last night. He is not too terrible."

"Bullshit," I say, using Megan's word against her. "Spill. You all are always yanking each other's chain and then I come down the stairs to you lost in your own little lust bubble tonight. They didn't even hear me until I was right beside them and cleared my throat."

"Well, we sang a karaoke song together last night, played pool, had some more drinks, and then when I dropped him off, we kissed." She whispers the last word.

I cup my ear. "You're going to have to speak louder. I couldn't quite catch that last word."

"You kissed Finn! Oh my God, how was it?" Gina squeals.

"Well, we both leaned in at the same time and hit heads. We joked at the other's expense about that. But then our eyes locked and then our lips followed suit. It was a beautiful kiss. But your brother pulled away and got out of the car to go inside. So, when he told me at the house that he was glad I came over to get you, I was confused because he agreed to do it again but then started joking around. I don't know if he meant to just hang out or if he meant repeating the kiss. He's doing my head in with his mixed signals."

"Why can't guys just tell us what they want? They put up this macho wall and then leave us to second guess whether they really like us or just enjoy having us there to play with," I say, pissed off.

"Saige. There is no way in hell that Declan isn't head over heels for you. No one has emotions that strong for someone unless they feel something true for them. You said he looked so distraught when you all looked at each other from across the road. He's probably so miserable not knowing what he did wrong," Gina says.

"Yeah, you and him are acting like idiots," Megan adds.

"Hey!"

"Just go to your man tonight, jump on top of him and shag his bones. Let your body express how much you mean to each other," Megan emphasizes.

"Yeah. I wouldn't exactly put it as eloquently as Megan, but yeah, go confess your love to him. It's awesome how amazing life is with the one you love by your side."

"I'm not sure jumping his bones is what I will do, but I will go talk to him tonight about everything. I just have to talk to Finn first."

"I may have to call it a night. I'm so tired," Gina says as she yawns loudly.

"I take it that growing a baby is tiring?" I ask.

"Girl, I'm lucky to make it to nine before passing out. And don't get me started on the morning sickness that hits all day."

"Eww! I'm never going to have a baby. Uh-uh! No way," Megan says disgusted.

"Just wait until I tell you all about giving birth."

"Oh no!" Megan plugs her ears. "I don't want to hear it."

"Well, I'll see you girls later." Gina gives us both a hug and I watch her walk to her car.

~

Megan and I go to her car an hour later. Without communicating verbally, we are on the same wavelength. Megan pulls up to the Tastee Freeze and we both order an ice cream. What's dinner without dessert, right? We head to the hiding spot we found when we were growing up together. It's an abandoned tree house in the woods outside the city.

We don't know who built it, but we came across it one day after school when we went exploring, because neither one of us wanted to go home to our parents. My parents were constantly fighting about this and that and hers were there but never really there, if that makes any sense. We soon made it our home away from home. We put posters up on the walls, wrote in our diaries there, and chatted until late, probably about boys.

When we arrive at the treehouse, it looks a little worn from the elements. Some of the wooden planks look like they need to be replaced, but all in all it is still sturdy. We climb up the ladder to get inside and laugh at how much harder it is to climb now that we are older and more out of shape.

We sit down next to each other on the ground and become silent. We are overcome with memories and emotions. When we met Gina our freshman year, we brought her back with us to this treehouse knowing she was going to be our third musketeer. We went through many breakups, life altering events, and the normal days of just wanting to escape for a while.

I run my fingers over our carved initials, and Megan grabs my hand. "It will be alright."

I squeeze back. "I hope so."

I lay my head back against the wooden wall and a tear escapes my eye. Megan lets go of my hand and throws her arm over my shoulder. I lean into her, and she wraps her arms around me.

"Just let it out. I know you don't like to cry or show emotion, but I know you are scared. I'm your safe space. Let it all out. Scream if you want to."

And just like that, the tears start flowing and I am sobbing uncontrollably. Megan never let's go and instead holds on harder. She starts running her hands through my hair and rocking us back and forth. When I can't cry any longer, I sit up.

"I think I need to scream now."

"Well, get at it then." She motions her hands towards the railing.

I stand up, walk over to it, and brace myself. I let out a weak scream.

"Oh, come on. You can do better than that." Megan joins me at the railing, and she screams louder than I do.

I grip the railing harder and scream as loud as I can.

"Felt good, didn't it?" she asks.

"Yeah. It really did. Okay, well, I should get back and talk to both Finn and Declan."

"Let's do it. Let's get you home to that fine brother of yours so you can see that handsome man of yours."

I brush my shoulder against hers. "I knew you liked him."

"Yeah, well, I have eyes. I still don't know where he stands, and I'm not going to throw myself at him. But I will not fight whatever happens."

We make our way down the ladder and towards the car.

Saige

When Megan drops me off, Finn is waiting on the porch for me and stands up from the wicker couch he was sitting on.

"Waiting up for me?" I ask.

He takes a sip from the beer in his hands. "I was beginning to wonder if you were going to show. Especially since you knew you had to talk to me."

"I'm ready to talk now. Is River home? He deserves to hear this too."

"He is. He's watching a movie with Gin on the couch."

"Well, let's go find him." I swing my arms towards the house.

I climb onto the porch, and Finn opens the door to me. When we enter the house, Gin and Riv both look over at us. River can see the looks on our faces, so he tells Ginny he will be right back. He kisses her forehead and follows us into the kitchen.

I ask them to sit down at the island bar stools and stand on the opposite side from them, leaning against the kitchen sink with my arms crossed. I look down at my shoes, afraid of how this might transpire.

"What's going on, Sis?" River asks.

A small tear escapes my eye. "Well," I say choking on my words.

I feel Finn's arms around me, and I look up at him. "Smalls, you are scaring us. What is going on?"

I fish the notes out of my purse and hand each one to my brothers. They read them and then switch. Bile rises in my throat, and I feel like I am going to pass out.

"What is this?" Finn asks, afraid of what my answer will be.

I glance at the letters. "Well, the letter in River's hand I found on my car when Declan and I had the date at City Lake. We had a picnic and then went hiking to the wildflowers. We kissed on the hike and then when I got back to my car, it was folded up and underneath one of my windshield wipers."

"The second letter I found last night. Finn, Megan, Declan, and I went to karaoke and then Declan drove me home. I told him I was going to come here and change into sweats and a tank top and then I was going to come over to his house. I walked out the door and locked it. When I was turning around, I saw the second note folded up underneath the welcome mat. So, I canceled with Declan because I was afraid and didn't want to bring him into this."

"This was Milo, wasn't it?" Finn is angry.

"I'm not sure." I lower my head again.

"It has to be fucking Milo!" He screams.

River looks at the door. "Will you be quiet? I don't want Ginny to hear and go into labor early. I will put tail on Milo and keep the neighborhood on patrolled watch, but I can't do a whole lot else since we can't prove it's him."

"Oh, it's him," Finn grits out.

"Is that why you were freaking out when you thought you fell asleep with your earbuds in, and your bedding was messed up?" River asks, changing the subject.

Finn looks away after getting caught talking to River about me.

I touch his arm. "It's okay. I heard you two talking about me when I was climbing the stairs to get ready for Ginny's appointment. Yes, I know I wasn't dreaming. I remember seeing the sunshine through the curtains, knowing I didn't get any sleep. The blankets were all on the floor and the pillows were crumpled into a pile on the side of the bed. I then heard y'all walking past my room talking about breakfast, and you were trying to shush the girls so they wouldn't wake us.

"After you all went downstairs, I put my earbuds in, played music and closed my eyes. I must have fallen asleep because I didn't sleep that night, with being worried about the two letters. When I woke up my earbuds were out of my ears and in the charging case in the bedside drawer. I didn't take them out and none of you did. The pillows were all under my head and the blankets were on me. I know I didn't dream it up."

Finn leaves the room, and River and I follow him. He climbs the stairs two at a time, and when I manage to make it upstairs, he is in my room going through my closet.

"What are you doing in my room?"

"Good thinking." River starts looking too.

"Good thinking? What is going on?" I stand with my hands on my hips.

Neither one answers me.

"Stop!" I yell, and they both jump. "Will someone please tell me what the hell is going on?!"

"If you think someone took your earbuds out and it was none of us, then someone was here and took them out when you were sleeping. We are going to see if anything was left behind by this someone," Finn responds.

"But River, Ginny and the girls were downstairs eating breakfast. There is no way someone could have come inside and went up the stairs without Ginny noticing."

"But we weren't downstairs. The girls couldn't make up their mind and I didn't want Gin making multiple meals, so I took them all up to go get McDonald's breakfast." River looks at me.

I shake my head. "But Ginny had breakfast made for me on a plate when I came down."

"It was McDonald's. She just moved it to a plate for you."

"Oh," I whisper.

"Can we please finish searching? I want to know who is sending these letters to our sister." Finn sounds annoyed that we are talking and not looking.

"How are you two going to know what's out of the ordinary? Why don't you let me check? It won't take long."

They sit down on my bed while I search my closet. Nothing is different other than the clothes Finn rummaged through. Next, I look through the suitcases, and they are empty. I look in the bedside drawer and under the bed. Everything looks normal. I start going through the drawers in my dresser one by one, and I freeze.

I get sick to my stomach and run to the bathroom to throw up.

When I walk back in, they both look at me worried. My face is pale, and my skin is clammy. I'm shaking and dizzy. They both stand up and come over to me.

"Are you sick?" River asks.

I shake my head. "No."

"What is it then?" Finn asks.

I walk to the dresser and reach into the drawer. I pull out the eggplant and garnet lingerie sets I showed Milo and throw them on the bed. I grab the letter out and hold it in shock.

River snatches it out of my hands, and he reads it while Finn reads over his shoulder.

"I didn't tell you everything," I whisper, holding back tears.

"What do you mean?" I can see the fire blazing in Finn's eyes as he grabs the letter from Riv to take a closer look.

You should always be showered with gifts.

These will look perfect on you.

Think of me when you wear them.

I hope to see these on you soon.

It's a date.

"I saw Milo today after Ginny's appointment."

"Where did you see him? Here or in Huntington?" River asks.

"Huntington. Ginny and I had pedicures and lunch in the square. I asked if she wanted to go shopping since I needed new clothes, and she said that she was tired, but she would sit on the bench and watch the people around her."

"I've never met another woman that loves to watch people as much as my Gin." River smiles.

"Go on." Finn sounds like he is going to combust if I don't finish my story soon.

"So, I made my way around the square and was just leaving the lingerie store when I saw him standing in the doorway. He said he was dating someone new and wanted to pick a few things up for her. These items were my size, and I was confused by that, but I thought maybe he just likes bigger girls. He grabbed those lingerie sets and said she would love them and then he bought them. And now they are here, in this drawer, for me, in your house. I can't stay here."

"Now, hold on a minute. I'm going to take these letters and see what evidence we can get from them. If we are able to connect them to Milo, then we will file a restraining order and I can work on arresting him. You aren't going anywhere. I can protect you when you are here," River says, and he leaves to go downstairs with the letters and lingerie.

"Finn, I can't stay here. I can't put Ginny and the girls in harm's way if this is Milo and he's malicious."

He pulls out his phone and waits for an answer.

"Declan, Saige and I are coming over."

He hangs up, grabs my suitcase out of the closet and throws it onto the bed.

"Pack some clothes and necessities. You're bunking with Dec."

~

Once I finish packing, Finn grabs my suitcase and my hand and drags me downstairs.

"Where are you two going?" Ginny comes out of the kitchen to ask. She is curious and hopes someone will tell her the truth because she knows there is something being kept from her, and she doesn't like it.

"Saige is going to stay with Declan for a bit," Finn responds while trying to yank me out the door.

I pull my hand away and walk to Ginny. "Ginny, do you really want to know?"

At that moment, River walks into the room, his work phone in hand, and sees what is about to happen. "Absolutely not!"

Gin ignores him and grabs my hand while looking at me. "Yes, I do. I know it is something serious and you all are afraid to tell me in fear that I'll go into labor, but remember what Dr. Walker said? He told me I need to deliver by Thursday, or he will induce me anyway because of the swelling. So, if I go into labor from you telling me then I don't have to deal with all the crap of inducing me."

"Okay." I lead her into the living room and tell her everything while Finn and River stand in the doorway listening.

"I understand why you want to go live with Declan for a while, but you don't have to leave if you don't want to. River can protect you."

I grab her hand. "I'm not going to put you or the girls in harm's way if this is really something. He's been in this house twice now, that we know of. I think it would be better for me to leave."

She pats my hand. "I understand. We love you and want you safe."

I hug her and get off the couch. I walk to River, and we say all we need to say with our eyes. He hands Finn the bag with the lingerie and notes in it. Finn promises to bring it right back, and then he grabs my hand, and we head to Declan's.

Declan

I've been waiting anxiously for Finn and Saige to come over. I pace the living room, making invisible marks on the hardwood floor.

I wouldn't have been worried or pacing if I didn't hear the tone of Finn's voice. It's just that he sounded angry, scared, and sad all at the same time. I pick up my phone to call Saige and then Finn, but neither answer.

I pace some more.

Knock. Knock.

I try to keep myself from running to the door and settle for a fast paced walk instead. When I open the door, I take a mental picture of the two of them standing in front of me. Finn has a suitcase in his hand and is pissed. I turn to Saige, and her eyes are swollen like she has been crying. She keeps staring at her feet and won't make eye contact with me at all.

"What happened?" I ask, getting closer to Saige. I tip her chin up and stare into her big, beautiful, brown eyes.

"Can we come in?" Finn asks, pushing the door open and walking through.

I grab Saige's hand and pull her through the doorway with me. Whatever this is, it has to do with her, and I want, no, need to know what it is.

I turn to Finn. "Okay, what is going on?"

He places the suitcase on the coffee table and pops it open. He then takes out an evidence bag and I see the colors of purple and red, but I can't quite make out what they are. He grabs three smaller bags out and hands them to me. I look down and realize they are notes, and I begin to read.

"Milo. Fucking Milo!" I shout to no one and everyone at the same time.

"That's why I tried to stay away." She explains that when she received the letters, she was scared of the threats directed at me and that is why she tried to let me go, and then she adds, "But that's not all."

I finally meet her eyes and see she is trying to find her voice. It comes out softly, and a few tears fall from her face, but she tells me about what happened to her this morning. Silence fills her as she thinks about how to word her next sentence. I reassure her, but I don't think I was prepared to hear what happened next. Finn hands me the colored sealed bag.

Milo stalked her in Huntington and pretended to have a girlfriend. All the while he was probably smiling to himself knowing that she just helped him pick up the lingerie that he would be delivering to her dresser drawer that morning.

I'll fucking kill him.

"Did he touch you or hurt you?" I let go of the anger quickly to make sure my girl is okay. She is all I care about at this moment.

"I'm fine. I don't think I was touched, but knowing he was in my room when I was sleeping gives me chills. He's invaded my space twice now."

"Where is Milo?" I say through clenched teeth.

"I don't know, but River said not to do anything. They are going to run a test on the lingerie and the last note and then they will try to build up a case against him. If we do anything right now, we can hurt the case and then Milo may never be punished."

"Now, I don't like this anymore than you do. I want nothing more than to pulverize the guy, but I'm not going to do anything, and neither are you. The best thing we can do is make sure our girl here is taken care of and that no harm comes to her. Are you willing to help?"

"I'd do anything for Saige. Is the suitcase here because you are going to stay with me?" I ask her, hoping her answer is yes.

"If you will have me? If not, then I will ask my mother."

I wrap my arms around her waist. "You are not going to live with her. You are going to stay here where you belong."

Her face brightens up, and she smiles at me.

"Well, I'm going to skedaddle. You two have a lot to catch up on. I will make sure to update you when River comes back."

I hear Finn retreat to the front door as I pull Saige close to me and taste her soft, full lips once more. When we pull away, I have a head rush.

"You are safe in these arms, okay? I will not let anything happen to you."

"I know. But I'm honestly more worried about you. It killed me to have to stay away from you, but I thought by doing so I'd keep you safe."

"Don't worry about me. I'll be fine as long as you are. Why

don't you go take a bath to relax while I get the guest room ready for you? Would you like a glass of wine to drink while you are in there?"

"Yes, please."

She follows me into the kitchen and watches me pour her a glass. I start to walk out of the room to go take care of the guest room when she grabs my arm to stop me.

"Declan. Thank you for taking care of me. I know you don't have to."

"Of course, I do. You mean the world to me."

And I walk away before I say anything more. She needs to relax and get some rest before we talk some more. I know she has to be exhausted, and now is not the time to be selfish and ask her to confess her feelings to me.

I grab her suitcase and walk into the room that will now be hers. I haven't even gotten around to cleaning this room, so I sit the suitcase on top of the dresser and go get cleaning supplies to make sure the room is clean enough for her.

~

When she comes into the room, she is only in a towel. She stops when she notices me.

"Oh. I'm sorry. I forgot my suitcase and I had nothing to wear."

"Don't apologize. It was my fault. I was hoping to have this room done before you got out, but I didn't. I just need to finish changing the sheets and duvet cover and then you will be good to go."

She mutters a 'thank you' and scampers back into the bathroom with her suitcase in hand. I stand up and adjust my pants. I hurry up getting her room ready. I want to be done and out of the room by the time she emerges from the bathroom.

~

I'm sitting on the couch with Luna in my lap eating leftovers when she comes out of her room. She's wearing a baggy t-shirt that is a size too big and yoga pants.

"Are you hungry?" I ask.

"No, I ate with Megan and Gina before I talked to River and Finn. What are you watching?" she asks, sitting beside me on the couch. The smell of her lavender shampoo fills my nose. I inhale deeply and immediately relax.

Luna jumps off my lap and wags her tail all the way over onto Saige's.

"John Wick is on. Do you want to watch it? If not, we can watch something else."

"No. John Wick is fine. Keanu Reeves is an amazing actor. I love his movies."

"I do too."

Halfway through the movie her eyes are getting droopy, and I start to feel her head drop onto my shoulder. I plan to let her sleep for a little bit right next to me until her head jerks upright, like her body reacts to the proximity between us.

"I'm going to have to take a rain check on the movie. I think I'm going to go to bed. I'm tired."

"Adrenaline will do that to you. I hope you sleep well."

"Me too." She blushes and walks away.

"Just remember if you need me, I am right down the hall from you. No matter the time."

She nods. "Thank you."

I watch her walk down the hall and then I hear her door close.

When the movie is over, I turn off the lights, lock the doors and check on Saige. I peer inside, but because it is so dark, I have to walk to the bed to see her.

I look down at her resting body lying in the bed. The blanket laying across her lower back exposes the lace bra she is wearing. She's a beautiful sight. Like a priceless painting just waiting to be put on display.

Her mouth is partially open but not quite smiling, and her cheeks are flushed with sleep. Her back is rising and falling slowly and soothingly. I can imagine lying in bed listening to her breathing and falling asleep to it every night. It would be like listening to a meditation CD at night.

She is there, waiting for me, calling to me, her lavender scent heavy in the bedroom. Gazing at her, I have this undeniable and primal urge to claim the beautiful Saige. I imagine her voice saying my name in a seductive way, which sends shivers down my spine. I would pull her into my arms and claim her mouth as my own. My heart stops, and it feels like a lump forms in my throat, just thinking of everything else I would like to do to her. I blink erratically and turn on my heels.

~

I lie in bed after the shower punching myself mentally for thinking of Saige that way and having to rub one out when I know this is a vulnerable time for her. It is around one in the morning when I start falling asleep and I hear her crying in the next room. I go back and forth in my head, not knowing if I should go to her. I make a split decision and jump out of the bed.

When I knock on her door, I hear silence on the other side. After a bit more knocking and not hearing anything, I figure she fell back asleep. It doesn't take very long after climbing into my king size bed to fall asleep myself. I'm soon startled awake hearing her screaming bloody murder from her room.

I run in to the room without knocking on her door and kneel by her bed. I run my hands through her hair, trying to soothe her with the pointer finger of my other hand, rubbing up and down her cheek. Her eyes shoot open, and she lifts herself up in the bed, turning her head side to side, not realizing where she is. I jump up off the floor and onto the bed and cup her face in my hands.

"Shhh. Saige, it's Declan. I have you, love."

Her body relaxes at the sound of my voice, and her eyes land on my face. "Declan?"

"Yeah. It's me. You are safe, my love. I won't let anyone hurt you." I wrap my arms around her.

She clings to me, and I feel wet, hot tears dripping onto my bare chest. I just hold her until she quiets down. She lets go once her shaking has stopped and starts wiping her eyes.

"Do you want to tell me about it?"

"It was just a nightmare. I'm okay."

"You know you can talk to me, right? About anything."

"I know. Thank you."

"Do you want to try to get some more sleep?"

"I think so. Will you stay with me?"

"Of course. Anything you need."

I help tuck her in and pull the covers over her. I sit down beside her on top of the covers, and she rolls over to lay her head on my lap. I run my hands through her hair until her body relaxes into a deep slumber.

My back starts aching thirty minutes later, and so I try to sneak out from under her. I almost make it until her hand shoots out and grabs my wrist.

"Don't leave me, please."

"I won't. I'm going to move to the chair in the corner while I keep an eye on you."

"While it is a beautiful red lounge chair, it does not look like a comfortable chair to sleep in. You can lay here with me."

"No, the chair is perfectly comfortable to sleep in." No, it's not. My back will hate me in the morning.

"I insist. This bed is big enough for us."

"Okay." I lift the cover up and slip inside. She rolls over and places her head on my chest.

"Is this alright?" she asks.

I curl my arm around her. "This is perfect."

It doesn't take long for sleep to take me again.

Saige

Wednesday

I wake up in the morning, or perhaps afternoon, feeling a heavy weight on me and hot breath blowing on my neck. I turn to see Declan's face pushed right up to my neck, like he is nuzzling it, and my hair is splayed across his face. His left arm is crushed underneath my waist and his right arm is laying on top of my belly. Close enough that the thoughts of his fingers tracing the outline of where his arm is floods me with heat. His legs are entwined with mine so I can't tell whose limbs are whose.

I grab his hand and slowly try to lift it off me. It only makes him tighten up his grip, but at least he moves his legs off mine. I really need to pee, and if he doesn't let go, our first memory of waking up together is going to be me peeing the bed.

I try to lift his arm again. This time I manage to get it off me, but when I try to sit up, I realize that my hair is not only on top of his face but underneath his head also. Why do movies make it so romantic? Either the man and woman wake up at the same time or at least it is easy for the woman to get out of the man's embrace. Well, that is not the case here.

I lay back down and start to work on wedging my hair out from under him. It takes some time, but I finally manage to do it at the same time that he starts waking up. I get up quickly and run to the bathroom before he fully wakes up.

I take a few extra minutes in the bathroom brushing my teeth, putting on deodorant and trying to brush the tangles out of my wild mane. I realize I am only in my black lace bra and matching lace boy shorts. Of course, my clothes are still in the bedroom.

I work up the courage to walk back into my room and see Declan laying in the middle of the bed with the sheet covering only his lower half. If someone was here with me, I would have begged them to pinch me. I still can't get over the fact that I am here at this moment and a half naked Declan is lying in my bed.

"Hello, gorgeous!" I blush at his words. Surprisingly, I don't feel the need to cover myself anymore. "Wipe up that drool, love, and come join me in bed." He winks at me, and I turn into a puddle right there.

I climb into bed under the covers he is holding up. I put some distance between us because I'm not sure how close is close enough for him.

"What are you doing over there?" He grabs my waist and pulls me flush to his. "That's better."

He smells my neck. "You smell divine. Lavender?"

"Yes."

"I think it's my new favorite scent." He starts running his fingers up and down my exposed belly. "So soft and beautiful."

I turn around to face him and look down as I run my fingers over his rock-hard abs. "So hard and handsome."

"That's not the only thing that's hard."

I tense up. "Oh." I'm filled with heat, shock, and a sense of excitement.

"Don't worry, Saige. I'm not going to have sex with you until you are ready. I'm going to go make breakfast." He plants a kiss on my cheek, jumps out of the bed in only boxer shorts, and walks out of the room.

After a few minutes, I walk to my suitcase and put on a pair of leggings and a button-down shirt I have for chilly days. I walk out of the room into the kitchen. Dec is bending down fishing a pan out of a drawer to cook with. I stop for a minute to admire his fine derriere.

"You're staring at me again."

"Yes I am." I look into his eyes, and he leans against the counter behind him.

"What are you exactly staring at, love?" He walks around the island, stops in front of me and places his hands on my hips.

"You are very good looking, and I couldn't help but check out your butt as you were bending down."

"I'm not the only one that has a great butt," he says while his hands travel down my hips to grab a handful. "That's right. I've been admiring you, also."

"Why me?"

He tips my chin up to meet his face and asks, "What did you say?"

I step back and place my hands across my chest. "I said, why me? Why do you like me? Look at you and look at me. You look like a Greek god and I'm just a—"

"Do not finish that sentence," he says through gritted teeth. "You are caring, curvy, and sexy as hell."

"I'm not curvy. I'm plus size and have rolls where curves should be. You could have any woman you want. Why did you choose me?" I pinch my waist and look down again.

"You see rolls, I see a beautiful body that needs to be worshipped. You think you are ugly; I think you are the most beautiful woman staring back at me."

He lifts my chin up and stares deeply into my eyes. "I have never had anyone that took care of me or cared about my well-being more than you. You are so special to me. I love you, Saige."

I look up at him through my eyelashes. "You love me?"

"Yes, I have loved you from afar since high school. I treated you like you were nothing but Finn's little sister. Little Saige. But I only did it because I didn't want to taint you with my world. My dad beat the shit out of me daily and my mom did nothing about it. I hardly ate, and I feared sleep because I never knew when Dad would come at me and beat me. Your house, your family, you were the only saving grace from my reality."

"You took care of me when my parents chose not to. You stopped me from making big mistakes, and you never asked for anything in return. You didn't think twice about buying me items for your house or making me my favorite meals when I came over. To you, it was no big deal. Just something nice to do. But to me it was like God blessed me with an angel to save me. You were that angel."

"Once we graduated, I thought about you all the time. I had girlfriends and friends with benefits. I'm not going to lie about my past, but I could never settle down with any of them because none could compare to you. Nothing could compare to what you did for me selflessly."

"You then blew into my world five days ago, and all of the feelings I had from back then just became so overwhelming that I told myself it was just lust or infatuation, because you are a beautiful woman. I tried to talk myself out of thinking it was love."

"Anyone would look at this and say, how could one know they love someone after only five days? Well, they can, and I do. I'm done admiring you from afar and lying to myself. I want to love you wholeheartedly right here and right now. I want to be there for you through the good and the bad. I want to be part of your past, present, and future." He leans down and whispers in my ear. "Is that alright with you?"

Declan

Her mouth is parted, and her lips are a deep pink color. Her eyes are wide, and she sucks in a breath. She nods. I rub my thumb on her bottom lip, dreaming of claiming them with mine again so I can see the red color return.

"I'm going to kiss you again," I say.

She doesn't move when I place a gentle kiss on her lips. When I pull away, she blinks as if she has snapped out of a trance.

Next thing I know she grabs the back of my head and pulls my lips to hers. Our mouth's part, and our tongues dance with one another as if they know each other's next move. Her hands wind around my waist to pull me flush against her, and my hands grab her ass. I give her a little squeeze wondering how empty they have been until now.

I push her into the pantry door and place one hand to the right of her head against the door, while the other slowly skims her curves, until I reach her jaw. I pull away long enough so I can give attention and care to the rest of her body. I rain kisses up and down her neck and feel her body shudder against mine.

"Declan," she moans.

I claim her mouth once more and feel her hands run up my chest and then rake back down past my abs. My body flexes underneath her hands, leaving a burning fire everywhere. My dick jumps, fighting to rip through my jeans. This time it's my turn to moan her name.

"Declan, I want you," she pants.

"Are you sure? I'll happily oblige, because I want nothing more than to claim your body, but I want you to be absolutely sure."

She nods. "Take me. Claim me. Make me yours."

She doesn't have to say it twice. Today I am going to feast on the woman I love. The woman who has had my heart for years. I grab her hand and lead her to my room.

She stops in the doorway. "I had a dream about this moment," she says as she takes in my large master bedroom. "But I didn't picture your room looking like this."

"What did you picture?" I ask, trying to rein in my primal urges, because I want to go at her pace. I want to show her that I want to love her and bring our bodies together as one. She isn't a quick lay to me, so this is a first. I know, deep down, that I will be sharing many things with her.

"Well, I thought your walls would be a typical beige color like most people who hate painting, or a very dark color. Like a masculine dominatrix color. You know, deep red, dark gray or black."

I laugh at the dominatrix comment.

"But your walls are painted a gorgeous teal, and you have a gray bed frame that has a headboard. I've never met a man that has a headboard, unless a woman bought the bed. And look at this artwork." She steps towards the abstract mountain canvases on the wall above my long dresser and takes in each one before moving to the other paintings in the room.

"This room looks nothing like the rest of the house."

"That's because this is the only room I have remodeled so far. When I'm through with it, this house will be brand new inside and out."

"I can't wait to see it when it is fully remodeled." She looks around some more and then freezes. Her brow furrows and she bites her bottom lip.

Saige

"Saige." He pulls me out of my thoughts. He is grinning at me, like he knows exactly what I'm thinking.

"What?"

"Get out of that beautiful head of yours."

"I asked to come back here for one reason and then I just made us stop cold turkey so I could check out your bedroom. I'm stupid." I'm so embarrassed.

He walks back over to me and lifts up my chin. "Don't call yourself stupid. It's okay. I told you I love you. I plan on spending the rest of my life making love to you. If you don't want to then we don't have to. If you want to talk about my wall color or bedroom decor, then we will."

"No! I do. I really do. You make me feel beautiful and safe, and I want nothing more than to have you take me to bed. I've been wishing for you to be mine since high school. I wished every night that you would finally notice me and that I would be yours."

Declan cradles my face in his hand. "I was always yours. I

was just too immature to realize it. You will also still be mine even if we don't have sex."

"No. Just listen," I sigh heavily. "I had the biggest crush on you in high school. I knew I was just Finn's little sister, and I thought you were only nice to me because of that. I didn't realize you loved me back then and the reason why you tried to stay away. There would be certain moments where I would be talking to you, and I wanted nothing more than for you to lean forward and kiss me or tell me I was beautiful."

"I watched you go from girl to girl, and I saw what your type was, and they were the furthest thing from me. But I would watch you. I'd watch the way you'd entwine your fingers with theirs; I'd watch the way you would caress their cheeks or place your hand on the small of their backs. I yearned for that with you."

"Then I came home after being dumped by a jackass and you came wandering up my brother's driveway. My palms were sweaty, my heart was in my throat, and I was so anxious. Because then, and now, I wanted to still be yours. You started flirting with me and then called me Little Saige, and I didn't know what to believe; the guy who just thought of me as a little sister and a friend or the guy who finally opened his eyes and saw me. So, I put up a wall with you because I would rather dream my life with you, than have my heart broken all over again, especially by someone I crushed hard on.

"So, I was defensive, but then you kept flirting with me. At the bar, the first night, my dream came true back in the pool area. You saw me, and my heart mended a few of its cracks. I held on to that, but I knew what you were like in high school, and I still didn't know if you were playing me and if I would be a part of your little game."

"Then, it was like fate stepped in because you rescued me from the pouring rain after I rescued Luna from being tangled in the woods. Our first kiss was so intense, and I pulled away because I wanted us being together to mean something. I didn't want to be another conquest."

Declan tries to cut in, but I stop him.

"I now know I wouldn't have been, but you have to see my luck with guys and know why I was so hesitant. I didn't know the Declan that's in front of me." I motion to him. "I only knew Declan in high school, and he was a known player."

He nods with his eyes downcast.

"Now, the football game was a fiasco, and I don't need to bring that one up since we both know what transpired that day. But our first date was magical. My heart was beating so fast when Leo called us soulmates. I was happy, but I also was afraid that you would go running for the hills. When you didn't, I immediately knew the kind of man you were. You are thoughtful, generous, caring, loving, and funny. The picnic and hike couldn't have turned out better if I planned it."

"We just mesh well, and I never feel more like me than when I am with you. You make me feel beautiful. I don't feel like I need to hide any part of me."

"That's because you don't."

"If you could change anything about me, would you?"

"What kind of question is that? Of course, I wouldn't change anything. You are the most amazing woman I have ever met. You are my Goddess, and I will worship you every day if you'll let me."

"It's funny you say that because the girls and I call you Adonis. He was the Greek god of beauty and desire."

"Well, if I'm Adonis then you are Aphrodite. Minus the fair skin and blond hair."

"They were lovers, you know," I say, gauging his reaction.

"I know." He winks and wraps his arms around me.

I take a deep breath and pause for a few seconds before saying with absolution, "I love you."

He freezes and slowly meets my eyes. "What did you say?"

"You heard me. I love you, Declan Wolfe."

And on that note, Declan cups the back of my head as his lips meet mine in a hurried rush.

"You have made me the happiest man in the world," he says in between the kisses.

I quickly try to unbutton the shirt I am wearing when strong hands stop me.

"If we are going to do this, we are going to take our time. I want our first time to be passionate. I want every emotion to be heightened. I want you to feel loved and cherished and feel it through every sense, every nerve, and every fiber of your being."

"Yes, sir," I say, blushing.

"Sir? I like that."

"Don't let it get to your head, big guy. Only in the bedroom will I be calling you sir." I place a quick kiss on his lips.

He pulls my hands away from the buttons and closes in on a kiss where our mouths become one. He pulls away only to pepper kisses up and down my neck, focusing on the area behind my ear. I grab him through the fabric of his pants; his breath hitches with arousal. The sound sends a shiver down my spine and heat pools below.

He pulls away to gaze into my eyes as his hands undo the buttons of my shirt in slow motion. I silently plead with him to rip the damn thing off, but I also enjoy the build-up of need for him and the burning desire that is shining in his eyes for me. When the last button is undone, he lets the shirt slowly slide off of me while his hands follow behind, leaving a trail of heat over every inch that he touches. I look up at the man that is gazing at me in my black lace bra.

"Beautiful," he breathes out while he uses his fingertips to trace up my arms slowly until they reach my neck. They then slide over each mound that is peaking from my bra.

His eyes darken and hunger shines through them as he squats down. I hold on to his shoulders as he pulls my leggings down. We start laughing when my leggings get stuck on my ankles and won't come off.

"How romantic is this?" I say as I have to lean back on his dresser and have him pull to finally get them off.

"It is always romantic when you are with the one you love," he responds and stands up. He throws the leggings on the ground and wipe his forehead with the back of his hand.

He lifts my body up off the ground, and I wrap my legs around him. He does it with such ease that it is like he is carrying a feather. I feel his tight muscles flex as he holds me, while one arm reaches around my back to unclasp my bra. I throw it over his head as he lays me gently on his bed like I am his most prized possession.

His mouth trails kisses across every inch of my body. He marks every curve, dip, and imperfection like he is memorizing my body, comparing it to a personal map so he can find his way back whenever he wants.

"I hope you aren't attached to these."

"Hmm," I say in an aroused haze.

My eyes go wide as he rips the lace boy shorts I am wearing into pieces.

He steps back to look at me. "My God, Saige! You are exquisite!"

This man will be my undoing, and I'm going to enjoy every minute of it.

Saige

Thursday

"How do you feel?" the sex god beside me asks.

I peel my eyes open and feel the sunlight on my face. Strong arms wrap around my waist and a nose rubs the skin behind my ear.

"You smell fantastic. Lavender and sex."

I giggle and turn around to find the biggest, sleepiest smile on Declan's face.

"So, it wasn't a dream?"

"No, love. Yesterday, last night, and this morning were definitely a reality. A wonderful, amazing reality," he says, cupping my hands in his and kissing them. "Come, you need sustenance to build your energy back up."

"I could go for round twenty," I say playfully.

Declan groans. "Woman, you are going to kill me. I would love nothing more than to have the exhilarating rush of riding you in every position again, but we need food."

He pulls back the covers and pulls me out from under them. I throw on my t-shirt and he throws on his boxers. We head into the kitchen only to see the mess of all the leftover containers that we ate from yesterday. I look over at him and see that he is looking at me. We smile at each other. I think about how we spent all day and night connecting in every sense. I can tell you he hates tomatoes on his sandwiches, but loves them in his salads, and that he has a birthmark above his left butt cheek in the shape of a star. He told me about his college days and his feelings towards moving back here to start his practice. He even admitted he felt a sense of relief when his parents died, but then cried minutes later. Not for them, but for him and all he had endured under the hands of the ones who were supposed to love him the most.

It was magical and exhilarating to learn about each other, and I hate to see it end, but he has to work sometime today, and I still need to talk to Anne Carter, the mayor, about a booth for the Bicentennial. But that can wait, because this man that is gorgeous and mine is going to make me breakfast. I hop onto one of the bar stools and watch him be in his element as he is cooking. When I'm done drooling over my man and the food is done, we dig into the pancakes, bacon, and eggs that he has made for us.

Once we are full, I try to get up to wash the dishes, but he tells me he will do them. I think about hopping in the shower, but I go into my room and grab some workout clothes to put on so I can walk Luna. Luna and I come strolling into the kitchen and I stare at Declan wiping down the counters.

"While you are cleaning up the kitchen, I'm going to take this girl for a walk. We will see you when you come home?"

"Are you sure about that? Milo is still out there and I'm not sure I'm comfortable with you walking alone."

I place my hand on my hip. "River has extra cars patrolling and we won't go far or be long."

He places a gentle kiss on my lips. "Yeah, okay. I'll only be in the office for a few hours. I'll be back by supper time. Please be careful. You have special cargo there."

"Hey!" I swat his arm.

He laughs. "I was talking to Luna. She has special cargo with her." He wraps his arms around my waist, and we lean in for another kiss.

~

I try to call Anne Carter while Luna and I walk around town, but I get her voicemail. I leave a message, giving her all the details and ask her to return my phone call. Luna and I make it to City Lake, after passing six different patrol cars, and walk on a few hiking trails, when my phone lights up with Anne's incoming call.

"Hello." I answer.

"Saige. It's Anne Carter. How are you doing?"

"I'm doing great. How about yourself?"

"Pretty stressed, but I always am when we are planning big events for the town. So, I got your message about wanting to do a clothing drive booth for the women's shelter in Huntington. It sounds like a wonderful idea."

"Oh fantastic!"

"Yeah. So, we will put the booth up in front of the library on the square and make a sign for it. You just need to have people there to man the booth."

"Oh, awesome. Yeah, I've got people that will help."

"Great. I'll have my volunteer office helpers make some flyers to post around town and also post it on the Bicentennial website."

"Is there anything you need me to do? I can do the flyers or the website."

"Oh, no. I have volunteers for that. You just worry about being there and collecting as many women's and children's clothing items you can and leave the rest to me."

"If you are sure?"

"I'm sure. I look forward to seeing you there and catching up."

"Yes. It will be great to see you. Thank you, Anne."

"No problem. You have a great day. Bye." She hangs up.

After setting everything up with her and feeling good about the booth, Luna and I make our way back home so I can shower and tidy the house up before Declan comes home. I even order from that Italian bistro that Megan, Gina, and I ate at so I could have food ready for when he comes home since he needs some groceries in the house.

After my shower, I start cleaning the house and hear the doorbell ring. I grab my wallet, thinking it is the delivery driver with my food. I reach the door and open it without checking who it is, and when I look up, I really wish I would have.

Declan

I can't wait to get home to Saige, so I may be driving over the speed limit on the way home, even though my office is only five minutes away from the house. After everything that has happened with her, I have vowed to kiss her every night, make sure she knows she is loved and appreciated by me, and love her the way she should be.

I pull up to the newly painted ranch style home with teal-colored shutters. I glance at the teal front door and smile, knowing my woman is on the inside and she is the reason why it is painted teal. It's her favorite color, after all. Hell, I decorated the master according to what I hoped Saige would like even before I knew what I was consciously doing.

I walk up the steps to the porch and touch the 'Welcome to My Home' sign. One day I hope to change it to 'Welcome to Our Home' with Saige as my wife and our baby in her belly. She would be sitting on the glider on our porch smiling at me as I came home from work.

When I walk into the house, I notice it is too quiet. I look for Saige in the kitchen and living room as I make my way to the back sliding door to let Luna, who is barking up a storm, into the house.

"Where is Saige, girl?"

Luna jumps on me and runs to the front door.

"No walk right now, Luna. Let's find Saige."

Luna follows me through the house barking and tries to get me to follow her back to the front door. When I can't find Saige, I grab my phone to dial River.

"Declan, how's it going over there?" I hear on the other side.

"Good. Hey, is Saige over there?"

"No. Isn't she supposed to be with you? Are you tired of my sister already?"

"Hardly. I just came home from work, and the house is clean, but she isn't here. I just wondered if she was hanging out with someone."

"She's not with me, and Finn is upstairs with the twins playing. Maybe she's with Gina or Megan?"

"Okay. I'll call Megan." Wild thoughts run through my mind, but I can't panic. She is probably with her best friends.

"Let me know if you find her."

"I will."

I hang up and dial Megan right away.

"Hey, Declan," her cheerful voice greets me on the other line.

"Is Saige with you?"

"No."

"Maybe she is with Gina."

"I'm at Gina's house right now and she isn't here. Is everything okay?"

"I just got home from work. The house is clean, and Luna was left outside, which is unusual, and Saige isn't here."

Panic is in her voice. "I'm on my way."

"No you don—."

"I said I'm on my way," she grits out.

Right when Megan hangs up on me, Finn comes barging in.

"What's going on? Did you find Saige?" Finn asks frantically.

"I don't know. She isn't here. I told her that I was going to go to work for a client for a few hours, and she said she was going to take Luna for a walk and then order food for us."

"Well, maybe she is off getting food."

"Maybe, but I had the car, so she would have had to walk. I don't know why she wouldn't have just ordered for delivery or taken Luna with her."

He jiggles his keys. "Well, let's go look. If we find her, we can just pick her up."

Finn starts heading to the door when I stop him.

"Wait. Let me call her first."

"Wait a minute. You called everyone else and didn't think to call her phone?"

"No. I just started freaking out when she wasn't here, so I didn't even think about doing that."

He sighs. "Well, we can solve this then." He pulls out his phone and dials her number.

After a few seconds, we both freeze and hear the faintest sound of her ringer somewhere. I know what we are both thinking, but we won't say anything until the phone is found. We both try to follow the sound while Finn keeps calling, and it sounds like it is coming from the kitchen.

When we make it to the kitchen, I know it isn't there, so we follow the ringing to the front door and locate her cell in the large planter. Blood is on the edge of the pot, and I know in my heart that it is Saige's, and she didn't leave willingly.

Megan barges into the house and nearly knocks Finn on the ground when she hits him with the door. Any other time this would have been funny, but right now I'm scared.

"What happened? Why do you two look white as ghosts?" She rushes the words out.

Finn rubs his shoulder, but neither one of us is able to say anything to her. Our eyes are glued to the planter with blood on it. She turns to look at what we are looking at, and her eyes go wide.

Gina comes into the house and looks at the scene before her. "What is going on?"

"I don't think Saige left this house willingly." Megan's voice is shaky.

"We searched everywhere and then I called her phone." Finn bends down to pick up the phone.

"Don't touch the phone! Whoever took her could have left fingerprints!" Megan yells and swats his hand.

Finn looks at her.

"What?! I watch a lot of crime shows. They always say not to touch things left behind," she says, looking back at him.

"We need to get River here now," Gina says with tears coming out of her eyes.

I snap out of it and say, "I'll go. This is all my fault, anyway."

"What?"

"How is it your fault?"

"Don't say that!"

I hear them say these things, but I'm already out of the door running to River's house. I pound on the door as hard as I can. River answers angrily. He takes one look at my face and looks behind me at Finn, Megan, and Gina standing on the porch before he takes off running to my house.

I walk back slowly, giving myself enough time to calm down, because being the way I am isn't going to help find Saige, and she needs me strong right now so we can locate her. When I get to the porch, Finn is filling River in on what happened, and he runs into the foyer of the house. He turns to look at the planter.

"I need my phone or radio so I can call it into the station," River says frantically.

"I already called," Megan says, and we all hear the sirens. "That should be them now."

The next few hours are crowded with police and crime scene investigators taping off and searching every square inch of my house. Finn, River, Megan, Gina, and Ginny are all gathered together going over all the details Saige has given them. I'm listening and not listening at the same time, trying to rack my brain with the guilt of how I wasn't able to protect her.

"I should have protected her." I mumble. "This is all my fault."

Finn grabs my shoulder and pulls me into a hug. "There is no use in blaming yourself. We all knew what was going on and we all did the best we could."

"Did we?" I pull away and look at everyone. "She was taken by that asshole! So, I would say we didn't do the best we could. At least I know I didn't." I turn away to wipe a tear that I try to stop from escaping and end up sobbing into my hands as I fall onto my knees.

I feel hands on my shoulders, but it only makes me cry harder. "If something happens to her, I'll never be able to live with myself."

"We will find her, Dec." River pulls me up to stand. "We will find her. The department put out an APB, and we won't stop until she is with us, and he is in jail."

"River." We lock eyes, and I scan everyone else. "I'm going to kill Milo, and I'm going to bring her home."

"As an officer of the law, I'm going to pretend you didn't say that, but as her brother, I say make him feel pain and then make sure he never wakes the fuck up again!"

All eyes go wide, and some mouths even drop. Ginny is the first to smile and nod. Finn walks over to River and slaps him on the back.

"Hot damn! I knew my brother was somewhere in that stick-up-the-ass exterior."

River clears his throat. "Well, let's get to work and find our sister." He claps his hands. "Chop! Chop!"

"And now he's back." Finn rolls his eyes.

Saige

A hand brushes across my cheek softly and a light campfire aroma is in the air. My head is pounding, and my eyes feel like they weigh fifteen pounds apiece. I try so hard to open them, but sleep pulls me away.

It only feels like five minutes later when I feel something push against my leg hard and a vanilla scent hits my nostrils. I try to wake up again, but my head tells me not to. It is still pounding, and I feel so heavy, like an elephant is sitting on me. My body starts shaking uncontrollably and nausea hits, but I try to put my mind over matter.

"Shouldn't she be awake yet?" The voice sounds familiar, like someone I know, but I can't quite put my finger on it.

"Give it time. She should be awake fully in the next thirty minutes or so."

Dear God, no!

MILO! I know that voice, it belongs to Milo.

Fight or flight.

Fight or flight.

Dark.

The third time I wake up, I feel like myself. I know whatever Milo gave to me it is out of my system. I have a pounding headache, but the shaking is over. I crack my eyes open to see if anyone is around me. I don't see anyone so I try to move my hands and legs to sit, but I can only move them so far before I feel the restraints tug. I lay back down, facing the wall, realizing that I won't be going anywhere.

"There she is." I hear a voice behind me.

I twist my head up off the cold cement floor to see the shoulder and arm of someone walking in through a doorway. Possibly the only doorway.

He crouches down and brushes a strand of hair off my face. "I was wondering when my girl was going to wake up."

"Milo." I twist my body and look up at his face. "Where are we? What's going on?"

He smiles down at me. "You don't remember?"

I lower my head back down to the cold floor to think, and my memories flood back to me. I remember taking a shower, cleaning, and hearing the doorbell ring. I remember just thinking it was the delivery driver bringing the Italian food I ordered. My stomach was rumbling, and I could just taste the fettuccine on the tip of my tongue.

I'm usually a cautious person and look to see who it is before opening the door, but for some reason I didn't. Maybe it was because I was one minute closer to Declan coming home and us enjoying a romantic meal together. I opened the door and smiled, but when I saw Milo, I knew that I had just made a grave mistake. A sinking feeling hit, and my stomach dropped.

He had this sinister look on his face, and the words he said are ingrained in my brain. "You've been a bad girl, and you need to be punished."

I tried to run, but I wasn't fast enough, as Milo had anticipated me trying to escape. He came up behind me, grabbed my arm and twisted it in front of my chest with his right hand as his left put a rag over my nose and mouth. That is the last thing I remember before waking up here.

I look Milo in the eye. "You showed up at Declan's and put a rag over my mouth."

Before I can add anything more, I cover my mouth with my hand and look around for something to vomit in. Milo places a bowl in front of me. He grabs me by the waist and helps me up onto my knees. I just dry heave since I haven't eaten since lunch when I was kidnapped. I have no clue what time it is or even what day.

"Chloroform," he says as he holds me up.

After I finish wiping my mouth with the back of my tied hands, I say, "Excuse me?"

He doesn't answer right away. Instead, he grabs scissors from his back pocket. My heart jumps when I think he is going to hurt me, but he cuts my legs and arms free instead.

"Chloroform. That's what was on the rag. I should have known you would put up a fight though. I had to throw myself on you as you were trying to fight me, and the drug didn't work as fast as I thought it would. But when I threw my weight on you, we toppled over, and you hit your head on the way down. Boom! Unconscious."

I lifted my hand up and felt the dried blood on the edge of my hairline and forehead. I hiss from the pain and realize that is what is causing my pounding headache.

"You don't remember that part, I take it?"

I shake my head. "No. But you should have known that you can't believe what happens in the movies. It's never as easy as they make it seem." I sit down on my butt and put my back against the cold wall.

"Yeah. Well, I have you now, don't I?" He brushes his hand along my jawline, and I turn away. "As you can see, your precious Declan is nowhere to be seen. No one will ever find you here." He looks around the room I am being kept in.

I look too. It's not a place I know, so I'm not sure if I am in Winter Springs anymore. It's cold like a basement, but it's small enough to be the size of a bedroom. Maybe a room in the basement? The walls are painted a robin's egg blue. The only thing in this room other than Milo and me is a twin-size mattress, blanket, and pillow on the floor.

"Where are we?" I ask him.

He jumps up onto his feet. "Oh no. You aren't going to get me talking and spilling all of my secrets."

"Why not? If you have me in a secure location and you say no one will ever find me, what are you scared of?" I egg him on.

"I'm not. I'm not scared of anything."

"Okay, then tell me where we are."

"We are at Quinn's family's farmhouse on the edge of town. Twenty acres of quiet. No one will hear you, even if you scream. No one has lived here in a long time, so no one will be coming by." He tries to walk out of the room.

"Wait! Quinn?" I stop him.

"Wow, you really are dumb. Haven't you gotten it yet?" I hear as the five foot seven, red haired bombshell walks into the room.

"I'm part of this."

"What the hell is going on? How are you part of this? I did nothing to you."

"You did something the moment your ass tripped back into Winter Springs. Declan is mine! I had him right where I needed him and then you came in and suddenly, he dropped me like I was nothing. But now you're out of the picture. Declan will have no choice but to choose me again, and then we will live happily ever after when you are dead." She sneers.

"Whoa! Whoa! I didn't say anything about death. I told you that you could have Declan and I would take Saige away from here and she will be mine," Milo tells her.

"Hey," I say. Milo and Quinn are arguing with each other, and my head is going in so many directions.

"Hey." I repeat myself.

"Hello!" I yell. They both turn to look at me. "You're telling me this has to do with me being with Declan?"

"Correct." Milo answers.

"Well, this has been fun." Quinn pauses. "Actually, it hasn't, but I have a man I need to go see and make him fall madly in love with me." She leaves with a smile plastered on her face.

"Milo." I speak his name calmly and quietly.

"I don't want to hear it. You are mine, and you are going to be with me. You will soon realize that you belong with me too, and you will eventually learn to love me."

"That's not love. How do you think this is going to work? You kidnap me and then you plan to run away with me against my will? I won't comply. What makes you think I won't tell the first person we see that you kidnapped me?"

"Easy. I told Quinn she could choose which one of your family members to kill if you don't. She could mess with Finn's rock-climbing equipment and make it look like an accident. She could kill River when he responds to an emergency call. She could even put something in Ginny's IV when she is sleeping after giving birth to your nephew. An accident can happen to anyone, Saige. Are you willing to risk it?"

"You are mental! You can't hurt any of them!" I yell.

He grips my chin tightly and forces me to look at him. "You do as I say, and nothing will happen to any of them."

He lets go and walks out of the room while saying, "I'll bring supper down in fifteen."

Declan

Friday

I roll over to the other side of the bed and inhale the scent of her shampoo that still lingers. The scent triggers happy memories I have had with her. Happy memories that have been stolen from me. I groan and climb out of the bed and look for something to wear in the duffel bag I was given ten minutes to pack since my home is officially a crime scene.

I quickly set off on a mission and arrive at the police station. River is giving a statement to the press when I pull up, and he gives me a backwards nod, signaling for me to go to the back entrance of the station. When I park, one of his deputies opens the door to usher me in as quickly as possible.

I sit down in one of River's office chairs with a cup of coffee in my hand, waiting for him to finish. The deputy tells me it will only be ten more minutes and that River will join me before he closes the door behind him.

"How'd you sleep?" River jolts me out of my thoughts as he shuts the door to his office.

"How'd you sleep?" I question him back.

"I didn't."

"Well, you have your answer." I sit the coffee on his desk and lean forward with my elbows resting on it. "So, where are we?"

"Well, I've been going through all the notes of everything Saige told all of us and I've run Milo in the system, but I don't have much. He has a few priors in the state of Indiana for being too rough with past girlfriends. All the charges were dropped though."

"How many and what happened?" I ask, angry that he is out on the streets after being abusive towards women.

"Plenty." One word that answers both questions.

I growl. "That is not the answer I was hoping to hear."

"It's not going to happen overnight. As much as we both want it to. But I did release a statement, and we have sent out a BOLO to all the surrounding police stations. Hopefully Milo will slip up and someone will spot him somewhere."

"What if we don't have time, River? What if he wants to hurt her or kill her?"

"I don't think that's going to happen," he says, leaning back in his chair.

"What makes you say that?"

"Well, from what we have gathered, he is obsessed with her. He will try everything in his power to make her feel the same way about him before he resorts to any of that. I know my sister; she will go along with him to try and give us as much time as possible."

"What if going along with him means letting him, you know?" I can't finish the sentence, but River knows what I was going to say.

"We hope that doesn't happen. I know this isn't helping you at all, but we need some piece of evidence to lead us to where they are. We have a warrant for his car and house. Now, his car has been missing since yesterday, but I have people going through his house very carefully. Let's see what they find before going crazy."

~

When I get in my car, I just drive. I have no destination in mind until I see City Lake up ahead. I pull into the parking lot and walk to the dock. Leo is there again with his tackle box and rod.

"Mind if I join you?"

He looks up and recognizes me. "Not at all. Sit. The fish are biting."

"I'm not really in a fishing mood."

"Then why are you here?" He shakes his head. "Scratch that. I know why you are here."

"Enlighten me, please, because until I came here, I didn't even know I wanted to be here."

"You came to think. I always do all of my best thinking while fishing," he says as he hands me a fishing pole.

Leo and I sit on the dock for an hour before my phone rings. I quickly pull it out of my back pocket, hoping it is River or anyone else that can give me an update, but I notice Quinn's name flash on the screen. I turn my phone off and place it on the dock beside me.

"I'm guessing that wasn't the person you were hoping to hear from?"

"Not even close."

My phone rings again, and I look down to see Quinn is calling again.

"You better get that. It could be important."

"I don't see how it could," I say as I let it go to voicemail and look out over the lake.

He clears his throat. "Look son, I know you are here because Saige is missing, and you were hoping to find some kind of answer. However, if you ignore things, then you might just let an answer slip on by. Anything could be relevant, and anyone could give you an answer, whether you know it or not."

"The girl who is calling was a bully to Saige in high school. Before Saige came back here, she thought we would be an item again since we were in high school. She's fun to hang out with, but I don't ever see a life with her."

"Then when Saige blew into my life, I was done. Saige had won me over in every way possible, and I found myself in love with my soulmate in just a short period of time. I never had any feelings similar to that with this girl."

"Quinn, the girl who called, continued to be nasty to Saige when she came back here. I don't think she ever mentally left high school, and I am too old for that. I want someone to love and love me equally, and I want to be a dad to the kids I have with the woman I love, not a parent to her, also."

"So, I don't see how Quinn's phone call could be important while Saige is missing. I need answers, yes, but I doubt she has the answer I need to bring Saige back to me."

Leo blows out a puff of air. "Well, you just said a mouthful. Quinn sounds like someone who wants Saige out of your life so she could have you. She feels threatened by Saige, so she is mean to her." He looks at me out of the corner of his eye.

I nod. "Sounds about right."

"I'd still take her call because she could lead you to—"

"I know. Answers."

He nods.

It was like Quinn could read my mind because as soon as I thought about calling her back, her name flashes across my phone. "Hello." I answer.

"Hey, cutie. How are you?"

"What do you think Quinn?" I roll my eyes, getting frustrated with the nickname.

"You're right. Stupid question. I was wondering if you wanted to meet somewhere."

"I don't think that's a good idea. I need to find Saige and put all my effort into bringing her back."

"Well, that's why I'm calling. I want to help you find her. Would you like to eat at the Italian bistro and then we can put our heads together and figure out where to go next or who to talk to?"

"I'm not hungry."

"You need to eat to build your strength. You don't want to run yourself into the ground before you even find her."

I think and look at Leo. He raises his eyebrow and nods.

Right then a thought pops in my head. Last night Saige ordered food from there, but it was never delivered. I need to know why. The police think it is irrelevant to the investigation, but I need to know, even if it does lead to a dead end.

"Okay. Sure. I'll meet you there in fifteen minutes."

Her peppy voice makes me cringe when she says, "Good. I'm so excited to see you."

I hang up and look at Leo. "Answers."

"Answers," he repeats.

I hand him back his fishing pole. "Thanks, Leo."

"Don't mention it, kid. Go bring that girl back." He pats my knee.

Saige

I wake up, cold and hungry, to another day, and the smell of the ocean fills my nostrils. I gag and bury my face into the blanket. I refused to eat the soup Milo brought down to me last night because it had shrimp in it, and I said I was allergic. He got mad at me and threw the bowl at the wall. I was in a trance watching it all run down the wall that I didn't realize he was yelling at me, until I feel him grab my chin and jerk it upwards in his direction.

"I said look at me when I am speaking to you!"

"Sorry, Milo." I want to vomit when I apologize instead of saying what I really want to say. But I know my only chance of my loved one's survival is if I do everything he says and pretend to dote on his every word.

"Why didn't you tell me when I went to cook supper that you are allergic to seafood?"

"Because I didn't think." I keep my voice at a whisper.

"That's right, you didn't."

I get angry and can't stop the next thing out of my mouth.

"You do know that a lot of people are allergic to seafood, right? You could have asked me if I was." He slaps me across my mouth and cheek, and the pain is excruciating.

"You know I could just have Quinn play eeny, meeny, miny, moe and see who she should kill to get you to watch that mouth."

I cover my cheek with my hand. "No, no, no! I'm sorry! I'll watch my mouth!"

"Just for that, I'm taking your blanket, and you will have no food tonight. Tomorrow is going to be a better day, because you are mine and you will not talk to me that way ever again! Do I make myself clear?"

I nod and curl up on the mattress in a ball trying to stay as warm as possible while I cry, until the tears stop coming.

~

I wake up, unsure of what time it is. I don't know if I have slept an hour, or eight, since the light was left on, and there are no windows in here. I roll over to my back and count the tiles on the ceiling and sing a few songs to pass the time to take my mind off of hunger and being cold.

I have to pee so badly that I pound on the door, hoping he will hear me and let me go. When I can't hold it anymore and realize that he won't come to relieve me, I walk to the corner, take my pants off, and pee on the cement floor. As much as I try to avoid it, pee splatters off the cement and on my legs. I pull my pants back up, grossed out that I have pee on my legs, pee on the floor, and dried seafood soup on the wall and floor across from me.

I lay on the mattress in a ball and cry again. I don't know how much more I can take. Eventually, I cry so much that I fall asleep, too exhausted to care anymore.

~

"Good morning, baby. How did you sleep?" My body stiffens at the sound of his voice.

"Good," I croak out.

"That's good to hear." He covers his nose. "It stinks in here."

I don't answer him, unsure on what to say. "I brought you your blanket back and some eggs for breakfast. Would you like to eat now or after you use the restroom and shower?"

"After, if that is alright? I really need to go to the bathroom again."

"Okay. He grabs my arm and leads me out of the room. I look everywhere, trying to finish mapping out how many rooms there are, how close I am to the stairs, and other details about the house. He pulls me into the bathroom that is located under the stairs.

"I thought you had to pee?"

"I do. I'm just waiting for you to leave." He stares at me. "I can't pee and shower on my own?"

"I'm not leaving you unsupervised."

"Can Quinn supervise me? She let me pee in privacy the other night."

"Nope. She went out to eat with your lover. See, I told you that as soon as you were out of the picture then he would forget all about you. I told you he doesn't love you."

I find all this hard to believe, but I remember that I have to make him believe I trust what he says is right, and that I am falling in love with him. "You did tell me that. I should have believed you. Can I please have some privacy? You can stand with your ear to the door and listen to me."

"No, but I will stand at the doorway and turn around while you pee and while you get into the shower. But you need to get over this privacy thing, because I have already seen you naked, and you will soon be mine."

I turn around quickly to meet his eyes. "You've seen me naked? How?"

With no reply, he walks to the doorway and turns his back to me. I sit down to pee with my eye on his back the entire time. I strip out of my clothes quickly and hop in the shower before turning the water on, because I don't trust him as well. When I finish showering, I realize there isn't a towel hanging up. I pull the curtain back a little and look around the bathroom for one, but I don't see it.

"Looking for this?" Milo walks towards me holding a towel.

"Thank you," I reply and try to grab it.

He pulls the towel back so it's out of reach. "You'll have to come and get it."

There is no way I will let Milo see me naked. I look around for something to use to cover up with and I find my clothes are still in a pile on the floor in front of the tub. I crouch down and put my arm out from beneath the curtain to get them. He sees what I am doing and kicks them out of the way.

"Milo. I thought you said you would turn around until I was ready to go back to the room?"

"I didn't say that. I said I would turn around when you peed and climbed IN the shower. I never said anything about climbing out."

"Can you please turn around?" I ask softly and sweetly.

"No. I already said I've seen you naked."

"Well, I like to first be with someone for a while before they see me naked. You understand?" I'm shaking with worry.

"Don't feed me that bullshit, Saige. I know you have screwed Declan. Get out of the shower," he says sternly. I don't move.

"Now!"

I jump and pull back the curtain. I try to cover myself as best as I can and climb out. He has the towel open, and I walk into it. He wraps it around me and rubs my arms, making me cringe. "See, that wasn't so bad." He plants a kiss on my cheek, and I scream internally but smile on the outside at him.

We walk into the room, and I almost gag at the smell. I place the towel over my nose to try to mask some of the stench. "You'll need to clean all of that up. I don't like slobs."

"I can't touch the shrimp. Remember, I'm allergic to it." He recoils his arm like he is about to hit me again. "I only say that because if I do, I'll have to be rushed into the hospital before I die, and then we won't be able to spend our life together."

He drops his arm. "That's true. Plus, I can't have you in a hospital with the police looking for us since they don't understand what is between us."

"Well, what if I tell the police that you didn't kidnap me and that I left on my own free will?"

"I don't trust that you would say that if you saw your family."

He hands me clothes to put on. My clothes from the dresser and closet at Declans. I pull on my underwear and pants under the towel so he can't see me. I, then, turn around to face the wall, drop the towel, and put my bra and shirt on. When I turn back around to face him, I get physically sick seeing the way he is looking at me.

I sit down on the mattress, and he snaps out of it and hands me the food. I take a bite of the egg, and it's so delicious that I have to tell myself to eat slowly.

"Good?" he asks.

"Yes," I say with a bite in my mouth.

"Yes, what?" His tone is harsh.

I look up at him with my eyes wide open and swallow. "Yes, thank you."

smiles and his shoulders relax. "You are welcome. Don't ever forget your manners around me. I'm doing a lot for you, and I expect to be appreciated."

I nod and turn my focus to the food in front of me. I take bite after bite, not even stopping to breathe because I don't know when or if the food will be snatched away from me again. When I decide to look up at where Milo is sitting, he is missing. I look around the room and see that the bedroom door is open, but Milo is gone.

I sit for a few minutes listening for any sounds coming from anywhere outside the room. There is complete silence, so I put the empty plate down and slowly get up onto my feet and inch towards the door as quietly as possible.

"Milo?" I whisper.

I inch closer until my hand touches the door frame. I peek around it.

"What are you doing?" I jump at the sound.

Milo comes barreling down the stairs with two buckets filled with soapy water and rags.

"Nothing. I called for you and didn't hear anything, so I was just looking for you."

I back away from the door frame towards the mattress, and he walks in and shuts the door. He places the bowl at the opposite wall and studies me. I guess he believed me because he hands me one bucket and turns away to start cleaning up the dried soup. I take that as my cue to clean up the pee in the corner.

Declan

I walk into the bistro and see Quinn sitting at a booth waving me over. She has a big smile on her face, and it takes every ounce of my being not to just turn around and walk out of the restaurant. -I walk towards the booth, fighting with myself, and slide into the seat opposite her.

"There you are cutie. I've missed you." She reaches over to touch my hand that is resting on the table.

I pull it back in disgust. "I thought you wanted to help me find Saige?"

"I do, Dec. I'm sorry you thought otherwise. Do you have any leads?"

I clear my throat. "Yes, we know Milo has her. We just can't find him, and we don't know where he has her."

She wiggles in her seat and clears her throat. "Is he working alone?"

I arch my brow. "Yeah. At least we think he is. I don't see why anyone else would want her."

The waiter comes over to take our order, and when he leaves, I excuse myself.

I walk up to the hostess stand. "Excuse me, miss."

The lady turns and smiles at me. Her gray hair covers part of her face and her eyes twinkle. "Yes. How may I help you, sir?"

"I was wondering who I should talk to about placing an order to go?"

"Sure, sweetie. That would be Roger over there at the bar." She points to a bald man who has his back to me.

"Thank you for your help."

I walk up to the bar, pull out a red upholstered chair and sit down. Roger turns around and smiles, making his lip ring glisten in the lighting. He is drying glasses, his arms heavily tattooed.

"Can I get you something?"

"Answers. I was wondering if you were the one who took an order on Thursday evening from a woman named Saige Wilson?"

"Name doesn't ring a bell. Let me check." He turns around to grab a leather-bound book and lays it down in front of me on the bar. "Wilson. Saige Wilson," he says as he skims down the list of names. "Nope. Nothing here."

"Can I see it please?"

He shoves the book to me. "By all means."

It didn't take me long to find it. But it wasn't under Saige Wilson, it was under Saige Wolfe. "Found it!"

Roger comes around the bar to see what I found. "Saige Wolfe? I thought you said Wilson?"

I look over my shoulder at him. "I did. Her name is Saige Wilson, but she used her first name and my last name for this order."

"I remember that call. Tracy took it and told me all about the lovely woman talking about how she was so excited about this date she had planned with, well, you."

I look back at her name on this list and see that her order was canceled. "It was canceled. Why was it canceled?"

"Well, I took that call. It was a few hours or so later and the person said that the plans had changed. I assumed you stood her up."

"I didn't. Can I see the timestamp?"

"Sure."

I look and recognize that the call was after Saige was taken, according to the CSI team. "Damnit! And you are sure a female called to cancel?"

"Yes."

The door chimes, and the bartender from Sherry's walks to the bar.

"Hey bro," she says to Roger. "What are you doing?"

"Helping this gentleman find out why this order to Saige Wilson was canceled."

"Saige?" She looks shocked.

"You remember her?" I ask.

"Yeah, we talked at the bar a few times and I brought you all drinks. You're the man she likes. Is she still missing?"

I nod.

"I'm so sorry." She pauses and looks at her brother. He shakes his head, but she ignores him and continues, "I can help you."

"How can you help me?" I ask her in a hopeful tone.

"I have special skills."

"What she means is that she can read people and do other magical things," Roger chimes in.

"Oh," is the only response I can give. "I remember Saige saying you read us."

"You don't believe me?" Becky asks me.

"It's not that I don't, it's just that I really need to find her, so if you really can't help me, please say so."

"I can help you," she says with certainty.

"Well, okay then. I will not turn down help to find her."

"Declan! Come and eat! The food is here!" Quinn yells at me from the booth.

Roger stiffens and looks at me with wide eyes.

"I'll be there in a minute, Quinn." I look back at Roger. "What is it?"

"That was the voice I heard that canceled the order."

"What voice?" I ask urgently.

"Hers." He points at Quinn.

"Are you sure?" Blood drains from my face as I glance over at Quinn.

"I'm positive. She has a distinct whine and tone to her voice. Like nails on a chalkboard." He shudders.

"If that's true then that means that Quinn is working with Milo, and she knows where Saige is." I'm shaking with anger.

Becky grabs my arm to stop me from stomping over there and doing something I shouldn't do. "Declan. Think this through. If Quinn is working with Milo and knows where Saige is then it doesn't help matters if you call her out on it. Go over there and act like the perfect date she wants you to be."

"How am I supposed to do that? Saige is out there with Milo doing God knows what with her and this bitch is involved! I can't just go over there and act like nothing is wrong." I know Becky is right, but I can't think straight right now.

She sighs. "Look, I'll go with you. You can say you bumped into me at the bar, and we are old friends. You invited me to join you two. If you don't do anything, she will come over here. I know because of the nasty ass glances she has been throwing my way, trying to warn me to stay away from you." She looks at Quinn and smiles while waving.

"Are you sure?" I relax a little.

"Of course. I'll try to get a read on her too." She turns to Roger. "Roger, call the police and ask for Chief Wilson. Tell him everything and tell him to get a car stationed here to follow Quinn. Maybe she will lead them back to Saige."

"I have to be there when she is found." I blurt out.

"You will be. Just call River after Quinn leaves the bistro. If she asks you to go anywhere else, just tell her we have plans."

"You're good at this, Becky. Maybe you should be a detective."

"Well, I actually help the police department a lot with sketches and different things. Let's go before Quinn blows her lid." She pushes me towards the table.

~

It took a lot of will power to get through the meal looking at Quinn, and having to pretend everything was fine, but having Becky with me helped a lot. She was in tune to my cues and knew when I needed her to take over the façade, or else I would say something wrong. I could see why Saige liked her and was drawn to her.

Once the meal is over, Quinn takes forever trying to not leave me and even tries a few times to get me to leave with her somewhere so we can go look for Saige, but I do what Becky said and tell her we have plans already, but that I would hang out with her another day. I swallow the bile in my throat as I tell her I'll call her tonight and thank her for wanting to help. She gives me a hug and tries to kiss my cheek before walking out of the restaurant, but I pretend I don't know she is going to and walk out of her embrace towards Roger at the bar.

Once I see Quinn walking to her car outside, I call River, and he picks up after one ring. I gather my keys in one hand so I can run out as soon as she leaves to follow her.

"I was waiting for your call. Is she gone?"

"Walking to her car now. Is someone posted outside to follow her?"

"Yes. I have two of my best guys in a white Ford Focus parked three cars behind hers." He must have heard my keys make noise, because then he adds, "Don't do anything, Declan. Do not get in your car and follow her. My guys will do it and report back where they have Saige."

"I can't just sit back and do nothing, Riv! I have to do something. I swore to protect her."

"Do you not think it kills me sitting behind my desk watching the car's tracker on my computer instead of being out there and following her to get that prick myself? It does! It fucking sucks, but you know that we have to follow the rules to a T so that they get put away for a long time and so there is no chance of parole."

I sit the keys down on the bar and slump into the barstool. "I know. I know."

"As soon as I find out anything, you will be the first to know. Okay?" There is a softness to his tone this time.

"Okay. Thanks, Riv."

There is a pause, and I think he has hung up, until he adds, "Dec, we will find her."

"But at what cost to her?" I hang up on him.

Roger and Becky are listening, and when I hang up, they both look at me with pity in their eyes. I exchange numbers with each of them, and Becky wraps me in a hug. They offer to go do something with me to take my mind off of everything since Roger is now off the clock, but I decline.

I head back to City Lake again, and not surprisingly, Leo is still there.

"Do you ever leave this dock?" I ask him as I sit down.

"I do. I'm only ever here when thinking needs to be done." He looks at me and smiles.

"What are you thinking about?" I ask for a distraction.

"The question is, what are you thinking about?"

"Not so much a question." I fill him in on everything that has happened since I left him last, and his face remains unchanged.

"Answers," he declares. "I told you that you could find answers."

"Yeah, but I need to know where Saige is so I can bring her home to me. I'm shattered without her."

Just then my phone rings. River is on the other end and tells me the undercover cops lost Quinn and haven't been able to find her. I hang up without answering and toss the fishing pole beside me into the water while screaming.

Leo stands up and touches my shoulder. "Have faith, son. You'll find your way back to each other."

"I know you mean well, Leo, but this isn't really what I want to hear. It's not helping." I don't turn to look at him. I just stand facing the water and the fishing pole floating in the lake.

He doesn't seem bothered by my frustrated tone. He pats my shoulder. "Sometimes the things we don't want to hear are really what we need to hear."

I turn to look at him. "I don't know what you mean. I really didn't need to hear that the lead we had is gone."

He sighs. "You want to hear that she has been found. You want to hear she is safe in custody, but she isn't. She was taken. So, think of answers that involve them. Think of what you know about Quinn and Milo, who their families are, what houses or buildings they own or visit frequently that can hide someone they don't want to be found. It could be anyone. Cousins, siblings, parents, even grandparents." He looks me straight in the eye. "Get it?"

I think I do. "Okay." I sit back down. "Let's think."

Leo sits down beside me. "You owe me another fishing pole when you find Saige."

Saige

"There's my girl." I look up at the man that gives me nightmares.

I can't believe I thought about running my hands through his light brown hair that cascaded around his face and that his blue eyes reminded me of a fantastic beach day looking into the ocean. Now all I see is this monster before me. He reminds me of Jekyll and Hyde or Two-Face from the comic books. Having to tiptoe around everything he does or says in fear of seeing the supervillain.

He hasn't hit me anymore today since I learned to play his game, but I know it could come at any moment. I have learned when to talk and not to talk, when to pretend to be into anything he says and thank him for everything he does for me. He's here at the house all day and will only leave me alone when I am napping, or he is cooking. The only saving grace is that he will let me use the restroom and shower alone now. Granted, he has to stand on the other side of the door and then will escort me back to the room right afterwards.

I've been trying to map out a mental picture of the layout of this basement every time I go back and forth between the two rooms with him. What I have gathered is that the main area is big and spacious. There are many boxes tucked away in the corner of the yellow painted brick room hidden under the wooden steps. An old baby blue Schwinn bike leans against the boxes, and from the looks of it, it hasn't been ridden in a long time. There are books piled on an old bookcase that lean against the wall that separates the bathroom from my new bedroom. On that same bookcase are board games that are covered in dust and an old glass vase with dead flowers inside. A nineties couch sits against the main wall that the stairs lead down to. I can't remember the color or what else is against that wall just yet, but I will. I have, however, figured out there isn't a window anywhere down here and the only exit is up the stairs. The only possible way to escape this hell is if River and the police find me or I can find some way to knock him out and get away on my own.

I look through the closed door at the wall with the image of the bookcase with the vase in my mind. I picture grabbing it and smashing it across his head. I would run up the stairs and straight out the front door without looking back. I don't care if we are in the middle of nowhere; I will run until I find someone. ANYONE.

My mind automatically goes to Declan. I wonder if he feels as lost as I do. Like he is missing a big piece of himself. And my poor brothers and friends. I think of what the stress of me being gone is doing to them all.

"Saige!" I jump at the sound of my name coming from his lips. "You weren't listening to me, were you?"

"No, sir. I'm sorry."

He smiles an evil grin and brushes a stray hair behind my ear.

"What am I going to do with you? I thought you were finally getting better, but it looks like you aren't."

"No! I am. I'm sorry. I'm just hungry and tired." I hope he will believe me.

He grips my chin and squeezes. "Well, if you would have listened, I told you I brought you lunch. It's a little late, but I had some things to do earlier."

I look down at the plate, not even really seeing what is on it, other than the gold and navy leaf design that reminds me of a crisp fall morning. I reach for the bottle of water and chug it down.

"Saige. Are you forgetting something?" I look into his eyes and see the monster coming out to play.

"Thank you." I whisper.

I can see in his face that he is getting frustrated. I put the bottle down and raise my knees to my chest with my hands lying flat beside each hip, ready to push me back as fast as I can to avoid being hit.

The sound of stomping down the stairs takes his attention off me.

"You are not going to believe the fantastic time I had with Declan today," she says as she opens the door to lean against the door frame.

I say nothing but make sure to look her in the eye and hide the emotion of what her being with Declan is doing to me. I will not give her the satisfaction of knowing she is under my skin. I can feel Milo's eyes boring into my face.

He must have been satisfied because he turns towards Quinn and smirks. "You're back early. Did he blow you off already?"

"No! We went to dinner at the Italian bistro and had a great time. I pretended to help him look for her." She points at me. "And

I was the perfect shoulder to cry on. He snuggled really close to me. I'm just back already because he apparently already had other plans with a girl named Becky who was there at the restaurant with some bartender."

"See, Saige." Milo gets my attention, and I look at him. "He has already replaced you with someone else. That is not someone who loves you."

"He is not replacing her with anyone other than me! Becky and her brother, the bartender, are his cousins. She's lucky she is his cousin because she is a tattooed quack. She kept talking to me about tarot and reading people. It took everything in me not to call bullshit on everything she said. But since she is his cousin, and I can tell they are close, I had to grin and bear through it all."

"She's not a quack. She is the real deal." I chime in.

"Whatever." Quinn waves me off. "All I know is that they had plans, but Dec promised to call me tonight. Maybe I should stay here and take the call just out there so you can hear the whole thing."

"Do what you want, Quinn. He won't believe that you are trying to help find me. He's much smarter than that. Maybe he already knows you are part of it." I quickly shut my mouth, regretting saying any of it.

Milo trains his eyes on her quickly. "Does he know?"

"No. There is no way. I said nothing and did nothing that could incriminate me."

"When he calls tonight, I will be listening to make sure."

"Whatever." She turns sideways.

I glance up and see a bobby pin poking out of her hair. I smile to myself and know I will get hurt after doing what I'm about to do, but it will be worth it.

"You are not that good of an actress. I bet he has contacted my brother and the police are already looking for you. All you are in his eyes is a gold-digging whore. He wouldn't touch you with a ten-foot pole," I say with the most strength I have had since being kidnapped.

"Shut your mouth, you bitch. He believed me, and I could tell he was eating out of the palm of my hand," she hisses out.

"Eating out of the palm of your hand? You really are delusional. People have been locked up in mental institutions for less."

"Look at you and look at me. There is no comparison. Soon he will forget all about you."

"And how long have you been trying to make him yours? Since high school?" I push.

"I was his high school sweetheart."

"That's true, but I have him and I've been back less than a week. You've had years, and he tolerates you. But me, he loves me. He said it so many times as we made love."

Her face turns red, and she lunges for me. I try to shield myself from her punches and grab the bobby pin out of her hair at the same time. It takes a while, but I manage to get one out when I grab her hair and flip her over, so I am on top of her. I get a few good punches in before Milo yanks me off of her.

He is livid and that anger is pushed only in my direction. Here is where I talk about getting hurt, but it is worth it. I just fought someone for a guy that wasn't Milo in front of him. I fought over the one guy he has tried hard to make me forget. This pain will hurt, but I will endure it. Because I will pick the lock on this door; I will escape this house, and I will be back with the people who love me while these two are put away forever.

Declan

River has been allowing me to stay in his house since Saige was taken. I can't bear going into that house without her. Luckily, Phoebe and Paige have fallen in love with Luna, and she is having the time of her life here.

When I come into the house with more clothes, I look up to see River, Ginny, and Gina sitting on the couch, Finn sitting in the chair, and Megan sitting on the arm of that chair.

"Good! You're here. Now River can let me know why we are all here," Finn says.

River clears his throat, walks to the fireplace and glances at the mantle. Pictures of the family are on there, and he is looking intently at the picture of Saige with everyone. He turns around and looks at all of us.

"Look. Saige is missing."

"No shit, Sherlock." Megan interrupts, and Finn looks up at her and tries to hide a laugh. River glares at her. She places her hands in her lap and looks down, trying to make herself look as small as possible. "Sorry. I'm a bitch when I'm scared."

"Don't apologize, honey. We all handle grief, fear, and all emotions in a different way." Ginny leans forward and touches her leg. She looks at River and gives him a look that tells everyone that they will be talking later tonight when everyone leaves.

"Please tell us what you were going to say. What do we know?" Gina changes the subject.

"So, we all know she is missing, and Milo and Quinn have her. What we haven't found out is where. I have invited everyone here tonight for us to put our heads together to try and figure out where she could be."

"Isn't that what the police are for?" Finn questions.

"Yes, Finn. That is what we are for. I have the guys in the office searching as much as possible. But I figured since you all went to school with both of them that you may know of a few places they go to or houses that are in their family that might hurry up the process."

"Well, Gina and I probably won't be much help. Quinn was a grade A bitch in school and tormented Saige to no end. The only words out of her mouth were meant to hurt Saige and anyone else who was below her. Milo was on the football team and wasn't part of the same groups we were in. Other than class, we never talked. Finn and Declan will probably be more helpful." Megan chimes in.

Gina adds, "I know nothing about either one that will be useful. Sorry."

"Finn, what do you know?" Ginny asks him.

Finn thinks for a minute. "Well, Milo lives in his own home here in town and so does Quinn."

"We checked both of their houses. Nothing." River lets everyone know.

"Milo's parents moved away, and Quinn's parents also live in town," Finn adds again.

"Checked."

"Milo owns the bookstore, a few actually, and Quinn works at…" He pauses, thinking.

"The mall. She manages the Ulta there," Gina says.

"Surprise, surprise. A perfect place for someone so vain," Megan adds.

I'm still standing in the foyer listening to everyone, pushing myself to join them, but I can't move or talk. I look around and realize the girls are gone. That knocks me out of the frozen state I am in.

"Where are the girls?" Everyone whips their head to me.

"What?" Ginny asks.

"Where are the girls? Phoebe and Paige?" I walk into the living room looking for them. "Are they upstairs?"

"No. They are with my parents. With everything going on and Jace coming soon, they are spending a few weeks with them."

"Grandparents?" I ask. Something important hits me.

She looks at me confused. "That's right."

"Grandparents," I say, sitting down on the spot on the couch that River has been sitting in. Everyone is looking at me, or at least I think they are by the feeling of eyes on me.

"Guys, I think he is broken." Megan chimes in.

Finn laughs out loud this time.

"Declan." Gina touches my arm and says in the soothing voice of a mother making sure her baby is alright, "Are you okay?"

I don't respond because I know the word grandparents is important for us finding Saige.

"Let's leave him alone for a little bit and see if we can come up with anything else," Ginny places her hand on my other arm and says to everyone else.

"Okay. Can anyone else think of anything else?" River asks, and no one can think of a thing.

I think back to my conversations with Roger, Becky, Milo, Quinn, and Leo. I remember Leo saying something about family homes.

I suddenly remember and jump up, scaring Gina and Ginny. "Grandparents!"

Finn jumps out of the chair and walks to me. Concern is on his face. "Grandparents?"

"Quinn! She has a family farmhouse outside of town. It belonged to her grandparents, but they passed away last year. She used to go on and on about how great it would have been to throw parties there when we were younger because it's in the middle of nowhere with acres of land. It's been abandoned other than family going out there to mow the lawn every once in a while, during the spring and summer. It's a perfect place to keep Saige!" I exclaim.

"By George, I think he's got it!" Megan yells and slaps Finn on the ass.

Finn turns around to look at Megan and smiles. She smiles back, and everyone laughs, myself included. River grabs his phone out of his pocket and calls into the department while looking me in the eye. "George, we know the location. It's Quinn's grandparent's farmhouse outside of town." He listens. "Yes, that's right. Can you send me the address when you find it? I'll meet you there." He hangs up the phone.

"Wait! His name was George?" Megan stands up and moves to Finn. She looks at Finn and he looks back at her. They laugh.

"By George, I think he's got it," Finn says and slaps Megan's ass.

Everyone gets it at this point, and we start laughing.

Gina comes to stand next to me with one hand over her belly and nudges me with her other arm. "You think those two will ever figure out that they love each other?" She looks towards Finn and Megan.

"I don't know. Look at how long it took me, and I actually knew I loved Saige."

"Yeah, but you were dealing with your own problems, and you only did it to protect her from them. You are good for Saige. I see a long future for you two."

I pull her in for a long hug. "I now know why Saige picked you two as her best friends. Thank you for being there for my girl."

She hugs me back. "You are welcome. Now, go bring our girl home."

"That's the plan."

River's phone buzzes, and he looks down. "I have the address." He starts walking to the door. "Coming Dec?"

"Hell yeah, I am." I walk towards him.

"I'm coming too." Finn yells. "Wilson brothers to the rescue!" He puts his arms around River and me. "I'm not a Wilson though," I correct him.

"You've always been a Wilson, man. You just need to marry my sister to make it official." Finn pulls me in with his arm.

I look at River, and he nods with a smile.

"Well, let's go unleash hell, brothers." I say as we walk out the front door.

~

When we pull up to the police station, it is all hands-on deck and crowded inside. Everyone is wearing a smile when we walk in, and people are slapping Finn and River's backs giving them encouraging words. We follow River to get fitted with bullet proof vests.

My phone rings, and I answer. Becky is on the other line. "Becky, I can't really talk right now."

"I know. You figured it out. Call Quinn."

"What?" I'm confused.

"Remember that you promised Quinn you would call her tonight?"

"Well, yeah. But I hardly think that is important right now."

"Please just do it." There is urgency in her voice.

"Is this coming from one of your special powers or whatever they are called?"

She ignores my question. "Promise me you'll call. Go outside and call her." She hangs up on me.

"What was all that about?" Finn asks.

"You remember Becky from the bar?" He nods. "Well. she knows things that others do not."

"Yeah, I know. What does that have to do with this?"

"Well, she told me to call Quinn like I promised her I would when we left the restaurant today. She sounded like it was important."

"Then call." River comes up behind us. "Becky has done many things for this station that are hard to explain. I believe anything that girl says. Call Quinn."

I nod and walk outside to the back parking lot so it is quiet. I pull up Quinn's number and dial.

Saige

Quinn's phone rings as soon as Milo hits me again. He stops to listen to who is calling her, motioning for her to leave the room so that he can continue.

"It's Declan! I told you he'd call me." She smirks at me and starts to walk out of the room. "Oh, just my friend."

I wait for another punch, but he walks out of the room. I hear whispers that I can't make out, and Quinn tells Declan to hold on. She asks what Milo wants, and I inch closer to the door frame to hear better.

"I told you that I want to be there while you talk to him. I want to make sure he doesn't suspect anything." He turns back to me and notices that I am in the opening of the doorway. He comes barreling towards me, and I back up into the room. "We will continue this when I come back down."

He is still angry at me, but Declan's phone call is more important right now. He glares at me and closes the door. I hear the lock click into place. I count to sixty ten times, hoping that it gives me enough time for them to be upstairs. I hold up the bobby pin and smile, hoping the things River showed me years ago would work.

I fiddle with the bobby pin in the keyhole more times than I can count, but the door won't budge. I get frustrated and lean against the wall, wincing in pain. My fingers trace the swelling and bruising on my body and I turn all my emotions into one. Anger is what I feel when I look at the bobby pin and the doorknob and say to myself, "One more time. I'm going to try one more time."

I walk back to the white wooden door and listen for any noise on the other side. It is silent, and I place the bobby pin in and twist it around. My tongue sticks out of my mouth in pure concentration. Finally, I hear the latch unlock, and I sigh in relief.

I slowly open the door to keep it from creaking and peek into the main room before opening it fully. I close the door behind me and lock it because if someone does happen to come down here, they might think I'm still in there and that could buy me some more time.

I edge into the big room next to the bookcase and grab the glass vase. I pull the dead flowers out and place them back on the dust covered shelf. I observe the vase and wish that it was a metal pipe or a baseball bat instead, but I know that it is the only weapon I have available, and I will use it.

I walk like a wolf, ready to strike my prey at any given moment. I step quietly and carefully. When I make it to the bottom of the stairs, I look up to the top and listen some more. All is quiet in whatever room the stairs lead up to. I take the steps one at a time with my hand gliding up the rail, the cool metal bar rubbing my palm.

When I reach the top of the stairs, I stick my head out into the room. It's still quiet. I inch into the room, my back against a closet, and take in the old eighty's kitchen. There are knives in a knife block near the stove on the other side of the room. I tiptoe to them. I open the cabinet above me and place the vase inside, on top of some plates. I look at the block and grab the biggest knife there is, contemplating grabbing a second one when I hear voices sounding like they are coming down from the top floor, the creak of the steps coming after. I run quietly to the closet and open it up to find a pantry staring at me. I rush in before someone finds me.

"I'm telling you, he knows something." Milo walks closer.

"What are you talking about? He doesn't know anything," Quinn tries to tell him.

They stop. "Then why did he ask where you are?"

"Maybe because he cares about me and wants to come visit. You are paranoid, Milo."

"I don't know. Call him back. I'm going to finish what I started with Saige."

"Make it hurt." Her voice is full of cheer.

I hear the creak of the steps going up to the next level as footsteps fill the kitchen. I track his heavy steps as he walks around the kitchen and hear the opening and closing of cabinets and the fridge. Oh, dear God! Please don't open the plate cabinet. Why didn't I hide it somewhere else?

He stops in front of the closet I am in. I try to calm my breathing and put my hand over my mouth. I'm shaking, and my breath is coming out raggedly. He stops for only a few seconds before his footsteps descend down the stairs.

I open the closet door and look at the bottom of the stairs. I can hear the keys jingling in his hand. I walk stealthily through the kitchen into the hall and hear Quinn talking upstairs. She is pissed and talking to herself. I pause at the bottom of the stairs and stare at the front door.

"SAIGE!" Milo's scream fills the whole house, and I startle.

I duck down as I hear Quinn yell down the stairs, "What's going on?!"

"WHERE ARE YOU?"

I look into the dining room that is beside the hallway and run in there. I place myself against the wall that hides me from the hallway.

Quinn runs down the stairs and into the kitchen and meets Milo there, because I hear him roaring out loud all the things he is going to do to me when he gets ahold of me. I stand in fear and start crying.

I will not be locked down there again. I will either get out alive or I will die trying. I just really wish I would have grabbed that second knife now because the odds are two against one, and I'm on the losing end even if I have a knife. I go over my options; make a run for it out the front door with them running after me, run upstairs as quietly as possible, or stand here and wait them out.

Without giving it another thought, I run to the old wooden front door and turn the knob. It's locked, and I look for the latch as I hear Milo screaming for me, his voice getting closer. I look over my shoulder down the hallway as I unlock the door and throw it open. I push open the screen door and take off down the porch and into the yard with Milo screaming behind me.

I'm running as fast as I can, my legs burning and my arms pumping. I throw a quick look over my shoulder to see only Milo chasing after me. I look forward and keep running, not knowing if I am running the right direction until my feet hit the gravel of the driveway.

The rocks bite into my feet, but I will myself to keep going as fast as I can because I can hear Milo gaining on me. I run and run, and the fear of not seeing the road yet is getting to me.

"Stop, Saige!" Milo yells, closer than earlier.

I ignore him and the pain my feet and legs feel. This is survival.

Declan

River is speeding through town, the lights and siren on, when my phone rings again. I look down and see who it is, about to ignore it when River looks over. "Answer it."

"Uh!" I growl out and push the green button that lights up on my screen. I place the phone on speakerphone and clear my throat. "Quinn."

"Hey, Dec! We were talking earlier and then you told me you had to go. Would you like to get together tonight at my house? I could make us some supper and we could watch a movie."

I look at River, and he nods his head, but I sigh, "Not tonight. I plan on searching for Saige until she is back with me." Silence on her end. "Anything else?"

"I thought we talked about hanging out again?"

"I said no, Quinn. Saige is the only thing on my mind right now."

"Declan, can't you see what's right in front of you? I thought you were going to get over that trash and realize you are supposed to be with me! You need me!" Anger is in her tone as she talks. I look at River, and he arches his brow. She goes silent, probably realizing the mess she made by letting her anger get the best of her and letting me know she has been pretending to help me all along.

"That 'trash' is more woman that you will ever be. She is beautiful inside and out. Goodbye, Quinn." I say calmly before hanging up. I look at River. "What's our ETA?"

He looks down at his computer. "Fifteen to twenty minutes."

"Can't this thing go any faster?" Finn chimes in anxiously.

River slams his foot on the gas, and the car revs up to speed us down the road.

Saige

At this point my whole body is screaming at me to stop, but the adrenaline keeps me going. I still don't see the road, but I talk to myself with encouraging words to breathe and run. A hand grabs onto my shoulder and pulls me.

Milo throws me down onto the gravel driveway and stumbles with me. I try to get back up to my feet, but he gets to me faster and uses his body weight to keep me down. He throws a punch at my right eye and pain explodes in my head. His legs straddle my hips, and he grabs my right arm with the knife and smashes it down onto the rocks again and again until the pain is unbearable, and I drop it.

He throws a punch at my ribs and continues to use my body as a punching bag. I move my hands around me, feeling for a weapon while my body and face are pelted with hits. I latch onto a pointed rock with my left hand and use my right to block the incoming attacks. I will the strength back to me and throw my left arm up. The rock slams into the side of his head.

He loses his balance and falls to the side of me, holding his head with his right arm. Blood is trickling down his face, and his hair is covered in blood.

"You bitch!" he roars.

I turn onto my belly, wincing, and see the knife ahead. I crawl towards it, rocks cutting into my body. Milo latches onto my feet as I reach as far as I can for the knife. My right arm is burning in pain as I grab the handle and try to kick out of his grip.

He pulls himself up using my feet and flips me onto my back to face him. He straddles me again smirking, thinking he has me and I am helpless. My hand, on fire, thrusts the knife upward, and I know I met my mark.

He looks at me in confusion and then falls onto the ground. I push him the rest of the way off and rise onto my knees. I roll his heavy body onto his back and stare at his eyes, hearing his last breath leave his body. My fist pounds into his chest and face, and I scream. I continue to pound and pound until my arms feel like limp noodles and I can't lift them anymore.

After resting, I weakly rise onto my feet. I can't put weight onto my ankle because of twisting it earlier. I limp slowly, every step pulsing pain all over my body. My right eye is swollen shut, so I blink the blood out of the only good eye I have to look at my surroundings. Eventually, I think I see the road ahead, and as I continue walking down the gravel road, the rocks continuously bite my feet.

Declan

River pulls onto the road that the farmhouse is on, and the sound of a car speeding down a road draws near. River and I exchange a look as he pulls into the driveway. There is a car barreling down the driveway towards a silhouette of a woman who is limping towards us.

It doesn't take long for us to recognize the silhouette as Saige, so River speeds up, throws the car in park and gets out. He raises his weapon and yells for the person in the car to stop. Saige looks behind her and moves towards the bushes that line the driveway. The car keeps aiming for her.

River yells a second time as they get closer, realizing they aren't going to stop until they hit Saige. He unloads the clip of his nine-millimeter through the windshield and hits the target. The car slams into the bushes, mere feet from Saige.

I jump out of the cruiser and take a look at her. I yell her name as I run to her, and she limps towards me. I take in the arm lifted to her chest, and the breath gets knocked out of me when I see her face. I place my hand on her chin, lifting it up so I can get a better look. She winces. I let go and pull her body to my chest, and she cries.

"I'm going to kill him," I say into her hair. She squeezes me harder, not wanting me to leave her.

The noise of all the other squad cars drowns out her sobs. River is yelling to everyone, and I think I hear the name Quinn. When they come into my peripheral, I can see that they are walking around the car that's now in the bushes. I hear Quinn's name again, but I ignore it. All I'm focused on is Saige's warm body pressed into me and her breathing that has calmed down.

River and Finn stop beside us. Saige pulls out of my embrace to turn towards them, a small smile on her bloody and bruised face. They give her a once over and notice the pain isn't only on her face. River pulls out his radio and yells for an ambulance to get here.

"Smalls," Finn says gently, wrapping a blanket around her.

"Hmm?" She looks at him, not letting go of me.

"Where is Milo?" River asks, talking as gently as he can. He puts his radio away.

"I killed him." She looks behind us and up the driveway. "He's lying in the driveway up that way." She points.

She turns her face back into my chest and cries again. I scoop her up and walk her to the ambulance that is pulling into the driveway.

Finn stands beside me as the paramedic looks Saige over. We watch River walk up the driveway with another officer. They stop and observe what I assume is Milo's body. River waves a few officers over, and the crime scene unit takes over as River walks back down to us.

"Is he dead?" a voice behind me asks when River steps in front of me.

"Yeah, Sis. He's dead." He walks over to Saige and puts an arm over her shoulder. She leans into him. "I'm so sorry I couldn't protect you." He kisses the top of her head.

She starts to say something back, but the paramedics tell us they need to take her to the hospital to be treated. River jumps up, and Saige lays on the gurney. She turns to look at us three standing beside her and smiles at us. They lift her into the ambulance.

"Declan," she demands, throwing her hand out to me. The paramedic has started an IV of pain meds.

"I'm coming." I climb in and take her hand into mine. "Don't think for one second you're leaving my sight." I kiss her hand and then push her hair back away from her face. "Sleep. We will be there soon."

Her eyes close and I take in her face and body. A small tear slides down my cheek and then I crack. My body is shaking with grief and happiness. I kick myself for not being there to protect her, I cry with relief that she is here with me, I yell because the asshole did a number on her, and I smile knowing what I need to do. At the end of my emotional rollercoaster, I glance over at the paramedic who just witnessed it all in its glory.

"Sorry, man! It's been a hell of a time."

"No worries, dude. You'd be surprised how many times I have witnessed this. Get it all out now because by the time she comes to, she's going to need you to be strong."

"Did she say anything to you? About what he did to her?" I'm scared of the response.

"He didn't rape her, if that's what you are asking." I nod and he continues. "But this type of physical and emotional trauma she went through is just as bad, no matter how many days she was held captive. Be gentle with her and let her recover at her own pace."

I nod again. I look at her and swear to myself and her that I will be there every step of the way, no matter how long it takes. I will replace the hits with loving strokes, the nasty words with kind, gentle ones, and the abuse with love. She may always hold on to this trauma, but I will make every moment from here on out a happy and joyful one. I will give her my whole heart; to have and to hold from this day forward. For better, for worse, for richer, for poorer, in sickness and in health, to love and to cherish, till death do us part.

I will give her my forever.

Saige

I wake up to all of my friends and family piled into the room with me. My right eye is still swollen shut and my body is in a lot of pain. It's so crowded, and my eyes roam frantically over all their faces, making sure Milo really isn't here. I am not surprised to wake up to Declan holding me in bed, but I am surprised to find my mom's hand holding mine and her head asleep on the bed. Seeing her hand intertwined with mine calms my racing heart down.

I rub my thumb across the back of her hand. She lifts her head and jumps up in surprise, saying my name. She brings attention to me from everyone in the room. The joy and squeals of everyone is a lot to take in, so Mom ushers them out for a few minutes and tells Declan to tell the nurses I am awake.

While the nurses and doctors are coming in and out, Mom turns to me and starts fussing before her face turns serious. She starts the conversation of our first heart-to-heart. We bring everything out in the open, things we have held onto and repressed.

I'm not sure it's something I should be dealing with after waking up, but the pain meds the doctor just administered still have me loopy, so it helps. We laugh, argue, cry, and hug at the end.

The doctors come back in after waiting for the meds to kick in and talk to me about my injuries. When they leave, Mom brings everyone back in. I look around but don't see Finn or Declan.

"They will be here in a few minutes, honey." Mom squeezes my shoulder.

"The booth!" I exclaim. I missed the Bicentennial and the booth to help the women at the shelter.

"Leave it to this one to think of others when she is hurt," River says.

Gina informs me that Mom was able to get the stuff for the booth and both her and Megan ran it. They were able to get all of the shelter's needs met and were even given monetary donations to buy special things.

"You guys are the best friends anyone could ask for." I tear up knowing they knew how important it was to me, so they made it happen.

The twins run forward and show me a pile of all the pictures they made for me since I've been gone. I have so many emotions running through my body, but I only show happiness and gratefulness to them.

"Auntie Saige?" one of them says while I'm looking at a drawing of me pushing the girls on the swings.

"Yes?" I look up into their faces.

"Did you have fun on your trip?" Paige asks.

I tense up. "What?"

Phoebe jumps on the bed, and I hiss in pain. "Your trip." Someone tries to get her off the bed, but I raise my hand to stop them as I listen. "Daddy and Mommy said you went on a trip, but your face and arm are cut up and bruised. Did you fall? Is that why you had to come back from your trip early?"

"I, uh, I…" I stutter, and my voice shakes.

"Okay, that's enough chatting for now. Come with Mimi. I will get you some candy out of the vending machine." Mom reaches for their hands and gives me a pity smile before walking out the door with them.

"Shit!" I yell and throw my head back onto the pillow. I throw my arm over my eyes, and my mind succumbs to the nightmare of Milo hitting me and me fighting for my life. Over and over and over.

"Hey! It's okay, love," Declan says, sliding onto the bed and wrapping his arms around me. I tuck in close beside him, not knowing when he came in. "You are safe. They can't hurt you anymore."

"I can't do this. I can't," I reply into my hand.

"It's okay, Smalls. We are here for you. All of us." Finn walks to the bed and grabs my hand away from my face.

I look around at Declan, my brothers, and my best friends, knowing if anyone can help, it will be them.

~

As I'm talking to Finn and Megan, I hear River and Declan arguing about where I should go once I'm discharged. My interest peaks, so I listen.

"She needs to be surrounded by family," River says sternly.

"She will be unless you don't plan on walking twenty feet across the street to see her. Besides, my house is one floor. She shouldn't be walking up the stairs to her bedroom."

"We can move the bed downstairs into the living room." River is serious.

I chime in. "River, I'm going to Declan's. You are not moving a bed down the stairs, and I am not living in a room where I'll have no privacy. I've been here for God knows how long, and I haven't had a private moment at all. My body has been poked and prodded more times than I can count. I am not climbing stairs anytime soon until all of this," I motion to my body, "is healed up. It hurts to just get out of the bed still. I have a cast on my arm and a boot on my foot. And besides, you have a newborn at home to take care of. You do not need to take care of me as well."

He leans down and hugs me. "Are you sure? No one will object to you staying with us."

"I'm sure. Give Ginny, Paige, Phoebe, and baby Jace some love from me. I'll see you soon. Promise."

He leans down and presses a kiss to my forehead before walking out of the room to go home to his beautiful family.

Declan climbs onto the bed with me and wraps his strong arms around my body. I smile at him at the same time Gina walks in with food in her hand.

"I figured someone would want a wet burrito and white queso with chips." Gina holds up a to-go bag.

"Oh my God! Gimme!" I reach for the bag and pull it open on my lap. The smell of Hacienda fills my nose. I inhale and moan in happiness.

"Remind me to never come between her and food," Megan announces to no one in particular.

"I did once, and I will not be making that same mistake again. The scars are still noticeable on my arm because of it," Finn tells Megan.

"Oh, hush. You would be excited too if all you had to eat was this nasty hospital food. Only thing that would make this better would be a margarita to go with this." I open the packaging of the burrito.

"Well, you keep making that noise and I will buy you all the Hacienda you want." Declan looks at me with hunger in his eyes.

I blush in response. "Promise?"

"As soon as you feel one hundred percent and the doctors give you the okay, you bet your sweet ass I am." He squeezes my thigh, and the heat spreads remembering just what those fingers can do. We lock eyes, and I know he is thinking the same thing.

"Muy caliente! I'm going to need a water sprayer when I'm in the same vicinity as you two." Megan pulls the collar of her shirt open and blows into the opening.

"What are you talking about?" I turn to ask her with a smile.

"Was I the only one that just watched them practically eye fuck each other just now?" She looks at Gina who turns her head with rosy cheeks. "Now Gina, don't be getting all shy on us. We know you know what I mean."

Gina snaps her eyes to Megan and tries to look at her with the same intensity but laughs. "It's kind of hard to hide the fact that you know what I mean." She motions to Gina's protruding stomach.

"Oh, that? Yeah, I just woke up one day and it was like this. Guess I should lay off the donuts." She rubs her stomach.

We are all looking at her rubbing her belly when she stops and looks up at us. "The baby just kicked!"

We all start talking over each other with excitement and want to feel her stomach when she chimes in again, "Saige, I think you should be the first one to feel."

I am honored that she is giving me this experience. "Are you sure?"

She walks over to me and places my hand on her stomach where hers was just resting. I hold my breath, afraid that if I breathe too loudly then I will miss it. I feel a quick ripple underneath my hand, and I look at Gina in adoration. "Was that a kick?" She nods at me. Megan walks up, and I start to take my hand off for her to have a chance. Before my right hand lifts off of her belly, I feel the flutter once more.

Megan feels the flutter a few times too, and even Finn walks over to feel.

I feel Declan's hot breath on my ear before I hear him say, "That could be you one day."

I smile, looking on at Gina's belly, agreeing with Declan in my head. The picture of me lying down on the chair on the back patio with my hands resting on my swollen belly. I watch Declan chase a child through the yard, and the sounds of laughing coming from them.

Saige

Three Months Later

I see the sign for Winter Springs up ahead, and my phone rings. I answer it on the car speakerphone. A deep, husky voice rings out through the car.

"Hey Mike, how's work?" I ask as I turn down the road to the house.

"Good. We miss you here though," my old boss from Just a Sip answers.

"I know. I miss you all too, but you know why I couldn't come back. My life is here now."

"Oh, I know. Speaking of, how is that fine specimen of a man doing? Haven't thought about leaving you for me yet?" He laughs.

I laugh. "No, I'm sorry. He's still straight and still very much mine. He's doing great. His practice has boomed lately since he's added nonprofit law on top of his other jobs."

"Well, tell him if he decides to bat for the other team to give me a ring. He can get my number from you."

I roll my eyes. "When pigs fly, Mike. When pigs fly."

"You can't fault a guy for trying when a man looks like him." He pauses for a moment. "So, the ladies at the shelter were asking about you."

When I called to tell him that I was quitting and not moving back, Mike took it hard. He then bounced back five minutes later when he told me I was too good for the place anyway and he could tell I'm happy now. As my only true friend in New York, he knew what happened between me and Philippe because he was one to witness some of the things he did, and he told me to run.

I, of course, didn't listen until it was too late, and he didn't let me live it down. After the breakup, he would come to the apartment every day when his shift was over to try and kick my butt in gear. I told him off every time, but he never faltered. He thought finding a rebound guy was the best way to get over a breakup. So, he would just tell me I was being a grumpy bitch and to put on a dress and go clubbing with him.

The last time I saw him, he was meeting me for dinner and drinks one night and I told him about River and Finn blowing up my phone about coming to the Bicentennial, and he practically packed my bag for me. I thought he was joking, but he was serious when he said he was buying me a plane ticket right then and that he would be taking me to the airport to make sure I left.

A month ago, I finally had the courage to tell him what happened to me here, and he cried with me, blaming himself. I promised him I was okay because I had been going to therapy every Friday afternoon, and my friends and family were here with me.

So now, every Friday afternoon after therapy, he calls me on my way home and asks how it went. We start out with 'I miss you' and 'how are you?'. He then tries to hit on Declan if Declan comes with me, and then we get to the important stuff. In a way, he's like my New York therapist after therapy.

"Tell them I miss them." I really do miss all the ladies at the shelter. Mike also volunteers there in my place. I think it started out as another part of blaming himself for sending me here. Layla, the lady in charge, didn't think it was a good idea at first, but once she saw he was a flamboyant gay man, he quickly became her best friend. The ladies took to him so well.

"I always do. Sarah and Jessica moved out. Sarah has a job now and found herself an apartment to rent. Layla agreed to babysit Jessica while she was at work, and I have never seen Sarah happier."

Tears fill my eyes. "Oh my God! That's fantastic! I'm so happy for the next chapter for them." Sarah and Jessica had been at the shelter the longest, at least they were there the longest for me. They had already been there a few months before I started volunteering.

"Now, on to you. How did therapy go?"

"Uh, it was actually good. I had to revisit the whole being taken and escaping today since it was my turn to share with the group. I couldn't sleep or eat last night because I was so scared it would have an adverse effect on me, but it was quite therapeutic. I came face to face with a few demons. I've still been battling a lot with the whole thing, and I've let go of a lot that I now know wasn't in my control or wasn't because of me."

"I've stopped waking up from nightmares where Declan would have to follow me into the bathroom so he could hold my hair back while I vomited. I'm going to continue therapy because it has helped talking to others that have been through the same or something similar to me."

"I'm happy for you, Saige. I know I haven't asked this since you told me what happened, but are you and Declan okay?" There is concern in his voice.

"We are good, great actually. He has been my rock through the whole thing. I have a red surprise for him tonight."

"Get it, girl!"

I look up and see Declan standing on the porch waiting for me.

"Well, I've got to go. Dec is on the porch waiting for me." My breath hitches finding Dec's piercing green eyes on me.

"Uh huh. Talk to you on Friday. Now, go get some."

I laugh.

I turn off the car and take the keys out of the ignition, grab my purse on the passenger seat and open the door. When I climb out of the car and close the door, I see that Declan is still staring at me, only this time he has a huge grin plastered on his face.

"Hey there, handsome!" I walk up the porch and give him a peck on the lips.

I start to pull away, but his arms bring me closer to him, and he kisses me again, his tongue asking my mouth for permission. I open and let our tongues do the talking.

When we pull away, he leans his head down so our foreheads are touching. He notices my heavy breathing. "Love, are you okay?"

"Perfect." I lean back and smile at him. I lean in for another kiss, and he takes it.

He lays his hand on the small of my back and walks us both inside.

I put my keys and purse on the wooden table by the entryway

and smile at the pictures of us in frames that are scattered across it. He found this table at an estate sale not long after I was admitted into the hospital. We worked together, sanding it down and repainting it in a deep burgundy color.

The planter with the plant by the entryway was thrown out as soon as the forensic team was done with it. Bless his heart, he has worked hard these six months to gut the whole inside of this place and make it our dream home. He didn't want me to have any physical reminders of my trauma.

"So, I was thinking we should go out tonight. I'll put on a suit, and you could put on a dress or whatever you want. What do you say, love?" Declan runs his hands through his hair, and his eyes catch mine.

"Actually." I step out of my shoes and look over my shoulder to see his shoulders sag. "I thought we'd stay in tonight." He looks at me in interest, and I grab a bag out of my purse. I look at him and smile when I pull out a red thong and bralette set and hold them up for him to see. "I could wear these."

He practically gallops to me and grabs me in his arms for a long, hot kiss. When he pulls back, his piercing green eyes twinkle in mischief. "Are you planning to have your way with me, Ms. Wilson?"

"Only if you have your way with me, Mr. Wolfe." He smiles and grabs my hand.

We walk down the hallway. The gray wooden floor is cool on my feet, and we walk past the room that was once my outdated bedroom but is now a library and Declan's at-home office. The teal walls are lined with black bookcases filled with books; some are his law books, but mostly they are filled with books for pleasure. The book that I was reading yesterday is sitting on the small round black table next to the high back purple lounge chair.

We continue walking to the master bedroom, and another teal room welcomes me in. The black king size bed is pressed up against the back wall and plants sit in the corner next to my bedside table. The curtains are open, and the light from the sunset casts a glow into the room.

I walk into the middle of the room with Declan still holding my hand and turn to see lust in his eyes. It sends heat right down to the spot just begging to be touched by him. I look at the lingerie set in my hand and throw it over my shoulder.

"Screw these." I pull him in and plant my lips on his full plump ones, inviting him to dance the dance our tongues know so well.

He pulls away before the kiss deepens. "Hey, I was going to enjoy peeling those off of you."

"Oh, shut up! You might peel the bra off but not the thong," I tease.

"What are you talking about? I peel off your clothes all the time."

"Oh, okay. Let's just have a look in my underwear drawer, shall we? It will show you a different story, seeing as though I only have maybe five pairs of underwear left." I poke him in the chest. "You, sir, are impatient and rip them off of me instead of pulling them off."

He shrugs. "That's true." He smirks and looks down at the leggings I'm wearing. "It's a good thing you just bought a new thong because you are about to have one less than this morning."

He grabs my butt and lifts me up to wrap my legs around him. We kiss passionately until he drops me on the bed and my hair falls into my face. The strong hand of his that has felt every inch of my body brushes the hair out of my face and lingers on the back of my head.

"Do you think you'll ever get tired of this?" he asks.

"This?" I shrug. "Eh, maybe."

I giggle when he starts to tickle me. "Maybe, she says. Is our bedroom game not enough for you, love?"

His eyes reel me in, and I'm the fish holding on because I can't wait to see what he has in store for me. "It could be a little spicier." I laugh because we both know that isn't true.

"Oh, yeah? Well, I aim to please, so let's make sure it's spicy enough for you."

He puts his hand between me and the mattress and uses it to lift and guide me up the bed until I am in the middle. His body hovers above mine and he leans forward to grab the straps that are under our pillows. "Give me your hands," his deep, husky voice demands.

Declan

She lifts her hands willingly, and I strap one of her wrists in tight, watching her for her reaction.

She looks at the binds on her wrists and then looks in my eyes.

"Are you alright?" I ask.

She nods.

"Is this okay?"

She nods again.

I sink into the bed. "Love. Look at me." She looks into my eyes. "I need you to verbally tell me if this is okay. I will not do anything with you that you aren't comfortable with."

She looks away to eye the restraints again. I watch her stare at them and make a decision myself. I lean over to grab her wrist and the bind when her voice stops me.

"No. Don't take them off." She faces me again. "I know you aren't him and this is for pleasure and not for capture."

I eye her suspiciously.

"Honest. I am fine. I want this. I want you and the pleasure you bring to me when I am tied up. I need the happy memory of being bound by someone I love to erase the memory of everything that is him."

I cup her face. "If this ever gets too much, just say the word. I will stop and release you immediately. Okay?"

She smiles at me. "I trust you, but okay."

I reach over and strap the other wrist in and she smiles at me the entire time. My hands glide down her arms, and I take in her round face, high cheekbones, pointed nose, full, pouty lips and her smile that can stop any man's heart. I drop one arm to the bed beside her face while my other circles the peaked nipple that is showing from under her shirt. The moan she lets out is music to my ears. I tease it for a few seconds before moving to the other side and giving it my attention.

I raise the bottom of her shirt until it is laying across her arms. I position it so that her eyes are completely covered, and she has to go by sense of touch.

I reach around her to unlatch the lacy bra she is wearing, and a sigh of relief comes out of her mouth when all of the hooks are undone. I lift it as far as I can over her shirt.

"I don't know if that thing tortures you or me more," I say, knowing she is happy to have the bra off.

"Try wearing these all day long where the straps hurt your shoulders because they have to hold the boulders you have been gifted with, and then we can talk," she mumbles under her shirt.

I laugh and push the shirt up so that her lips are visible through the neck hole. My lips reach hers in a soft kiss. She tries to arch up to deepen it, but I pull back. "No." I growl.

I lean down so my lips tickle her ear through the fabric of her shirt. "Patience, Saige." She squirms.

I lift up and use my pointer finger to trace patterns across her stomach and back up across her breast and hardened nipples. My mouth claims one while my hand massages the other. I give a little flick of the tongue, and she arches her back, pushing her breast into my mouth more, encouraging me. I hum at the same time I pinch her other nipple in my hand, and her body reacts just the way I want it to.

I trail kisses down the mound of her breast, across her belly, and right to the spot above her pubic bone. She jerks her hands to reach out to me but doesn't get very far with the restraints holding them in place. I lift off the bed, and a groan escapes from her mouth but stops abruptly when she feels me grab her leggings to pull them off.

It takes me damn near five minutes, or close to it, to just get the things off, cursing that they are annoying but relishing in what they make her ass look like.

I growl, knowing I am hardening with every minute, and I won't be lasting very long with her.

This is why I take my time getting her ready before I even grant myself any pleasure. Although, giving her pleasure is not anywhere near a bad thing to me. I smile and look down at the strip of fabric that covers her most sensitive area.

"Ready, love?" I ask and she responds in a breathy yes. I hook my fingers around the band on her hips and rip it apart. She gasps and starts breathing harder.

When I'm done, her thong is in tatters in my hand. I toss it on the floor, giving my attention to my goddess who is lying naked in our bed.

"You know you could have just taken them off me. They were my favorite pair," she says, and I can feel her eyes roll beneath her shirt.

"I could, but what would be the fun of that?" I press my face to her sex and inhale deeply.

I press a kiss before she can respond and lift my head to look at her face. "Beautiful."

Not a second later, I grab the back of her legs, lift them up over my shoulders and lick up the middle of her core. Her body arches in ecstasy, and the sweet music of her moans fill my ears once more as I feast on her.

I lick and nip and bring my thumb up to rub her clit. My finger rubs, flicks, and pinches, making her breathing heavy. I lift my head up to watch her body when I slip in a finger to replace my mouth.

"So wet. So ready."

She moans at my words. I add another finger and pump faster and harder, teasing her clit with my mouth and tongue before she screams out my name. She rides out her orgasm on my fingers, her juices coating them. And I watch her reaction, making my dick twitch and strain against my pants. I lap up the cum that is dripping out of her.

I rise and lean over her. "Open your mouth," I demand.

I insert my fingers into her wide mouth. She closes her plump lips around them and sucks.

"See how good you taste. How addicting you are. I'm never going to be able to get enough of you, love."

I sit back down on the edge of the bed and place her leg in my lap. I trace circles across her ankle while I pull the restraint up and latch it. I lean across her restrained leg to grab the other restraint. I latch her other leg and kiss her ankle before sitting up.

I stand up at the end of the bed and discard my clothes onto the floor while staring at her tied up in bed. My dick jerks and I grab my phone out of the pocket of my pants on the floor.

"Say cheese, love." I snap a picture of her.

"Don't you have plenty of pictures of me on your phone?" She mumbles under her shirt.

"Yes. Doesn't mean I don't need another one."

"One of these days I'm going to snap a picture of you tied up on this bed with a ball gag in your mouth."

I laugh and toss my phone on top of my discarded clothes. "I'd like to see you try."

I step at the end of the bed and touch her ankles. She sucks in a breath, anticipating my next move. I run the tips of my fingers up to her thigh as I kneel on the bed between her legs. I slip two fingers back into her, finding her still wet and she moans. I pump in and out slowly, frustrating her as she tries to ride my fingers. I pull my fingers out and hear her groan. I laugh as I grab her butt and lift her hips. I don't have to say anything because we both know what's coming next. I thrust into her, and we both cry out. My primal instincts taking over as I fuck the woman I love.

Sweat is running down my brow as I thrust in her deep and fast. Her grip tightens on the restraints and I watch her knuckles turn white. Her breath gets shallow and her walls squeeze my dick. My thumb finds her clit in between our bodies and I rub until the sweet sound of her screaming my name comes out.

As she rides out her orgasm I pull out, my dick throbbing from the absence of her body. I unhook the leg restraints. I twist her onto her left side and straddle that leg while holding her right leg by my waist. I line myself up and thrust in for deep penetration. My hands caress and wander around her body, stopping at her ass and breasts.

I feel her move with me. knowing her orgasm is done. "Come for me Dec." she urges me on.

And what the goddess wants, she gets. I come for her.

~

The doorbell rings, and Saige rolls out of my arms. I get out of bed and look for my pants. I almost fall over trying to put my leg into my pants. I hear her laugh behind me as I sit down on the edge of the bed. Saige's arms wrap around my neck, and she kisses me just below the ear. A shiver rolls down my spine, and my dick twitches for her again.

"If you keep doing that, I'm going to say screw the pizza delivery guy and take you every which way till Sunday," I growl.

She pulls her hands away. "As much as I want you to take me again, my body needs to recover and I'm hungry."

"I thought so." I stand up and button my pants. I lean down and plant a kiss to the top of her head. "Be right back."

I head to the front door, grab my wallet out of the bowl on the table, and open the door to a teenager.

"I got your pizza, Mr. Wolfe." He smiles and gets the pizza out of the warming bag.

I take the pizza from him and place it on the table beside me. "And I got the money for you, Trevor." I begin to hand the money to him but quickly pull it away. "But please, call me Declan." I then hand the money to him.

He nods. "Got it, sir."

I chuckle. "Please don't call me sir. I'm only twenty-seven and you're making me feel old."

He laughs and walks down the porch. "Sure thing, Mr. Wolfe." He throws his hand back in a wave as he heads to his car.

I close and lock the bolt before snatching the pizza up. When I get into the kitchen, I grab two beers out of the fridge and head back to the bedroom.

Saige is still laying on the bed naked with her phone in her hand. "Your pizza, my dear."

Her phone flops onto the bed, and she rises onto her butt and crosses her legs. "Great! I'm starving."

I watch her lean forward and snatch a slice out of the box and take a bite.

"So, I wanted to ask you how therapy went." I eye her, looking for any hints on her face.

She finishes swallowing and places her unfinished pizza back into the box. "Good." She smiles. "More than good. I feel like myself now, and I was able to tell my entire story without stopping or having horrible flashbacks. I mean, I still get flashbacks, but now it's like I'm watching it from the outside looking in instead of reliving it over and over again, if that makes any sense?"

I nod. I can't lie and say that I understand her because I have never experienced what she has. I wouldn't know where she should be at mentally if I didn't go with her to see her therapist periodically. The therapist has helped me find ways to understand and help her throughout this process. It has been the best thing for us.

I learned that every woman or man that goes through this grieves differently, and most partners don't even try to find a way to help them grieve the way that they need to. But I made a vow before we left the hospital that I would do everything in my power to help her in whatever way she needed. So, when she asked me to start going to therapy with her, I jumped at the chance.

I can't say I'm a saint because part of me wanted to know what was going on for my own selfish reasons. She wouldn't open up to me at home and would just brush it off like it was no big deal. But as someone who has memorized every part of this girl, I knew she was lying and hiding it from me, which was her prerogative.

I am glad to be in the loop with her now, and I think she feels the same. But that's for her to say because I can't read her mind. I'm just thankful she has opened up to me and let me know things instead of running away and bottling it in.

"What are you thinking about over there?" I zone back in and see her staring at me, eating her pizza once again.

"Honestly, I was thinking of when you first started therapy and didn't tell me anything."

She looks away. "I know. I'm sorry."

I grab her hand. "Hey." I squeeze her hand. "Look at me."

She looks me in the eye. "Don't ever apologize, alright? You have nothing, and I mean absolutely nothing, to be sorry about. I just hated not knowing what was going on with you because I wanted to help."

"I know. I'm…" she starts saying but stops. "I'm glad I finally was able to see that in all the bad that was going through my head. I couldn't have gone through any of this without you."

"Sure, you could. You are the strongest woman I know." There is not a doubt in my mind.

"Thanks. I'm glad you came with me because I'm not sure what would have happened had I not opened up and brought you with me." She looks down at the pizza.

"Love." I lift her chin up, and her eyes land on mine. "Let's not dwell on that. I am here and so are you. I will continue to go with you, and you will continue to go alone, okay? No matter how long it takes. I'm not going anywhere. You're stuck with me."

She nods and smiles. "Good!"

"Now, eat your pizza before it gets cold." I smile back.

"You know, I quite like cold pizza." She raises her eyebrow at me and smiles.

"You are insatiable, woman." I growl, and she shrugs.

I close the lid on the pizza box and throw it to the floor. I grab her by the waist and lay her flat on the bed. A smile is plastered on both of our faces as I lean down to kiss my love.

"Ready for round two?" I smirk at her.

"Round two? More like round one hundred!"

Saige

Mid-December

I roll over and wince in pain after another all-nighter with Declan. To say we are well is an understatement. It's been eight months since the horrible ordeal happened and Declan and I professed to never go a second without the other knowing just how we felt about one another.

When I moved in with him, I thought it was a temporary fix until I got better. What a stupid fool I was for believing that. I'd gladly be a stupid fool any day to bask in this happiness day in and day out. We make each other laugh; we smile, and we joke with each other. We live in the moment and never take a day for granted.

I feel for him in the bed, but my hand lands on the cool bedding beside me. I peek my eyes open and look for him in the room, but he is not here. I notice that his suit is missing from the hanger on the back of the closet door.

I'm surprised he left for work without waking me up to give me a kiss goodbye. I groan, lay my head back down and shift my body until I get into a comfortable position. I close my eyes and tell myself that I can take ten more minutes to rest before I need to start my day.

The bedroom door bursts open, and I jump up, a scream leaving me. I grab the nearest weapon I can find beside me and lift it up to protect myself.

"Well, we have officially become official! I found one of your hairs in my ass crack in the shower this morning." Declan takes one look at me and laughs. "What are you doing, crazy?" he asks.

I'm sure what he is seeing is crazy. I'm standing on the bed with a pillow in my hand, raised in a defensive pose. My hair is wild and, in my face, and I'm trying to tame it by blowing it back, which is only making it worse.

"Well, I thought you left and someone broke in. I wanted to protect myself." I push my hair back with my hand.

He walks over to me and grabs the pillow. He throws it on the bed and laughs some more. I swat his arm.

"And you thought a pillow would save you?" He helps me off the bed.

"It was the closest thing to me that I thought to use."

He pulls open my bedside drawer and points inside. "And you didn't think to grab your gun?"

"Well…I…Uh. I actually forgot it was in there and I just grabbed the first thing I could when you barged in here."

He grabs my waist and pulls me to him. He kisses the top of my head. "We need to practice with you. That way if an actual intruder comes in here, that will be the first thing you grab."

I look up at him. "Yeah. You're right."

I push off his chest. "Wait a minute. What did you say when you came in here like a psycho?"

He thinks for a moment. Then, he wraps both hands around my waist and smirks down at me. "I found your hair in my ass crack while showering. We are officially official."

"And a hair in the ass crack is what makes us official?" I raise one eyebrow.

"Yep. I find your hair on blankets, in the bed, threaded in my clothing, even on Luna. But now, one has weaseled its way between the cheeks."

"Okay. Quit talking about hair in your ass." I laugh. "But why did you have to barge into the room like your ass was on fire? You scared the shit out of me. I thought you had left for work already."

He leans over and kisses my forehead. "I'm sorry I scared you. I wouldn't have left without letting you know. Let me make it up to you and take you out to dinner tonight."

"Are you going to be able to get away from the office tonight to even do dinner?" I ask, knowing how many dinners he has missed because of work lately.

When Declan expanded his business months ago, we never thought just how much time it would take from him. We aren't complaining because business is booming, but it does make seeing each other daily harder. When I was going to therapy multiple times a week and writing my book, it worked out, but now that I have less therapy sessions and the book is done on my end, it's been harder to find things to do to keep myself occupied.

"I'll only be in Huntington today, so I will be home." He checks his watch. "But I need to leave in fifteen minutes, or I'll be late getting there with traffic." He gives me a gentle kiss on the lips, and I pull him in to deepen it.

I follow him into the sage colored kitchen as he starts the coffee before walking to the stainless-steel fridge to make his lunch. I grab the watering can off the counter and go to the sink to fill it up.

"Do you have therapy today?" He looks up after spreading the mayo on his sandwich.

"Not today. I'm going to see her Wednesday to discuss if I still need it. She is leaving it up to me, but I think I'm ready to stop." I pause and then add. "I'm going to go visit the shelter today. I submitted my book to the agency last week and they emailed me last night saying everything looked perfect, so I have some free time now."

"Look out world, here comes your next best seller," he says to no one in particular. "It was a fantastic read. I'm not a big reader, but I couldn't put yours down."

I knew he meant it. He hasn't stopped raving about it to everyone he sees since I let him read the finished product. He spent every night in our library reading it as I tried to keep busy while waiting for his opinion. I might have even made a permanent line down the hallway pacing back and forth waiting for him to finish. He put it down and just sat there for a few moments before making eye contact with me. His smile lit up the room before he jumped out of the chair and wrapped me in his arms. He is my number one fan, and he proved that to me over and over that day.

I put the watering can down when he gathers the mugs from the white cabinet above his head and pours me some coffee. He adds cream and sugar to mine and hands it to me. I lean against the marble countertop and take a sip of my French vanilla light roast coffee.

He chuckles at me.

I smack his butt. "Don't make fun of my coffee preference."

"I wouldn't dare. I made that mistake months ago and never again. It's just funny that you basically drink sugar and French vanilla coffee creamer with a little bit of coffee." He pinches his thumb and pointer finger together.

He pours the rest of his coffee in the pot into his thermos. "Compared to your Satan's chokehold you got in that thermos."

He laughs again. "Don't hate on my black coffee. That's why we have his and her coffee pots."

"That's true. We can't share everything." Declan leans against the counter beside me, and we both take a sip of the coffee, allowing the silence to fill the room for a few seconds. "I think I'm going to see if Emma is hiring at the shelter. Give me something to do with these long days you have been having."

"They'd be lucky to have you. You love volunteering there, and I know you like getting out of the house. Sounds like a win to me."

"Now, let's hope they have a position for me."

"They'd be stupid not to, love." He leans over and places a kiss on top of my head. He hesitates for a few moments before adding. "I'm proud of you, you know?"

I place my mug on the counter and smile up at him. "Thanks."

"I'm serious. You have come so far. You are the strongest person I have ever met."

I raise my eyebrows at him. "I don't know about the strongest. There were a few times that I wanted to give up. The nightmares were so bad I couldn't sleep at night for months, the fear of going anywhere without you or those close to me and having flashbacks anytime you or another man tried to get near me. I really thought I was okay in the hospital, and then we came home and boom, I was a mess."

"Love, you were still riding the pain meds, and you constantly had people coming and going while you were in the hospital. You then came home to just me, no one waking you up in the middle of the night for hospital care, and you went from heavy dosed medication to Ibuprofen. It was a big transition. But you got through it."

"Because of you," I add.

"No. Because of you with the help of your therapist and everyone that loves you." He gives me another squeeze. "I hate to cut this short, but I need to leave for work. I will text you on my lunch break so we can decide on where to meet for dinner. Deal?"

"Deal." I give him one last kiss and then he is out the door.

Saige

When I walk into the shelter, I'm greeted by warm smiles from the employees and the ladies living there. A few of the kids run up to me and beg me to play with them, which I promise to do later once I finish the job I need to do. I show them my bag full of crafts and goodies for them, and they squeal in delight as they run back to the playroom.

I find Emma in the kitchen getting lunch ready for the families here. She greets me with a smile, apologizing for not hugging me as her hands were otherwise indisposed. She introduces me to some newer volunteers in the kitchen, and I make small talk with them and the other workers I know while she finishes with her duties.

After washing her hands, Emma grabs my shoulders and leads me out of the kitchen and into her office. I take a seat across from her desk and wait for her to get seated. She hesitates for a few moments with a look on her face filled with curiosity and remorse.

"It's okay. You can ask me the questions that are going through your head."

Her shoulders relax. "Okay." She clears her throat and leans her elbow on her desk. "Well, first, I wanted to ask you how you are doing?"

"Great! I'm still in therapy once a month, but we are going to talk about stopping it in a few days. I can talk about it and think about it without emotions overpowering me. I can't say where I would be without my support or if the circumstances surrounding my kidnapping were different."

"What do you mean?" she asks in confusion.

"Yes, I was kidnapped, and yes, I was beat and fought for my life, but I'm alive and other things didn't happen to me. I've learned to think about the good instead of focusing on the bad." She eyes me. "My therapist has helped me a lot."

"Good. If this is still too soon, you can volunteer in a few more months." Her motherly instincts kick in.

"No, I'm good. Honestly. I wouldn't be here if I didn't think I was. The ladies here deserve my full attention. I'm here for them and with fresh eyes."

"Okay. Well, let's find something for you to do here." She goes to stand.

"Actually, I would like to talk to you about something else. I was wondering if you had a position available. I would really like to work here full time or even part time. My latest book has been submitted and my therapist thinks it will be a good idea."

"As a matter of fact, I do. I have a full-time position available. You'd do everything you do when you volunteer, but you'd also provide crisis intervention, practical support, emotional support, and education to these ladies. You'd also provide case management, counseling, and advocacy to the ladies and children. It'll be a ten a.m. to six p.m. job."

She reaches into the file cabinet behind her and hands me a paper. "Here is the application with a few more job descriptions for you. Why don't you look it over, and if you feel like this is for you, then fill it out and give it to me at the end of your shift today, okay?"

I look at the application and then look at her and smile. "I will."

"We have a few other applicants, but we will look at all the applications and choose the best one that seems to fit the position and this facility."

I am nervous that I might not get the job, and my face must show that because she then adds, "If we don't choose you, you can still volunteer. We would hate to lose you."

"Okay. Thank you." She nods.

I follow her out of the office and into the dining room.

She turns to me. "Okay. When they are done eating, you can clean the dining room and wash the dishes. You can also do some laundry and crafts with the kids. Sound good?"

"Perfect. I was hoping to have time with the kids today." I smile.

She smiles back. "I know. I saw your craft bag at the front door when we walked by."

"Thank you, Emma."

"Anytime, Saige. Thank you."

When Emma walks off the kids who were watching come running over to me asking to do crafts. I promise them to do crafts after I clean the dining room and dishes. They moan and groan, and I chuckle silently. "Patience, guys. I promise we will get to them. I just have to get these things done or else I will get fired and then I won't be able to come back and do crafts again. Go play, and when I'm done, I will find you."

They walk away still groaning but quickly recover once they make it to the playroom again. Laughter quickly fills the room. I head to the kitchen and grab the cleaning supplies out of the closet.

~

Before I know it, the dining room is cleaned, and the dishes are all on the rack. I'm drying my hands when I feel a tug. I peer down and find the cutest hand holding onto my pant leg. A little girl with caramel skin and the most beautiful black ringlets falling around her face is staring at me. I scoop her up, and she smiles before laying her head down on my shoulder.

"Where is your mama, little one?" I ask her while rocking back and forth with her in my arms.

"Maia! Maia, where are you?" I hear the voice yelling out in the dining room.

The little girl lifts her head and faces the sound. "Is that your mama?"

"Mama." She responds.

I carry her from the kitchen and into the dining room. The woman turns to face us, and relief washes over her face.

She runs over to us and grabs Maia from my arms. "Oh, thank God. I was so worried. I turned my back for a few seconds, and she was gone."

"She was just supervising me washing dishes." I look at Maia. "Weren't you?" Maia smiles.

I look at her mom again. "I'm Saige."

"Jacklyn. And Maia you already know."

"Yes, I do." I motion to the papers in her hand.

"Applications?"

"Yes. I'm trying to apply for jobs so that I can get us a place to stay and get us back on our feet."

"Well, I can watch her, if you like. I was just about to start some crafts with the kids."

"You don't have to do that."

"I want to. I even have something that she can make for you while you are busy. We will be in the playroom if you need us."

"Thank you. That will be a great help." She hands Maia back over to me.

When I watch Jacklyn walk to a table and sit down to start filling out the applications, I turn with Maia and walk in the opposite direction towards the playroom. The kids look up quickly once they hear my footsteps enter the room.

All in unison they yell out about crafts and playing with them.

"Alright. We can make some crafts now. Everyone sit in a circle, and I will let you know what we are making." They scurry into a circle and all sit, patiently waiting for me to start. "We are all going to make snowmen today since Christmas is coming up."

The older kids quickly go to work making theirs while I show the little kids how to make them. The toddlers get more paint on me than the snowmen, which somehow turns into all the kids making my face look like one. Laughter fills the room, and soon, moms come in to see what the commotion is about. A few of them smile and a lot of them join in on the laughter.

When the laughter dies down and my face is finished, the kids grab their artwork and show their parents what they have done. They all start trickling out of the room while I gather the supplies up and clean the mess we had made. A body jumps onto my back, and I smile when I turn my head and see that it is Maia again.

"Horsey." She grabs my shirt in the back and pushes her hand forward trying to get me to go.

I make sure she is holding on tight and sitting in the middle of my back properly before I start walking around the room on my hands and knees. Every once in a while, I will put my hands behind me to hold up her legs while I lift up onto my knees like a horse rearing up. I let out a 'neigh' and then drop back down. She giggles and squeals in delight.

After twenty minutes of playing horsey, she climbs off my back and runs out of the room. I slowly get off the floor, cursing my knees and hips for hurting as I try to chase after her. I round the doorway and find her climbing into her mother's lap. I watch the two of them interact, and my heart fills up with joy from the adoration they have of each other. Jacklyn looks up and sees me watching them, and she smiles at me. I smile back and walk towards them.

"Saige, thank you for taking the time to take care of Maia. You don't understand the year we have had." She starts crying and tries to stop by covering her mouth with her hands.

I grab her hand and pull it away from her face. "You don't ever have to hide your pain. Not from Maia, and especially not from me."

She cries more, and I take a seat next to her and wrap an arm across her shoulder. She leans into my embrace with Maia still sitting in her lap, sucking her thumb. I hold her until her sniffles recede, and she lifts her face up to wipe the last of her tears.

"Thank you for that. I've been holding it all in since we got here, too afraid to let any emotion out." Her red-rimmed eyes look into mine. "Do you know why I'm here? I'm not sure if you are privy to my file."

"I don't know. I'm just a volunteer, so we just help out without knowing anyone's story, unless they share it with us."

"I want to share if you want to listen."

"Of course," I reply.

"My boyfriend, Maia's dad, has been in our life for six years. He was sweet and caring in the beginning. He slowly became controlling, but it was in small increments, and I didn't even notice I was being controlled until it was too late. He used emotional abuse to get me into his grasp, and after Maia was born, I looked different.

"I got the mom belly that some women have the luxury of losing. I tried to lose weight by eating better and working out, and when that didn't work, he used his emotional abuse to make me feel like the ugliest woman in the world. I starved myself, or he did, I can't remember. I lost sixty pounds by barely eating, and I was skin and bones. I lost all the muscle in my body, and I believed everything he said.

"He hated that Maia got all of my attention with nursing and her just being a newborn, and that was when the physical abuse happened. But after the controlling and emotional abuse, I let it happen because I believed I was just as worthless as he made me believe. I believed I deserved to be punished for not giving him as much attention as he wanted.

"He never touched Maia and never hit me in front of her, but she heard the words he said to me. She heard her father calling me worthless and worse. She watched me wither away while still providing for her. I secretly started to hate that I had her because I couldn't find joy in motherhood anymore."

She started to cry again. "It wasn't until my mom came over for an unexpected visit, did I see what had happened. My mom saved my life and hers." She motions to Maia.

"Mom got me out of there that day, and we moved in with her. She put meat back on the bones, and I found joy in life and motherhood again. It only lasted a few months because my mom passed away. He found us and killed her while Maia and I were sleeping. I found her in her bed, and blood was written on the wall saying, 'If I can't have you, neither can she'.

"We took off right away with just the clothes on our backs and came here in fear for our lives. This place has been a Godsend, the people here as well."

I reach over to grab her hand. I give it a little squeeze. "Thank you for trusting me with your story. You have been through a lot and came out so strong. I am always here when you need me."

"I appreciate it. Can I ask you a question?" She is nervous.

"Yes. Of course."

"What happened to you? I heard some whispers about you when you were gone and then the stories have gotten worse since you got back today. You don't have to share if you don't want to, but if you do, then I'll listen."

I think long and hard. "Well, what exactly have you heard?"

"That you were kidnapped. It was on the news." She is still nervous.

"That's true. I used to live in New York. I had a controlling boyfriend there, and when I found out he cheated, we were over. I took it hard and eventually came to visit my family in Winter Springs for their Bicentennial.

"When I got here, things were going well. I caught up with friends and family, and I started falling for the boy next door that I wanted in high school. A lot of things are involved with that, but I won't bore you with the details.

"I met a guy at the bar on my first day back, and he seemed like a good enough guy that I agreed to go on a date with him. Before the date happened, he showed up at a football game I was at and was possessive, flirty, and gave me stalker vibes. My friends picked up on it too, but we chalked it up to him just coming on strong. I should have picked that up as my first red flag.

"I started receiving notes in random places. I woke up one day with things in different places than they were when I went to bed. He found me in Huntington in front of a lingerie store of all places. He said he was buying things for his girlfriend, who just so happened to be my size. I still was stupid to not say anything to others even though that should have been red flag number two.

"Eventually, the red flag number three came soon when I found said lingerie set that he bought in my drawers in my brother's house, along with the last note. My brother is a police officer, so he called it in and took the notes to the station, but it was too late. This guy had his sights set on me, and I was his.

"He took me one evening, and it wasn't pretty. I thought it was just him, but there was also this girl that was obsessed with my boyfriend. I was hit and treated horribly until one day I was finally able to escape. I won't go into those details, but I had to fight for my life, and thankfully I was the one to live.

"It took almost a year of therapy and a long hospital stay, but I am here now and better than ever. But I want you to know that I know what you're feeling when you feel like you have been so defeated that you don't want to go on, and then one day you wake up and say, 'I am a woman, and I am powerful. I am a warrior!'."

"Thank you for sharing your story. It helps having someone that has also gone through something traumatic to understand you. Someone who has come so far that you know you will be okay because they are." She grabs my hand and squeezes it like I did hers.

"If you ever need someone to talk to or even someone to watch Maia while you are at job interviews and such, please don't hesitate to call. My phone will always be open to you," I reply.

"Thank you, Saige." She puts Maia down and pulls me into a hug.

I pull away first and smile at her. I bend down to give Maia a hug also before standing back up. "I'm going to go talk to Emma and head out of here. I will have her give you my phone number."

"Okay."

I grab my bag and walk to Emma's office. I wave goodbye to a few people on my way and then stand in front of her office door, composing myself. I knock on the door, and Emma's voice calls for me to enter on the other side.

"I filled out the application." I pull it out of the bag and hand it over to her.

"Good." I sit down across from her. "You're hired."

Shock fills my body. "What? I thought I had to fill the application out and then you would choose the best applicant?"

She smiles. "I only said that because I wanted to be absolutely certain you were ready. I already thought you were perfect for the position before you even asked for a job. You are fantastic with all the residents, and you do your jobs well. You always go above and beyond what is asked of you."

I smile back and feel my cheeks flush. "Thank you. You won't regret it."

"I know," she replies. "Well, if you have time, I can show you to the office you will use and go over the paperwork and the ins and outs of everything."

"Absolutely." I stand up and open the door. "After you."

~

I start the car and the air hits me in the face. I turn the radio on, and the sound of 'I Am Woman' by Emmy Meli fills the car. Before I know it, I am belting along.

The song is like an anthem to women everywhere. There is so much that has happened in my life in just a year and a half that would have made almost anyone give up. But I held my head high and persevered. I am so blessed right now. I wrote a second book, moved back home, I have a new job, a handsome boyfriend and fantastic friends and family. What more could a woman want?

Saige

I stop by Mom's on the way home, and she greets me with a smile. Mom asks me about jobs, therapy, and Declan and I. I'm open and honest with her, and I am grateful that I can be. Eight months ago, this wouldn't have been possible. We are still mending our relationship, but I have high hopes for us.

"I'm seeing someone now," Mom blurts out.

"Seeing someone? Really?"

"Yeah. John. My neighbor. I really want you and your brothers to like him."

I take her hand in mine. "Are you happy?"

She nods.

"Well, then that's fantastic." I smile at her. "I want to see you happy, and if he makes you happy, then I'm sure I'll like him."

"Thanks, sweetie. I have some other news." She gets up from the couch and walks towards her bedroom.

"What news?" I yell down the hall.

A black Labrador puppy comes running out of the room and

down the hall towards me. I crouch down and pet it. He jumps up and licks my face, and we fall over backwards.

I try to get up, but the puppy keeps pushing me back down.

"I think Mom needs to get her money back on those obedience classes. Midnight still chews on all of my shoes and poops in my closet." Finn walks out of the spare bedroom and leans down to help me up.

We all walk back to the living room with Midnight following us. His tail wags, and he yips a few times before jumping into Mom's lap and settling down.

"He just doesn't like you," Mom replies. "Maybe he is just trying to assert his dominance over you and telling you he should be the only kid in the house."

Finn has been in Winter Springs as long as I have. He said it is because he hasn't had a job offer yet, but River has already let it slip that he has turned down two offers. I know the reason why he declined the offers was because of me. He wants to keep an eye on me.

"Mom, I told you. I don't live here. I'm just waiting for a job offer to come through, and I'll be out of here and out of your hair."

"Waiting. Hmm? I know for a fact that you have had offers, but you turned them down," Mom adds.

"What are you talking about?" He looks at me, a blush creeping.

"Finn, I wasn't going to bring this up, but since Mom has, why are you turning down offers?"

"I don't know what you are talking about."

"Finn Wilson, don't you lie to me. I am your sister and you, my brother, have a telling face when you lie. So, I know you are lying right now."

He sighs, and his shoulders slump forward. "I couldn't leave until I knew you were alright."

"I never asked you to give up your jobs to be here for me."

"You didn't have to. I'm your big brother, and you are my best friend. It's my job to be here and take care of you."

"Finn, I am a grown woman. I can take care of myself, and I have plenty of people here to watch over me. Mom, Declan, River, Ginny, Megan, and Gina are all here. You didn't need to stay for me. I know how much you love your job and being out there. You must be itching to get back out in the field."

"You didn't see what you looked like after the whole ordeal with Milo. I couldn't leave you." His voice raises.

"No. You are right. I didn't see myself because I lived through it."

"Just listen to me." He growls in frustration. "We had to watch you go through it and not be able to do a damn thing about it. The whole time you were gone the constant fear of you being killed and raped constantly filled our minds. We worried that we would never see you again.

"Then we found you, and when we saw you, you were bloody and bruised and your face was so swollen that if I didn't know you inside and out, I wouldn't have recognized you. We had to see the struggle you had with Milo in the driveway where we couldn't tell what blood on the gravel was yours or his. Then we watched Quinn steer the car in your direction trying to murder you in front of our very own eyes.

"We watched your helpless body lie in that hospital bed while we heard about all of your injuries from the doctor. We watched you come home and pretend to be strong, but we heard from Declan that you weren't sleeping at night because of the nightmares. How you would flinch away from him if he touched you a certain way or said something to you that triggered a memory.

"It was fucking torturous to see and hear you go through that. I had never felt so helpless in my whole life. So, that is why I am here and not there. I am here to make sure my sister is safe and loved and okay before I even start to think about leaving. Got it?"

All I can do is nod as tears roll down my cheeks. I reach for his hand. "It's been eight months. I am okay, I promise. Go live your life doing what you love. Unless there is something else that keeps you from leaving, like a certain someone?"

Mom turns abruptly to look at me, "Someone!" She turns back to face Finn. "Who is this someone?"

Finn sighs. "No one, Mom. Saige doesn't know what she is talking about." He eyes me.

"My mistake," I say and then catch Finn's eye. I mouth 'we will talk later', and he nods.

Declan

I finish up with my client early and sit in the office to work on some paperwork before it piles too high. After pushing through for two hours, my finished pile is taller than my unfinished one. I count and see I only have two more files to go and debate on finishing them or stopping early and surprising Saige at home so we can drive together instead of meeting at the restaurant.

My phone beeps, and I find a text from her, like she knew I was thinking of her. I open the message and see her nude body in the bathroom with the caption, 'Wish you were here to shower with me'. I adjust myself and turn off the computer because there is definitely no way I can concentrate after that.

On the car ride home, I think about what outfit she may wear. Will she wear the leggings that make her ass look like a ripe peach that's begging to have a bite taken out of it, or will she wear a dress so that her thick thighs are showcased? I smile knowing my girl looks hot in anything she wears, and I am a damn lucky man for having her love me.

She asked me one day, in the beginning of our relationship, why I liked her. 'Why someone like me could love someone like her'. I thought at first it was because of the trauma she went through, but I know her well enough to not believe that in its entirety. I remember her friends Gina and Megan and even her brothers telling me about her self-love. I remember her telling me about Phillippe. So, I knew she was actually asking me why I loved her because, to her, she was fat, and I was fit.

It didn't take me but a moment to respond to her. "While you see fat, I see the most beautiful girl in the world. There is nothing sexier than the woman standing in front of me. Your thick thighs, big booty, side rolls and stretch marks on your hips are what makes you, you. You see fat, but I see a woman that has more than enough for me to love, to cherish. I worship your body, and I'd gladly eat every inch of you up.

"You wonder why I chose you over a skinny girl like my exes in high school? Well, I never believed in society's standards on how a woman should be. Because while I was dating them, I was in love with you. I have been in love with this body since the first time I laid eyes on you.

"Some men like skinny women. Their bodies are like a highway because it gets them to the end result faster. I like your body because it's like a country road. Curves, dips, mounds, valleys, all of it because it's the most surreal scenic route. A country road is a road to take your time on and enjoy the scenery before you get to your destination."

I guess the answer was good enough for her, or I proved how much I loved her body, that she never asked again. But I will gladly prove it to her over and over if I need to.

Ten minutes later Saige's red Ford Explorer sitting in the

driveway welcomes me as I park my black Ford f-350 beside it. I hop out of the truck and run up the porch steps to unlock the front door. I swing the door open wide and yell, "Honey! I'm home!"

A naked Saige is sitting on the recliner, legs crossed at the knee, facing the front door. She drops her top leg down and plants it on the floor. Her legs slowly spread apart, giving me a view of her wet opening.

A smile creeps on her face. "Took you long enough."

Saige

"Here I thought I was going to have to take care of myself." My hand slowly crawls down from my thigh to my core.

"Don't." Declan growls out as he walks to me.

My hands stop what they are doing, and I wait patiently for what's coming next.

He lowers down onto his knees, his face aligned with the one place I want him to touch. "Allow me to apologize."

He buries his face into me and inhales my scent.

"Ah." I moan out as he slowly licks from the bottom to the top of my slit.

He continues his torture with his tongue as his thumb flicks my clit and rubs it in circles, adding pressure.

It doesn't take long for me to come undone.

He raises his face to look at me, my juice glistening on his mouth. "Did you shower alone, love?"

I shake my head, my eyes closed, enjoying the sensation of pleasure this man can bring to me.

"Good." His thumb leaves, and my body is left wanting.

He rises to his feet, grabbing my hands to pull me up.

"Let's go kill two birds with one stone." He tugs me behind him to the bathroom.

I watch him tug his shirt off, his perfectly sculpted body out on display to me. He goes for his belt, and I stop him.

"Let me."

I place my hands on his hips and use my tongue to guide my face from his chest to his abs as I lower onto my knees in front of him.

"Christ, woman! The things you do to me." I look up and meet his dazed eyes.

My hands find his belt, and I slowly unbuckle it. Never breaking eye contact with him, I pop open the button and lower the zipper.

"It's only the beginning. You haven't felt anything yet." I say as I pull his boxers down and grip his cock in my hand. "So ready for me." I look down at it, and it jerks in my hand.

"Always, love," he says, his voice deep and husky.

I lick the veins on the underside and swirl my tongue over the sensitive tip, licking up the pre-cum. My jaw relaxes as I put my mouth over him, swirling my tongue over the tip once more before taking as much of him in as I can. My head bobs up and down, his cock hitting the back of my throat. Tears well up in my eyes, and I choke a little.

"Fuck!" His hand fists in my hair, pushing my head to meet his bucking hips.

He pulls back abruptly and pulls out of me, fisting himself.

He grips my chin and rubs his thumb across my swollen lips. "As much as I would love to come inside this beautiful mouth, we need to shower and take care of both of our needs if we are to make our dinner reservation."

"We could always skip it and order in." I look into his green eyes.

He growls, and a shiver runs up my spine as heat floods my lower belly. "Aren't you a bad girl? But no, we are going out tonight."

He leans sideways to start the hot water and then pulls me to my feet, his mouth claiming mine immediately. Without breaking the kiss, he turns us so that my back is facing the shower, and he guides me into it. The hot water rushes over my body, and I break the kiss when my back hits the wall.

Declan raises my hands above my head, using one of his hands to keep it there. His mouth plants kisses on my face and neck before coming back. His unoccupied hands grope my breast, causing my already hard nipples to turn rock solid. I wrap my leg around his waist, and he drops his hand from my breast to place my leg where he wants. He thrusts into me, both of us crying out.

We both dance in movement with each other, bringing pleasure until we both scream out with our releases. We don't move as the waves crash over us. My body relaxes from the exhaustion and chemicals it just released, and I feel sated.

Declan is the first to move, dropping my leg from his hip and pushing me into the water. He plants a kiss on top of my head before he squirts shampoo into his hands and massages them throughout my hair. He rinses it out while I lay my head back to keep the shampoo from getting into my eyes. His hands are massaging my head again, this time with conditioner.

Once it is rinsed out, I step behind the stream of water and have him lean his head forward. I shampoo him and rinse it out, running my fingers through his hair. His hands roam my naked body, and I smile knowing I feel the same way; I can't keep my hands off of him either. I reach for the loofah on the hook and suds it up with his body wash and wash every inch of him, allowing my fingers to glide over the skin that's washing off. He shivers from being ticklish but also from enjoyment of my hands on him.

"Now, it's your turn." These are the first words being spoken since we had sex.

He takes the loofah from me and rinses it out before placing it on his hook. He grabs my loofah off my hook and squirts some of my body wash and repeats the same thing I had done to him. I shiver the same way, and we smile at each other.

When we are both clean, I turn the water off and turn around to face Declan, who has a towel wrapped around his waist. He holds a towel out for me. I walk to him, and he wraps the towel around me, rubbing my back and arms, trying to dry me off.

Our foreheads rest against each other.

"Do you think it will always be like this?" I ask him.

"I hope so," he replies.

"Me too." I lift my head to kiss his lips before leaving the bathroom.

He follows me inside the room. "I know you. What's wrong?"

I turn to face him while sliding my thong on. "Nothing."

He gives me a look, and I sigh. "It's just that everything is going good."

He raises his eyebrow. "And?"

"A little too good to be true. Don't you think so?"

He pauses a moment before coming towards me. He grabs my hand, and his piercing green eyes bore into my soul. "Trust me, love. For me, this isn't too good to be true. This is endgame. I'd marry you in a heartbeat if you would let me."

I suck in a breath and hold it.

"I'm just going at your pace. I have all the time in the world."

I let out the breath and look down. "I love you too, and I know in my heart that you are meant to be mine. I'm just afraid that something bad is going to happen and this dream I'm living is going to shatter."

He lifts my chin up to look at him again. "Don't worry. I got you and I'm not going anywhere."

Declan

We arrive for our dinner reservation and are quickly seated. A waiter comes over right away, and we both order a cocktail and look at the menu. I glance at Saige from behind the menu and see worry lines on her face.

"Saige."

She looks up and places her menu on the table. "Yes?"

I reach out, and she places her hand into mine. "It's alright, love. I'm happy you shared your feelings with me. Good or bad, I want to know everything, okay?"

She nods, and a small tear slides down her cheek. I lift my hand to brush it away.

"I just feel like I ruined the mood because I told you I felt like it's too good to be true. Now I'm at this wonderful, nice restaurant with the best guy I know, and I can't help but wonder if I made this awkward and screwed it up. I feel nervous like all eyes are on me, and I can't be myself right now. Even this dress feels like it isn't my own."

He stands up. "Come on." He gives me his hand.

I stand up. "What are we doing?"

"We're leaving." I throw the money down for the cocktails we haven't got yet.

"No! We can't leave!" She's shocked.

"Of course, we can. We are going home to change and then we are going somewhere that is a comfort for you. I never want you to be in a position where you feel awkward and uncomfortable."

We walk out of the restaurant, and when we get outside, she turns to face me. "We can go back in. You took the time to make a reservation here, and I'm ruining it."

I cup her face. "Look at me." She doesn't look. "Look at me, Saige." She meets my eye. "I love you. I want to be where you want to be. If you are uncomfortable there, then we need to be somewhere that makes you comfortable. We can make reservations here anytime. You are all that matters to me."

She wipes her tears away. "Okay. Are you sure?"

"One hundred percent sure."

She leans into me and wraps her arms around my waist. "You are too good for me, Declan Wolfe."

I wrap my arms around the back of her head. "You are equally as good, Saige Wilson."

I kiss the top of her head. "Now, where would you like to eat after we change out of these clothes?"

"Um, can we just eat at the Main Street Cafe and then walk around the square taking pictures with the Christmas decorations?"

"Sounds perfect."

"Can we not change though? We are wearing perfect picture clothes, and I'd love to show you off."

"As you wish. But, love, it is I that will be showing you off. You, in that dress, look sexy as hell." I look her up and down and lick my lips.

She laughs, "Let's go, Casanova."

~

It takes only ten minutes to get to Main Street, and the entire town is there. An older couple leaves, and we slide into their booth.

"Well, look at you two, looking all fine and shit." We glance up to see Megan pushing her way into the booth seat across from us.

"Thanks. We were going to go to Cavanaugh's, but we decided against it." Saige tells Megan.

"Sure. Who would want to be at that fancy smancy place when you could be here?" Megan replies, gesturing around the cafe.

I can see Saige moving in the seat, her nerves getting the best of her.

"I messed up the reservations by mistake. I thought it was tonight, but I accidentally made it for next week."

Saige looks at me and smiles. I give her hand a squeeze under the table.

"Whoops. You're not supposed to do that, big guy," Megan says with a chuckle.

She turns to Saige. "I feel like it's been forever since I've seen you. We should hang out soon, you, me, and Gina. That is if she will leave Scarlett with Jeff for the day. Baby girl is three months old already, and Gina has been with her all day, every day."

Saige looks at me, asking me with her eyes if Megan can join us. I nod.

I clear my throat and ask, "Megan, after we eat, do you want to join us going around the square? That way you can spend time with my love here."

"Oh, I don't know. I don't want to impose on your date." She looks at Saige.

Just as Saige is about to say something, Finn squeezes into the booth with Megan and pushes her over to the other side.

"Oh, you know what they say. Three is a crowd but four is a gathering." Finn interrupts.

"And who invited you?" I ask Finn.

"I did. Did you not hear me clearly just now? Or do I need to spell it out for you, Mr. Ivy league."

I roll my eyes as the waitress comes over. We all put in our orders and chat until our food arrives.

When our bellies are full, I pay the check, and we head to the square.

Saige

"Oh my god, I'm so full you could roll me like an Oompa Loompa." Megan groans while rubbing her tummy.

"Well, then come here Violet. Let's roll you around," Finn adds.

"And here I thought only Saige got my movie references," Megan replies.

"Must be in our genes," I say. "Movie references we get."

"That we do, Sis."

I glance over to the square and see Santa sitting on a big red chair and a line of children are waiting to see him. "Oh, look." I point at him. "Let's start this fun off by sitting on Santa's lap and telling him what we want for Christmas."

"Really, Saige? Aren't we a little old for that?" Finn groans.

"Speak for yourself, old man," Declan chimes in.

"Last one to the line is a rotten egg," Megan yells behind her as she runs to Santa.

I look down at the heels I'm wearing and curse myself for not going home to change at least my shoes. Declan rushes after her, and Finn stays behind with me. We both walk to Santa and watch Declan beat Megan and hear her threaten to castrate him. We start laughing.

"I took a job."

I stop in my tracks. "You did?"

"Yeah, it starts the day after New Year's Day for a few months. They wanted me to leave before Christmas, but I wanted to spend it with everyone this year. So, they pushed it back for me."

"I'm glad you are going to be able to spend Christmas with us. Who hired you and where are they sending you?"

"It's a third-party affiliated with National Wildlife Magazine. They want me to go to Colorado and photograph the Rocky Mountain National Park. I'll be staying with a friend there, but it's good money and you know how much I love nature."

"I do, which is why I'm so happy for you." I notice he is looking at Megan. "Have you told her?"

He looks back at me. "Told who?"

"Megan. Don't you both have something going on?"

"No." He pauses and looks at me. "How do you know?"

"Because you are my brother, and she is my best friend." I touch his arm. "You need to tell her. She deserves to hear it from you."

"It's nothing serious. We've only been on a few dates is all. But when I'm with her—"

"You feel like all is right in the world?" I ask, knowing that feeling all too well.

"Yes. But my line of work doesn't allow me to have a serious relationship. What woman would want to only see the guy she's dating for four months out of the year?"

"The kind that loves you and feels the same way. Plus, there are plenty of ways to see each other often. She could go with you. Megan is adventurous too. Maybe not as adventurous as you, but still," I say.

He sighs. "I'll tell her I'm leaving, but a few dates are not enough to tell her I want to be with her, but I will be away three-fourths of the year. I respect her too much for that."

"Okay. Let's go over there. Declan and Megan are getting impatient with us."

He chuckles. "Okay."

We walk over to Santa and realize all the kids are gone. It is a school night, so I figure all the kids are home doing homework and getting ready for bed.

"Woo wee, big man. You smell those rotten eggs?" Megan waves her hand in front of her face.

Declan pinches his nose. "Yep. It will take months of showers to get rid of that stink."

"Hardy-har-har," I say, walking up to them.

"We already took a picture with Santa together. Now it's your turn together. Then we will get one of all of us." Megan hands the picture of the two of them to me and I smile at the picture.

"This is fantastic!" I say.

"And you thought it wouldn't be?" Declan asks me. "Just look at us and our smiling faces."

Declan and Megan smile at me.

"Let's go, Smalls. Leave the egos behind." He drags me to Santa.

"Ho, ho, ho," a jolly voice comes from behind the beard.

I sit on Santa's leg and Finn takes the other one. We smile as the elf helper takes our picture.

"What would you two like for Christmas?" he asks, his voice jolly.

"I would like for my new job to go well and Christmas with my family to be one to remember," Finn answers him.

"I think that can be arranged." He smiles. "And you, Saige, what would you like for Christmas?"

I look at him in shock. "How do you know my name?"

He looks around to make sure no kids are around and then pulls down his beard. "It's me, Leo."

I fling my arms around him. "Oh, Leo! This makes this even more special."

Finn jumps off his leg so that Leo and I can be alone.

I met this man once on the dock and then we have run into each other once a month. We always stop what we are doing and talk for hours at a time, catching up on what the previous month had brought to us. I feel a deep connection with him and talking to him is so easy that I don't hold anything back and neither does he. I know deep down that we both needed to know each other and be in each other's lives for our own personal reasons.

He wraps his arms around me. "I pray for you, sweet girl. Every day I pray for you."

"I know you do. I pray for you too," I reply softly.

"I guess this is our once-a-month meetup."

"As much as you being Santa is a perfect meetup for this month, I'd like to meetup more than once if you'd like to."

"I'd like that more than you know. It's lonely being an old man with no more family."

"Declan and I are hosting a Christmas party at our house, and I'd be honored if you would join us. We will be your family from now on."

A tear trickles out of his eye, and a big smile is planted on his face. "It would be my pleasure."

Declan comes over to join us. With my arms wrapped around Leo, Declan stands behind him. With his hands on Leo's shoulders, we show our brightest smile while the camera snaps a picture. Finn and Megan join us for another picture, and I tell Leo the time and day of the party. We walk away with the photos in our hands.

Declan slings his arm around my shoulder, and we look at the pictures until we come across the sleigh on the other side of the square. Finn has Declan and I climb in first, and he pulls a camera out of his pocket to take a picture of us.

"And here I was thinking you were happy to see me." Megan jokes with him.

"I'm always happy to see you." He winks at her.

Declan and I jump off, and I grab Finn's camera to snap a picture of him and Megan. Just as Megan is about to climb down, Finn touches her arm to stop her.

"Can we talk?" he asks, and she nods.

"Let's go get everyone hot cocoa." I grab Declan's sleeve and pull him away.

When we are standing in line, Declan asks, "What's that about?"

He nods to Finn and Megan having an intense conversation.

"I'm sure Finn would like to tell you himself." I try to change the subject. "Want to get the small or large cocoa?"

"Large, and don't change the subject on me, love. I want to know what's going on from you."

"Finn is leaving after New Years for a job," I say, hoping he will be satisfied with the answer.

"That's good, right?" I don't answer. "Why isn't that good?"

"No, it is good. It's just that Megan and Finn have something going on. To what extent, I do not know. But he wants to tell her he is leaving, and he has been fighting with himself because he really likes her, and she likes him. But he respects her enough to not leave her here waiting on him since his jobs keep him gone for months at a time."

We order four large cocoas and sit down on a bench to sip ours while we wait for them.

"I see why we need to wait. If you could tell me all of that then I'm sure he has a lot more to say to her."

"That's why we are here waiting."

He puts his arm around my shoulders, and I snuggle into him, trying to take in as much of the warmth as I can. I really should have changed my clothes. Even with warm tights on my legs, I am shivering.

"We need to leave soon, or you'll freeze to death." He tries to take his jacket off, but I stop him.

"Let's go look at more decorations. They'll join us when they are finished."

We walk around some more and take pictures with Olaf and the Grinch before Megan joins us.

"Where's Finn?" Declan asks.

Megan shrugs before adding, "We had a talk about him leaving, and he said he needed to walk for a bit, but he'll join us soon."

I walk over to her and hand her the cocoa. She takes a sip, and I nudge her with my shoulder. "How are you?"

She tries to shrug it off. "I'm okay."

"Don't lie to me, Meg. How are you doing?" I stop her in her tracks.

She sighs and in a quiet whisper says, "I don't know. I like Finn and we have no commitment, but when he told me he was leaving, my heart sank. What does that even mean?"

"I don't know."

"And that's the thing. He leaves at the end of the year, so there's no time for us to figure this out."

"That's plenty of time, Megan."

She groans. "That's what Finn said too."

I look at her questioningly. "He told me that he respects me enough to not let me stay here waiting on him, but if I wanted to try then he would try. He then added that we have time to figure this out before he leaves."

"Then promise me this. Don't clock out." She tries to interrupt but I continue, "I know you. You clock out when anything gets hard. Stay with this. Stay with this until New Year's Eve and decide then. Do you think you can do that?"

"I won't promise anything because I don't know if I can keep it, but I will try."

"Good enough for me," I reply.

"Besides." She chuckles. "Finn is a whole lot of fun in the bedroom."

"Gross." I cover my ears.

"And in the shower." I pretend to heave.

"And basically, anywhere really."

"Okay, now I am going to barf," Declan says behind us.

We all laugh, and I throw my arm around her and pull her forward. "Let's go."

Declan and I show Megan the Olaf and the Grinch, and we

take more photos with them. Well, mainly Declan takes photos of us with them. We have a great time just being present and enjoying each other's company.

We start walking past the sleigh and we're almost at Santa's station when our names are called out. We look around to find the person responsible and find Gina pushing a stroller with Jeff. We join them, and I peer down into the stroller and take a peep at the beautiful sleeping Scarlett.

"We heard from Finn that you were out here. We would have been out here earlier, but Scarlett was fighting nursing and her bedtime. But now that she is asleep, we decided to get some sleeping photos of her and Santa together."

"You'll love Santa this year. It's our friend, Leo, and he'll be wonderful with Scarlett," Declan tells her.

"Gina, Saige and I have decided that next week we are going to have a ladies night, and we want you to join us," Megan tells her.

"I need to buy items for the Christmas party next weekend too. Would be great to get your input," I add.

"Oh. I'm not sure Scarlett would let me. She's nursing and still needs me," Gina says nervously.

"Jeff could watch her. We'd only be gone for a few hours or so," Megan says, knowing nothing when it comes to babies.

I pull Gina into a hug and whisper into her ear. "You do what is best for you and Scarlett. If you still want more time with her before you leave her, then take it. If you want to get away from the house for your sanity for a bit, then do it. You are the mom and only you will know what you and her need."

"Thank you," she whispers back to me.

I squeeze her hand. "Well, you better get going before she

wakes up and instead of a sleepy baby, you have a terror in a baby doll's body."

We walk back to the cafe and notice Finn is standing with River. Finn's hair is disheveled like he has been running his hands through it too many times. Out of worry or something else, I wonder. River is in uniform, leaning on the bar talking in hushed tones to Finn so that no one else around him can hear. River pats Finn on the back as he has the last word, and he turns to lean his back on the bar and stare out the wide-open windows. His eyes land on mine, and a giant smile forms on his face.

Declan and I walk to the front door with Main Street Cafe written in cream-colored letters. A bell chimes when we step in, and I see a group of teenagers sitting in the same booth we had left earlier. The boys have their arms slung across the red leather seats and the girls snuggle into their chests.

We walk up to my brothers and greetings are given. I hear the tone of Megan, and I look over at her. She is nervous and fiddling with her thumb nail, not making eye contact with anyone.

She clears her throat. "Well, it's been fun, but I should get home."

We all look at Finn, and he says nothing. Megan turns and walks abruptly out.

Declan hits Finn on the back. "You're a fucking idiot if you don't go after her."

Finn hesitates a moment, looking at all of us, and then runs out the door, the bells jingling loudly after him.

"I wonder how that will turn out?" River asks, all of us staring out through the windows.

"They're good for each other. They just don't know it yet," I reply.

Saige

One Week Later

I'm touching up my makeup in the bathroom when my phone rings. I put the eyeliner down and answer it, finding Megan on the other line. She goes on and on about begging Gina to come out with us before I stop her. "I need to get off here. I'm still getting ready."

She scolds me and tells me to hurry up because she is leaving to get me soon.

I pick up the eyeliner and finish my eye. I reach over to the Lazy Susan holding my makeup and find the mascara. I apply it to one eye before Declan comes in through the door and leans against the frame, watching me.

"May I help you?" I ask, applying the mascara to my other eye.

"Just watching my beautiful love do her makeup." He smiles at me through the mirror.

My eyes travel over his naked chest and down to his gray

sweatpants. I always wondered why women went crazy over men in gray sweatpants, but since being with Dec, I now know. They don't hide the package at all. If anything, they sculpt it.

"What you doing, love?" I look back at his face in the mirror. A smirk appears.

I smile back. "Just my handsome man and the package he delivered." My eyes dart down and back up to his face, my smile growing.

He looks down and laughs. "Is this why you love these pants so much?"

I nod. "It sure is."

I grab the red apple lipstick and put it on. When I am happy with the finished product, I add, "By the way, Megan and I are going out tonight. Gina might join us as well. We are going to grab drinks and then buy supplies for the Christmas party."

"Sounds perfect. I was actually going to see if Finn wanted to go to the bar myself."

I turn around and place my hands on my hips. "Declan Wolfe, don't you dare show up to the bar while we are there."

He walks to me and wraps his hands around my waist.

"I wouldn't dream of it, love." He gives me his world famous smirk. His hand grips my chin, and he runs the pad of his thumb over my lips. "But since you won't let us join you girls, can I ask you for something in return?"

"You can ask anything. I just might not grant it." My voice deepens seductively, and I see the lust in his eyes.

Still rubbing his thumb over my full red lips, he says, "I'd love to see these cherry red lips wrapped around my dick and you on your knees pleasuring yourself."

I pulled my face away from his hand. "And what, may I ask,

do I get in return?"

"Anything, love."

"Are you sure? Anything?" I ask, my eyebrows raised.

"Yes. Anything. You want the world; I'll give it to you. You want to be queen, well then baby you already are. You are my queen, and you rule over me always. I'll get on my knees and worship you right now."

"Queen sounds good."

He drops down to his knees and looks up into my eyes, his devilish smirk playing on his face. "Well, you can't have royalty without a feast."

I look at him questioningly.

"Hold on to the counter." He grabs my leg at the same time my left hand grips the counter.

I use my hand and the counter to hold me up as he lifts my leg and throws it over his shoulder. He kisses me in my sensitive area through my underwear and I gasp at the feeling. His fingers push the fabric away, and a growl leaves his throat. I shiver at the sound, and heat pools in my belly.

"Exquisite as always, love." I feel his breath on me, and goosebumps appear everywhere.

Before I know it, I am coming undone all over his face and he's holding on, letting me ride out my ecstasy on his fingers and tongue.

When I come to, he stands up, and I give him what he asked for. My red lipstick smears all over his dick, and I swallow his cum.

I reach for the toilet paper to wipe my lipstick off him.

In a growl, he says, "No, leave it. I want to go out tonight knowing I am marked by you because you own me every which way."

He helps me stand, and I stare at myself in the mirror. Most of the lipstick is gone or smeared on my upper lip and chin. I reach for the makeup remover and clean up the wonderful mess we have made. I touch up the foundation and lipstick and blow a kiss at the mirror. I fluff out my hair and walk out, humming a tune.

~

Megan rings the doorbell ten minutes late. She comes in, following Declan. I grab my ID and debit card, stuffing them in my leggings, and lean on the barstool, zipping up my black knee-length boots. I start walking to the coat closet and reach for my black wool coat.

"Seriously, Saige!" I hear behind me. She whispers something to Declan that I can't quite hear. They both start laughing

I turn towards her as I say, "What? Is this not okay?"

"Look at us. Look at what we are wearing," she says in between laughs.

I look down at my outfit and then look at hers.

"Okay, so either we have been friends for too long or you are my long-lost twin sister and we have twin powers," Megan announces.

I laugh this time. We are both wearing leggings and black knee length boots. Our shirts are the identical Coldplay t-shirts we bought when we saw them a few months ago. The only difference in our attire is the different coats we have on.

"Well, we might as well be sisters." I head over to Declan, give him a goodbye kiss and head to the door. "Let's go, twin."

Before I fully leave, I peek around the door from the outside. "Oh, and Dec? I better not see you out."

He salutes me. "You got it my queen." He points to the door. "Better catch up or your twin will leave you."

I blow him a kiss and head outside. Megan is sitting in the driver's seat of her car, the music blaring already. I chuckle and walk to the car, opening the door and getting in.

"So, if you are driving then I get to choose the tunes." I reach for the knob to change it.

Megan slaps my hand away. "Driver picks the music. Shotgun shuts his cakehole," she declares.

"Jerk," I tell her.

"Bitch," she replies.

We eye each other and I know she is thinking of those Winchesters like I am.

Megan searches for the right channel, and the sound of 'I'm Not Pretty' by JESSIA fills the car.

We look at each other and belt out the lyrics.

~

We pull up to Hacienda to grab food before heading to the bar. When we walk in, Gina is already there. We take one look at her and then look at each other. We cover our mouths, trying not to laugh. When we can't hold it long enough, we let it out, and Gina looks up abruptly at us with a confused and embarrassed look since all the tables around are staring.

"Will you two sit down and tell me what the hell is so funny?" her authoritative voice rings out.

We sit down across from her and point out the fact that all three of us are wearing the same clothes. Gina is also wearing the Coldplay shirt we all saw in concert, and black leggings with black knee-length boots. She chuckles, and when the waiter comes over, we ask him to take a picture of all of us. He snaps a memory we don't want to ever forget. I send the picture to their phones while we order food.

The chips and white cheese dip, our margaritas, and Gina's water is delivered. When Megan gives her a hard time about getting water, I understand her hesitation. Gina knows that it's okay to have a little bit of alcohol while nursing, according to the CDC, but she doesn't want to take a chance. She has read everything she knows about babies, hours and hours of research.

When I ask her about Scarlett and Jeff, she lights up talking about them. I smile in return, happy for her happiness and thinking about how happy I am with Declan. I look over at Megan with a smile on my face and see her faking hers. She's fidgeting in the seat and playing with her hands.

I nudge her with my elbow. "Hey. What's going on?"

Gina also looks at her with worry, and she looks up with the fakest smile we know. "Nothing. I'm so happy for you both. You, with your husband and my niece, and you, with a blooming love of your own. I just worry that I'll never have that. You guys seem so sure in your love life and mine's a mess."

"I love Declan, yes. But I worry every day that he'll find someone better. I worry all the time that it's too good to be true, and I'm ready for the other shoe to drop with some kind of disaster," I admit.

"Yes, but everyone around you can see how in love he is with you. I don't think this is a phase. I've heard him tell you that you are endgame. And you and Jeff have been together forever, and you are perfect for each other," she says, frustrated. "And what do I have?"

Gina stops me from saying something so she can get a word in. "Jeff and I are far from perfect. We fight and we have questioned if we should stay together at times. Hell, there was a point in our marriage where we were very close to ending it all because I had just had the third miscarriage and the emotional toll on me was severe."

"He wasn't there for me like I thought he should be, and I blamed myself for them, so I couldn't see why he would want to stick around. It almost destroyed the marriage I knew. I was dealing with numbness, disbelief, anger, guilt, sadness, and major depression. I looked at him and saw him going through life like everything was great and he didn't just lose a child. I hated him and hated myself more."

I reach across and grab Gina's hand. I give it a reassuring squeeze. "See Megan, everybody is a mess. Relationships can be messy. No one is perfect. Some people are just better at pretending than others."

Megan asks me in a whisper, "What about you and Declan? Is your relationship a mess?"

"Not messy, per se. Our relationship is great. It's me that's the mess. I keep thinking how it is too good to be true. I keep waiting for something bad to happen, something to swallow me whole and spit me out like it has time and time again. I think about whether I deserve him."

"So, you're self-sabotaging your relationship?" she asks curiously.

I look at her and notice Gina is listening intently.

"I wouldn't say self-sabotage. More like I've been wronged too many times that I don't trust myself to know right or wrong in a relationship."

Gina replies this time, "You'll know. There will be a moment, and you'll know." She then talks to Megan. "Meg, love will come to you. I feel it here." She holds her fist up to her heart.

"You're a fantastic friend to us and a wonderful aunt to Scarlett. There is no way a guy won't see that and fall madly in love with your crazy ass."

Megan holds her glass up and makes a toast. "To being a crazy ass and finding someone to love me."

I clink my glass with hers. "To finding my moment."

Gina joins in. "To strengthening my marriage and being the best mother I can be."

We each take a drink.

The rest of the dinner goes smoothly. We each eat in silence, enjoying the feast set before us. When we are finished with the food and our margaritas, we moan and groan about eating too much.

We load into the two cars and head to the store in hopes of finding supplies for the big Christmas party. The tunes are blaring, and Megan and I are singing off key. We turn left into the parking lot of the Hobby Lobby and park. Gina pulls up beside us and we all hop out.

"Good thing I have a fifty percent off coupon. I don't even want to know how much this is going to be," I say, peering into the two full carts.

"We could have started at Walmart or Target first. Would have been cheaper there," Megan tells me.

"Would have been, but Declan says since it's our first party since getting together he wants to go all out. Besides, these things will last more than one party, whereas the plastic ones from Walmart will break before the end of the evening."

"That's true," Gina adds. "When we had the baby shower, we tried to go as cheap as possible, remember? Things broke by the end of it and other things, like the balloons, wouldn't even inflate because they were old or had holes in them. We ended up throwing everything away at the end. One hundred dollars went…" Gina makes a popping noise and pretends to throw-something in the trash.

We move up in line with only one lady in front of us.

"I remember that. I have a feeling many parties are going to be held at your place," Megan replies.

"There better be more parties. When I get Scarlett off the boob, I plan on making up for all the chances I missed having adult conversations," Gina admits to us.

"Yeah, but by that time this one might already be with child," Megan points to me.

"Hardly." I scoff. "I've got to have my moment with Declan, beg him to marry me, and then have a baby after we are married."

The lady in front of us leaves, and we push the cart to the cashier. We load all the items up, and I pull out Declan's card to pay. We leave the carts inside the store and walk all the bags to the trunk of Megan's car.

Gina exchanges hugs with us and leaves to get home to snuggle and feed her daughter. Megan and I hop in the car, blast some more tunes and head back to Winter Springs to visit our favorite bar, Sherry's.

We take the long way so we can look at all the Christmas decorations. One of the houses we come upon has music in sync with the lights. Megan pulls over and parks so we can listen to a full song while watching the lights. They have decorative faces on the fence singing the songs, and the whole house lights up with the different beats. It isn't the first one we have ever seen, but when you see them, it's just so hard not to watch and feel the Christmas spirit.

Megan starts driving again, and we are too busy rocking out that I don't realize the house, Quinn's grandparents' house, is coming up. The car starts speeding up, letting me know Megan realizes it at the same time.

"Slow down." I tell her.

She whips her head over to face me and pulls over. She unbuckles and shifts in her seat so that she is facing me.

"Listen, chick, I'll whip this mother around and we will go another way, so we don't have to go by it," Megan says with a strong conviction.

"By it, you mean the farmhouse I was kept at?" I ask, amused that she won't say it.

"Well, I certainly didn't mean Old McDonald's farm of fun, now did I?" I laugh at her response.

"Let's go," I whisper.

"Okay." She shifts back, puts the car in drive and starts to whip it around.

I place my hand on her arm. "Stop!"

She puts her foot on the brake quickly, and we both lurch forward.

"What!" she yells back.

"I didn't mean to turn around. I meant let's go by it," I admit to the both of us.

"Are you sure? Like really sure? Wouldn't you rather do this with Declan?"

"Yes, I'm sure, and no, I don't want to do this with him. He would coddle and protect me the entire way, and that's one of the reasons why I love him, but I think I need someone to just sit back up and allow me to do this my way. You know?"

"Okay then." She turns the car to go back in the right direction, and we head towards the house. "Bitch, I'll gun it. Just say when."

I don't answer her because a few seconds later the driveway comes into view. The memories come flooding back, and it feels like the last stage of healing washing over me. The car turns and we are driving on gravel. The big white farmhouse is right there in front of me, the windshield being the only thing between it and me.

I look at Megan. "How?"

"I knew you needed more than to see the driveway to get through this. You needed to see the house. You needed to see it in its entirety." She glances out the windshield at the house. "Doesn't seem like much, does it?"

I lean over to hug her and then get out of the car.

I stand in front of the car, the headlights casting my silhouette onto the house, making it look much smaller than it is. I stare at my silhouette and think about how I came here that night weak and fragile, feeling smaller than a little mouse. Unbeknownst to me, I built my strength until I was willing to fight for my life and the life I deserved.

I give myself only a few more minutes to look before I turn around and walk back to the car with my head held higher than it has ever been.

Declan

Finn and I are taking another shot when River sits down, slapping us both on the back. I almost spill the shot but manage to keep it upright. I pour the contents into my mouth. Finn on the other hand has spilled his entire shot down the front of his pants, looking like he pissed himself.

"Shit!" he yells out while River and I laugh. "Anyone got any extra pants in their car. I can't stay here looking like I peed myself. It'll ruin my street cred."

River scoffs. "What street cred?"

"You know," he answers.

"I don't know. Do you know, Riv?" I say.

Emphasizing the p, River answers, "Nope."

Finn looks at both of us. "I don't even remember what we were talking about."

River and I chuckle. I tap him on the leg with the back of my hand and mouth, "Watch this."

"We were talking about you and Megan. How you want to be

with her but are afraid of telling her about your feelings."

"We were?" He thinks for a moment. "Well, that can't be right because I did tell her I wanted to be with her and that we would figure it out with my job. She was the one that wasn't sure about me and wanted time. I've given her until I leave and now, I'm just miserable waiting for her."

"And say she does want to be with you, how would that work out?" River asks him.

"Well, we'll talk about it. I don't know if she would come with me or if she would stay, and I'd visit whenever I can."

"Well, it'll be hard for her to come with you since she is a teacher. It's not like she could teach for a few months, quit and then continue the pattern over and over again with each one of your jobs," I add.

Finn puts his glass down and gives me a look.

I throw my hands up. "I'm just saying that you need to think about it all. Both of you are important to me and Saige. We want to see both of you happy in whatever way that is."

Finn nods. "I know. I thought I'd find her at the Christmas party and talk about it more. See if we can come to a conclusion before the end of it."

"Good." River slaps his hand on the table. "So, Declan. How is it going with Saige?"

I lift my drink up to my mouth and take a big gulp. I answer after I swallow. "Good."

He raises his eyebrow and looks at me. "Good? Just good?"

"Yeah, good." I go to take another drink and realize that my glass is empty. "I'll be right back. I need another."

I hear whispering behind me and know that Finn and River are talking about me as I walk away. I walk up to the bar, and Becky shoots me a look.

"I'll be right there, D," she says.

"Take your time."

A few minutes later, she sidles up across the bar from me. "Another?"

"Yep."

"Leave Saige at home?" she jokes with me.

"Nope. She left me at home, so I decided to drag her brothers out. I'm starting to see that might not be a good idea."

"Why not?"

"I probably shouldn't share this with you. How much do I owe you?"

"I'll put it on your tab." She stops me as I start to walk away. "By the way, she will have her moment."

I look at her, try to decipher what she means by that, but she quickly turns around and walks away to another patron. I face the boys and head towards the interrogation that's about to happen.

I settle into my seat. "So, what did I miss when I left?"

They both start talking at once, and I have to stop them so I can hear anything they are saying.

"One at a time."

"I was saying," River looks at his brother, "more like questioning what is going on. Usually when you are asked how you and Saige are, you get all gushy."

"I still am gushy, it's just that…" I let out a deep sigh, "You know how much I love your sister."

"Yes." Finn leans closer.

"Well, the other night when we were at the Main Street Cafe, Saige and I had other plans to go to a fancy restaurant on a well needed date. My plan was to come home with my ring on your sister's finger."

"Hey!" River slaps me on the back.

"Wait a minute. You said your plan was to come home with a ring on her finger. At the cafe she didn't have a ring on her finger, and you two didn't tell anyone you were engaged," Finn says suspiciously.

River's smile fades, and it dawns on him suddenly when his eyes go wide.

"That's right. I did say that. Before we went to that restaurant, she was asking questions, like if the relationship is too good to be true, and she was saying that she was waiting for the other shoe to drop. She was all nervous and such, and the ring in my pocket was burning a hole through my leg, but I knew that I couldn't ask her to marry me unless I knew that she was one hundred percent ready and not waiting for something bad to happen still."

"I know my sister, and I know she would marry you right here in this bar if you asked. But I think you did the right thing waiting to make sure she knew that she was ready," River says with certainty.

"Agreed," Finn adds.

"She has been through a lot, and I want her to share her life with me with no doubts about any of it."

"Well, cheers brother. It will happen," Finn says as he clinks his glass with mine.

"I know," I reply, taking a drink and setting the empty glass down on the table. "Well boys, it's been a good time, but I should probably head out before Saige and the girls get here."

I stand up and pull my wallet out of my pocket.

"Scared of our sister, Declan?" River says with a chuckle.

"Hell yes I am," I reply.

"Me too," Finn adds.

"Aw, hell. Even she scares me too," River admits.

I chuckle and go up to the bar to pay Becky my bar tab. I tell her to keep the card on file for Saige and Megan for when they come in. She winks and gives me a thumbs up.

I head out to the parking lot, and the idea of needing to get Saige's Christmas gift pops into my head. I quickly curse myself and take a detour to the mall in Huntington.

Saige

Megan and I pull into the parking lot of Sherry's. River and Finn's vehicles are here, but I don't see Declan's.

"Finn's here," I say, preparing Megan.

"I know. I saw the jeep," she says stiffly.

"If you want to leave and do something else, just say the word. I don't want to go anywhere that makes my best friend uncomfortable." She relaxes at my words.

She finds a parking spot and parks. She sighs. "I appreciate that you want to look out for me, but I'll be alright. It'll be okay." She turns to me. "Promise."

"Just say the word in there anytime and I will walk out with you."

She smiles wickedly. "It's a good thing I'm wearing boots then, because 'these boots were made for walking and that's just what they'll do' if your brother makes this night fucking awkward."

I slap my palm against my forehead. "Out of everything, that is what pops into your head?"

"No. It was either saying that or saying that I planned on getting drunk girl wasted and having sex with your brother over and over until we forget our little problem."

I roll my eyes. "You can't escape it. He's leaving the day after New Year's."

"And you can't escape finding out why you think your relationship with Declan is too good to be true."

"I'm not. I know he loves me; I know I love him. I also know life has never been easy on me in the romance department, so I'm afraid there is some red flag I'm missing."

We get out of the car, and Megan throws her arms around my shoulders and puts her face in front of mine. "Here is what I know. He is not like the others, like Philippe or even Milo. For one, you two have a history. You didn't with the others. Two, anyone can painfully see that he is irrevocably in love with you. No doubts from anyone on the outside."

"Three, if I remember correctly, you told everyone you were going to give up dating for a while. You didn't go looking for love, love found you. You didn't force yourself to fall. You tried to stop yourself from falling. But you fell! You fell in love!"

"Why deny yourself an opportunity to be with someone for the rest of your life because you are afraid? Love is about taking chances. It's about going in blindly and trusting your love is so strong that you can withstand anything."

"He has always been there. He was there when you tried to push him away. He was there when you were taken by Milo. He was scouring the town searching for you. He even came to rescue you. If he wasn't truly in love or didn't want to be with you, then he wouldn't have gone through all that trouble. He would have thrown his hands up when you came home from the hospital having nightmares and yelling when he would touch you. He could have easily walked away when you had months of therapy or even when you went missing. He stood up for you in the beginning and wanted you as soon as you came back home."

I pull her in close and give her the biggest bear hug I can muster. "Thank you. I needed that daily dose of a wakeup call. You are one hundred percent right."

She pulls one arm away, and we head inside, our arms linked around each other.

The wooden door scoots us inside to a crowded room. The stools are lined with locals talking and munching on peanuts. The tables are filled as well, some people we know and others that seem like they aren't from around here. We eye each other, trying to figure out what to do. Many people are standing around the tables waiting to be seated.

We are about to give up when part of the crowd opens up and I spot my brothers sitting at a table with four chairs. I look at Megan to see if she notices and is okay with it. She looks back at me and nods.

We head over to them and have to shoulder through some people who won't budge who think that we might be trying to cut in line. A few give us dirty looks, but I just smile at them. I can hear Megan behind me telling them to take a picture if they want to keep staring or telling them to chill the hell out. I laugh under my breath at her responses.

I finally reach the empty chair and ask if it is free. My brothers look up and sigh in relief when they see Megan and me.

"Thank God, you are finally here. We have been hounded for

an hour for these chairs and the table. I was going to hurt the next person who asked," Finn says dramatically.

We sit down, and Megan takes a look around before asking, "Who the hell are these people?"

"The town decided to host a Christmas parade tomorrow for the county. The inns are filled. Some of the townsfolk had to turn their homes into a bed and breakfasts just to fit all the people." River sounds stressed and frustrated.

"So, I guess that you have been busy then?" I ask him.

"That's the understatement of the year," he says in one breath.

"I knew about the parade, but why is everyone staying here? The other cities aren't far away. They could have just stayed home instead of crowding up our establishments." Megan gives the patrons of the bar a good look.

"I asked the same thing when they started filling in right after Declan left. Apparently, the mayor wanted the parade to be around nine and suggested people stay here because we have plenty of room." Finn rolls his eyes.

"Revenue to the town and all that," River answers.

"Well, thanks for saving the seats. I wonder how soon we will be able to get drinks." I look around and estimate it will take a long time.

"Not very long at all if you are friends with the bartender and she sees you come inside," Becky says behind me. She's holding a tray of four beers and shots and sits the whole thing down on the table. "Here you go. Drinks are on Declan. He left his tab open for you ladies, so I figured he wouldn't mind adding two beers and shots."

"Not at all. I really appreciate this," I say back to her.

"Just whistle when you need more. The money will be great,

but the attitudes of some of these people…"

After the mugs are empty and the shots have gone down, we end the night an hour later. Megan and Finn don't stop eying one another, and River and I exchange looks every time we notice. They never once talk to each other, unless it is in a group conversation. But we never say anything. They are grown adults and need to work it out on their own.

When Megan and I load into her car, we see Finn and River sitting in their vehicles waiting for us to leave. "Protectors through and through," I say to Megan. We drive for five minutes before Megan interrupts the silence.

"You don't have to say anything. I know. I should have talked to Finn."

"I wasn't going to say anything. You two are adults," I say.

"I promise to talk to him at the party. That'll give me a few days to prepare."

Saige

I wake up at six to prepare for the Christmas party. The turkey goes into the oven, the ham into the crock pot, and I make an apple pie and cheesecake. I walk through the house looking at all I need to do, kicking myself for not preparing sooner. I know If I just leave my house as it is then no one who comes this afternoon will care, but I need to clean for my sanity.

I grab any items around the house that don't belong and put them in their proper place. I sweep, vacuum, and mop the floors. The counters, cabinets, sinks, tables, and dressers are all wiped down. I fold the blankets thrown on the couch and recliners and clean the bathrooms top to bottom. It takes all of three hours to clean what I need to clean.

After glancing around the house and inhaling the smell of cleaning supplies, I grab all the items to decorate the house. I grab the ladder out of the pantry and fold the garland over my arm. As soon as I lean over on my tiptoes to tape one side of the garland up, the doorbell rings. Gina, Jeff, and Scarlett come walking in with goodies in their arms. Jeff drops the items onto the counter and runs up to help me. Declan follows them into the house carrying Scarlett in her car seat.

"Love, I told you to wait, and I'd help you hang everything up." He hands Scarlett over to Gina and grabs the other end of the garland.

"I know. I just thought I'd get started before you got here." I climb off the ladder and walk over to Gina.

I give her a hug and get Scarlett out of her seat. I inhale her baby smell, my ovaries bursting with excitement.

"Let's get you ready. The boys can handle the decorating." Gina tries to usher me down the hall.

"Are you sure? I kind of have a vision about how the decorations should look," I say, unsure about letting them decorate for me.

"We got this, love. You have told me your vision a billion times since you bought the decorations. It will look just like you want it to. Go spend time with Gina and Scarlett and get ready. It will be beautiful. I promise," Declan assures me.

Gina and I head down the hall into the bedroom. Scarlett is snuggled on my chest, and I'm blissfully happy cradling her.

"How can you go anywhere or do anything with this girl? I could just do this all day and be content," I question.

"It's difficult. There is no feeling like a baby that loves you and relies on you unconditionally. They are so trusting and comforted that they just drift off peacefully in your arms knowing they will be safe. It's just so pure," she tells me with adoration written all over her face as she glances at the sleeping baby in my arms.

"I can't wait. If you and Jeff ever need a babysitter, Declan and I would be ecstatic to watch her." I lean down and plant a kiss on the top of Scarlett's head before handing her over to Gina.

I walk into the closet and glance at the outfits. I pull out two and bring them into the room to ask for Gina's opinion. She chooses the deep purple, V-neck dress, and I walk back into the closet to put it on. I grab my black flats and step into them.

When I come back into the room, Gina looks up at me. "That dress was made for you."

"Thanks." I give her a twirl. "Time for makeup."

I head towards the bathroom, and Gina yells for me to do a glam look.

~

When I come back into the bedroom, Gina is nursing Scarlett. "Does that hurt?"

"It did at first and it does if she doesn't latch well." She looks up at me. "Oh Saige, it's perfect."

I leave Gina to finish nursing Scarlett and walk down the hall. I stop in my tracks and glance around at the fully decorated house that is better than my vision was. Finn, Mom, River, Ginny, and the kids are already here. They are all moving food around to organize, and Mom is putting the turkey back into the oven after basting it for the last time.

Excitement overcomes me as I look forward to celebrating this time with those close to me.

I clap my hands and walk into the room. "Okay. What needs to be done?"

"Nothing, dear. We've got it all. Just waiting for the turkey to be done in thirty minutes and then everything is done. Why don't you have a drink and relax before the rest of your guests arrive?" Mom suggests.

"Would anyone like a glass?" I ask. Ginny and Mom do, so I walk into the kitchen and grab a bottle of wine. I pop the cork and pour three glasses.

Jeff comes in and grabs a few beers out of the fridge.

"Gina will be out in a few minutes. She had to nurse Scarlett," I tell him.

"I figured as much. Thank you for hosting us today. It's probably the first real event we've been to since she was born. I forgot just how much I crave these kinds of things until they are taken away."

"Well, I told Gina, and I'll tell you. If you and Gina ever need a date night, Declan and I would be happy to watch her for you."

"We'll be happy to do what?" Declan asks, coming into the kitchen.

"I told Jeff we'd be happy to watch Scarlett if they want a date night."

"Oh, for sure. I love that little doll baby." Declan smiles.

"I appreciate that. We will definitely take you up on that," Jeff says gratefully.

I take the wine out to Mom and Ginny and pick Jace up. I sit down on his blanket and grab his colorful ball. I point and say a color, and he babbles a few words that are recognizable. He quickly loses interest and grabs his fire truck to push around. I sit and watch him until Ginny calls my name, and I tell Jace that I'll be right back. I find Ginny in the kitchen with Mom.

Mom has just taken out the turkey, and Ginny is checking on the ham.

"Everything alright?" I ask them both.

"We were wondering if the turkey and ham looked done before we cut them up and put them on the serving dish," Mom comments.

I grab the meat thermometer out of the drawer and check the turkey's temperature. I grab the butcher knife and slice into the breast, and the meat is tender and juicy inside. It is cooked to perfection. I cut a small piece off of the honey ham and put it in my mouth. I moan as the mouthwatering flavors fill my senses.

"These are great, but you two do not have to cut them up and put them on the serving dish. Let's have the guys do it," I declare, and they agree.

With the men in the kitchen cutting the meat, I lay out the veggie and fruit trays and take the cheesecake out of the fridge. The doorbell rings, and I wipe my hands on a rag and stride to the door. When I open it, a group of smiling faces greet me. Megan enters first with Becky and her brother Roger behind her.

"Leo is here too. He is out in his car gathering up gifts," Megan remarks when she puts mashed potatoes down on the table.

"Oh, Leo," I say before pulling the door closed behind me and finding him at his car with his hands full.

"Leo, what are you doing?" I ask while grabbing gifts from him.

"You didn't think I'd come here without gifts for you all, did you?"

"Yes, I did. We didn't tell you to bring any."

"I know, but I couldn't pass on the opportunity to bring you and Declan and all of the kids some. It's only ten gifts."

"Only." I scoff. "You did not need to bring Declan and me anything. Your presence alone is a gift."

"I know I didn't, but I wanted to. You and Declan have brought so much love into my life. I was alone and sad until you two. Now, I have family and laughter. So let me spoil you, alright?"

"Alright. Well, let's get these inside." I usher him in front of me.

He drops the gifts under the tree, and with everyone in the house, we let the festivities begin.

I glance around at all of our loved ones who have come over to celebrate Christmas together with love and laughter. Hours tick by, smiles are on everyone's face, the food is almost gone, and our bellies are filled.

I spot Declan by the sliding glass doors in the living room holding my nephew and kissing his cheek. He talks to him in hushed tones near his tiny ear. He looks up at my mother, brother's and Ginny, and his smile lights up the room.

I notice snow starting to fall behind him and cover the ground like a beautiful fluffy blanket. My nieces are running around outside with Luna chasing after them. They are all bundled up in their coats, hats, and gloves. Their faces look up to the wondrous sky. They open their mouths and stick their tongues out to catch snowflakes.

Arms wrap around my waist and pull me back inside. I turn and look into the piercing green eyes I always get lost in.

"Where did you go?" he asked me.

"Nowhere. I was just watching everyone I love and filled up with so much warmth."

"I figured. Your whole body lights up when you are happy. Your eyes squint and sparkle, your cheeks get rosy, your little dimple by your mouth pops out, and you shiver, just once, like you get goosebumps down your spine."

"My, aren't you observant?" I tease him.

"I can keep going." I don't say anything, so he continues, "I notice how you get this line down your forehead when you are angry or are concentrating really hard. I notice that you still watch Grey's Anatomy, even though you complain after every episode that it's not the same anymore."

"Well, it's not since Shonda left. The fantastic stories aren't there anymore, and all the characters I love have left," I explain.

"See. I love that you throw yourself into your books. I love that you have to toss and turn for fifteen minutes before you can go to sleep. I love that you are mending a relationship with your mom and have the kind of relationship with your brothers that many siblings would dream of having. I love that you don't take things for granted. I love that you work with women who have struggled in life under the hands of a man."

"I love how in just the small amount of time you have been back into my life; you have evolved into a new woman. You are confident, sexy, and smart. You know what you deserve, and you push for it. You went from baggy shirts and sweatpants to form fitting clothes."

"That's because I feel beautiful, and you make me feel beautiful. I'm done hiding my body to appease society's standards," I admit.

"I know, and I love you for being you. I notice you. I see you. And I love every inch of your body." He kisses my nose after every sentence.

When he is finished, I have tears rolling down my cheeks. I'm pretty sure this is the moment I have been waiting for. Megan gave me a slap of reality days ago, but here is my man standing in front of me, making sure I know that he knows me inside and out. Making sure I see the love he has for me in its entirety. Making sure that I have no reason to doubt anything about the sincerity of our relationship. Making sure I know he was always meant to be mine.

I am going to marry this man. I am going to be with him for the rest of my life. We are going to live happily ever after with kids and Luna. I vow to make sure he knows every day how much I love him and how thankful I am for him.

"I want to spend the rest of my life with you!" I blurt out.

"You do?" he asks with a smile forming on his face.

"I do. I have no doubts that we will be epic for the rest of our lives." I smile back at him.

He pulls me into his arms and seals our words with a kiss.

~

Megan, Ginny, and Gina join me on the outdoor couch outside. We are all bundled up in our snow attire, and the guys' inside are probably calling us fools behind our backs. We have a bundle of blankets thrown across us, and we are all huddled together with hot cocoa in our hands.

"We will have to do this again," Gina says, sipping her cocoa.

"Well, it'll have to be next year because I'm going to be exhausted for the next six months," I admit.

"Well, you still have one month before New Year's Eve." Megan laughs.

"Crap, you're right!" I groan.

"It'll be fine. Today turned out perfect." Gina pats me on the leg.

"And we will help you prepare. Actually, we should all go out and let the guys decorate again. They did a wonderful job," Ginny declares.

"Yes! We should do that!" I exclaim. "The house turned out

perfect."

"I wonder what the guys think about us being out here?" Megan asks, looking behind her into the house. I look into the house with her.

Finn, Jeff, River, and Declan are all leaning on the counter in the kitchen, beers in their hands. I see Megan and Finn make eye contact, and she looks away quickly.

"I take it the talk with Finn didn't go well?" I grab her hand.

She turns to face the backyard once more and sighs. "No. He really wants to do this job, and I'm so happy for him because it sounds so exciting and adventurous, but I can't just quit my job and uproot my life to go with him, especially since this is so new. I could see quitting if we were serious and had been together for a while."

"What about long distance? You could do that and still be together," Ginny adds.

We all look at Megan quizzically. She gives a pause and answers. "How would any of you feel only seeing your man three to four months out of an entire year? It sounds horrible to me! I just want a normal relationship with someone who loves me as much as I love him and where we equally sacrifice, not just one of us."

"You love him?" Gina looks at Megan with sadness in her eyes.

"I think I do. I mean, our story is similar to Saige and Declan's. I've liked him since high school. I just never told anyone."

Gina and I look at each other and ask, with our eyes, if either one of us knew. We both shake our heads.

"And when he gave me a chance, I was ecstatic. It's sort of

funny how we bicker like cats and dogs when we are with others because we push each other's buttons. But when we are together, alone, he is so in tune with me and my needs. He makes me feel like I am the last woman on Earth. I want to hear what he has to say or where we will go together next, and I yearn to see him again when he drops me home. It's hard to explain, but I've never felt anything like this with any of the other guys I've been with. Call it love, if you will, but it doesn't matter now. He's leaving and I'm stuck here."

"It's all my fault," I admit. "I'm the one that told him to leave and go work again because he didn't need to stay around here for me anymore. I'm sorry."

"No. It's not. It's no one's fault. Time's never on my side. End of story."

"Bullshit!" Ginny exclaims. "I'm sorry, but bullshit."

"I agree." Gina nods her head at Ginny.

"I'd have to say I agree too," I tell Megan. "You are funny, beautiful, and kind. You have a heart of gold, and you will find someone to love because time is always on your side, just not on your time."

"Thanks, girls. I need that kick in the ass to get me out of this pity party. Maybe I'll turn into Julia Roberts from Pretty Woman and find some man to take my puny teacher's salary and make me rich," Megan lifts her head up and tells us with a straight face.

Gina, Ginny, and I burst out laughing.

I wrap my arm around her shoulder. "I'm sorry, but no!"

Her shoulders sag and she lays her head down. I think we have hurt her feelings until giggles come from her. They soon turn into fits of laughter, and we join her and laugh again.

Saige

Christmas had come and gone. Declan and I opened the gifts that Leo had made for us. What we never knew was that he was an artist and his painting of us together is hanging up above the fireplace mantel. I called him up that day and begged for him to come over and celebrate Christmas, but he refused. He wanted us to celebrate our first Christmas together because the first time is always special. I did get him to compromise by coming over that evening for supper. I made his favorite food, fettuccine alfredo, and we shared a bottle of wine.

Declan and I gave him a new fishing pole and a trip to the ocean. It was the one place he and his wife, Lucy, never got to visit due to money, and we thought he would enjoy it. He was grateful but said he would only go if we went with him. It was a promise we agreed to.

Declan and I exchanged gifts too, and it's safe to say that we know each other very well. The home décor is on the walls already, and today I laid out the red, V-neck dress from Torrid, black flats and diamond heart necklace he gave me to wear for our New Year's Eve party. His bar cart is put together and filled next to the wall in the living room, and his new watch and black suit are laid out as well for tonight.

I'm in our room when Declan walks in, flips me around and pushes my back against the closet door. I grip his bicep.

"Why, hello there, gorgeous!" he growls.

"Hello, handsome." I run my hand down his arm and place it over his growing bulge. His cock jumps in my hand and he moans. "How may I help you?"

"I think we should take advantage of the fact that no one is here and it's the last day of the year."

I lick my lips, and his eyes dart to my mouth. "Oh yeah?"

He nods, his eyes not leaving my mouth. In one swift movement, he slams his mouth on mine, our tongues doing their familiar dance. My hands go to work unbuckling his belt, and his hands are gripping the hem of my shirt, breaking our kiss only to pull it over my head.

With his belt undone, I unbutton and lower the zipper of his pants. He unhooks my bra, and I pull my hands away to get my bra off before taking him out of his boxers. I grip him in my hand and lower down onto my knees. I look up at his piercing green eyes filled with lust and place my mouth on the tip, swirling my tongue over the opening. I run my tongue from base to tip on the large veins on the underside of it.

Moans escape him like encouraging words to my ears. I fill my mouth with him, bobbing up and down. He takes his shirt off, and I lift one hand up to run it across his abs. They flinch under my touch.

He fists my hair, and I grip his hips to keep a steady rhythm. I hum with him in my mouth, and a deep, primal growl fills the room. I shiver as heat fills my entire body. He pulls me to my feet and lifts me up. I wrap my legs around him and kiss those delectable lips that beg to be kissed.

Instead of taking us to the bed, he walks us out of the bedroom and into the living room before laying me down on a blanket beside the tree. The lights are off, and the curtains are closed, letting the soft glow of color from the tree bounce off our faces.

"You really planned this, didn't you?" I ask him.

A 'shh' escapes his mouth before he claims my mouth once more. He peppers kisses down my cheek and to that little spot behind the ear. I shiver, and he continues kissing down my neck, across my collarbone and over my mounds. He takes his time giving pleasure to my breasts while my nipples turn rock solid. I reach out to find his swollen cock and stroke it while he pays me attention.

He leaves my breast to trail kisses down across my naval and sits up to unbutton my pants. He stops every once in a while, letting out moans from my hand gliding up and down his shaft. My pants slowly unzip, and he pulls them off me, leaving me in only my underwear.

A twinkle in his eye lets me know that these will be going in the trash too. I gasp as he rips them off me, and my hand leaves his cock as he backs himself up to lower down on his stomach. He licks my slit and finds my bud. His tongue flicks it and sucks while he inserts two fingers into my opening, feeling my wetness. Pushing in and out and curving his fingers to find my spot inside. He continues his torture, and I scream out his name. He lifts up to watch my face until the high leaves.

A smile plays on his face. He flips me over onto my stomach and lifts my legs up onto my knees. With my ass raised in the air, he smacks it. His hand rubs across the area to soothe, and he comes closer. I feel him push inside until he is balls deep. He starts out slow until he can't hold out any longer. His hand winds through my hair once more, pulling it so my face is lifted. He slams inside me, and we both moan out loud. Another smack hits my ass, and I sigh when his palm rubs the area.

"Good girl. You like it rough, don't you?" He smacks my ass once more.

"Yes!" I yell in between breaths.

He pumps harder and faster, and we move together. When I think another orgasm is going to hit, he shifts our position once more.

I'm straddling Declan and looking down at his beautiful face. His hands are groping my breasts, pinching my nipples ever so often. The friction is rubbing my sensitive bud and I'm so close to coming. He grips my hips and slams into me, letting me know that he is also close. We move and grind and soon ride our orgasms together.

I plop on the ground beside him, and we lie there together, letting our heart rates go down. It's quiet except for the heavy breathing, and I look over and find him watching me.

"I love watching your chest go up and down, seeing the flush all over your body. Knowing that it's me that gets you going," he admits to me.

"I cup his cheek. "Always, my love. Always."

"I love you so much. I can't wait to spend the rest of my life making love and growing old together," he declares to me.

"I am excited for our future too. After holding Jace and

Scarlett and watching you with them, I want nothing more than to be your wife and have your babies," I tell him.

"Good." He leans over to kiss my lips once before getting up to go to the bathroom. I hear the water run a while before it turns off, and Declan walks out of the hall with a wet rag to clean me up.

~

Ginny, Megan, Gina, and I leave the house at seven p.m. to grab a bite to eat. Declan, River, Jeff, Finn, and the kids all say bye to us and promise to have the house ready by the time we come back. We all pile into my SUV and go on our way.

When we get to the Italian bistro, we all order a glass of wine. I look up and find Becky coming out carrying our salads, breadsticks, and alfredo sauce.

"What are you doing here?" I am surprised to see her here.

"Oh, just helping doofus out over there." She points to her brother behind the bar. "Our uncle owns the restaurant now, so when they are short staffed, he calls asking if I want to come in and make some extra cash, and I usually do."

"That's probably why I couldn't get a hold of you today. I wanted to see if you were coming to the party tonight."

She shrugs. "Probably not. I already made plans tonight. Sorry."

I break off a piece of a breadstick and dip it into the alfredo sauce. "Well, hey! When do you get off? Maybe you can join us for dinner."

"Sorry." She glances at the others. "Plans." She turns around and walks quickly through a door to the kitchen.

I look at the girls after watching her leave. "Well, that was weird."

Megan and Gina shrug, and Ginny goes back to eating her

salad. Thinking they all are being weird, I watch them for a while, but no one looks up to make eye contact. Instead, they all are busy eating the salad and breadsticks. I chalk it up to them just being hungry and enjoy my salad too.

The waiter comes back with our food, and that's when they all want to talk.

All at once I hear:

"So, what is your New Year's resolution?"

"What are you hoping next year brings?"

"What is the one thing you hope for in your future?"

I look across to Ginny. "You go first. They seem like roughly the same question, but what is your New Year's resolution? What are you hoping next year, and the future, will bring to you?"

"Me?" She points to her chest.

"Yep," I say.

She clears her throat. "Okay. Well, my resolution is to lose the baby weight."

"Here, here." Gina raises her glass.

"I hope next year, and the future, brings me and the family love and happiness," Ginny continues.

"Okay, Gina. Your turn," I say to her.

"Baby weight, same as Ginny. Then, I hope next year brings more parties and fun for all," she replies.

"Like a big celebration party," Megan adds, and Gina nods.

"Megan?" I ask.

"No resolution other than someone bringing Betty White back, and next year I hope to find love."

"You deserve love," I tell her.

"We all deserve the love we want," she replies. "Okay, Saige. Your turn to answer now."

"Well. My New Year's resolution is to build myself up more instead of tearing myself down. I hope." I pause. "I hope that a marriage with Declan and kids is in our future."

"So, if he was to ask you, you'd say yes?" Gina pushes.

"Of course. I know I'd been confused before Christmas, but I think it was more of a "me" thing then an "us" thing. But since the Christmas party, there isn't a doubt in my mind that I want him to be my husband."

Ginny looks at both Megan and Gina and says, "Good. I always knew you'd both end up together."

"You did?" I ask her with interest.

"Well, River told me about your crush way back when, and when Declan moved back home, the first thing he asked River was a question about you, not Finn. I found that odd since I knew you didn't date. So, I observed. He liked to move conversations around to find out something about you. And it wasn't until you came to visit that I really knew. He never took his eyes off of you, even when we were getting in the car, and he was outside. He'd watch you walk to the car and wouldn't take his eyes off until we drove off. Your brothers and I all agree that he is smitten with you, and you are equally smitten. Your cheeks pink up when you talk about him."

"Well, then." I say, covering my cheeks. I just can't believe he likes me and has liked me. I'm a lucky girl.

Megan grabs my hand. "I speak for every girl at this table. He's a lucky man to have such a wonderful bitch like you."

"Here, here." Gina raises her glass. Megan and Ginny lift theirs up next to hers.

I raise my glass and clink it with theirs. "Thanks, ladies. I love you all."

~

We climb back into the car for one last stop. I pull up in front of the treehouse, and Ginny is confused as to why we are here. We tell her that it is time we indoctrinate her into our club.

Megan, Gina, and I should have thought it through because four grown girls trying to climb a rope ladder in dresses on the last day of December is not smart. We lift each other up the ladder, sometimes using our shoulders to push the butt above us up.

When we finally make it to the top, we sit on the floor breathing hard. Gina starts laughing, and we all join in.

I have my knees against my chest, and my head is resting on them. "Whose brainless idea was this?"

They all look over at me and in unison say, "Yours."

"True." I clap my hands. "Well, let's do this so we can get down and get to the party."

Megan pulls out her nail file and hands it to Ginny. Gina shines the flashlight onto the piece of wood that our names are written on.

"Time to add another name," I tell Ginny, and she smiles before looking at the wooden plank again.

She leans forward and uses a nail file to carve her name under ours. When she is done, I pull out my cell phone and take a picture of it. I send it to each one of them before we descend the ladder. We walk arm in arm towards the car like links on a chain necklace.

Declan

The guys and I stand back to look at our handywork. The only people we are waiting on are Saige, Megan, Ginny, and Gina. Becky, Mrs. Wilson, and Leo came over once we finished cleaning. The food is cooked, and the decorations are put up.

I add my own twist to the decorations by having Mrs. Wilson and Becky lay rose petals down from the front door to the Christmas tree in the living room. All the guys, including Leo, put the 'Marry Me' sign together and in place, and I decorated the bedroom for the after party.

A beep from my phone tells me there is an incoming message from Megan.

"Megan says that they are leaving the treehouse now and are about ten minutes out."

Saige's mom jumps with glee. Leo yells, "Woo doggie," and slaps his knee. He laughs happily in the recliner. Finn and River smile and walk over to slap me on the back, asking if I am ready for this. Becky and Jeff are leaning against the wall with smiles on their faces, trying to stay out of everyone's way.

I excuse myself to the bathroom quickly to get rid of the nerves. I do my business, and as I am washing my hands, I give my reflection a pep talk. I adjust my suit and make sure everything is in order before walking out.

Finn is outside the door and gives me a hard time, saying that he heard me talking to myself. I punch him in the shoulder and tell him to shut up, but he keeps pushing. I know why he is doing it. He is trying to distract me, so the nerves don't get a hold of me again.

We all are talking together, counting down until they get here, but I can hardly pay any attention. I think about all the time we have spent together and all the time we will spend if she says yes. I think of what her face will look like after she sees I'm about to propose.

"Don't worry. Won't be long now, son." Leo pats me on the back.

I glance over to him. "It's these damn nerves. They are going to make my heart jump out of my chest and run away."

"Nerves are good. They tell you how much you care for her. Why, when I proposed to Lucy, I thought I would have a heart attack before I got the chance to ask her."

"How did you propose to Lucy?" I ask him.

"It was October of 1964. I was twenty-one years young. I took Lucy to the movies to watch 'My Fair Lady'. It wasn't my cup of tea as it was a musical, but she was looking forward to it. She watched it and I watched her the whole night. When it was over, we went walking. 'I Want to Hold Your Hand' by the Beatles was playing from somewhere and I remember thinking that if I don't do it now then someone else will do it tomorrow. She was a catch, you know? So, I dropped down right then and there on the sidewalk and asked her. Tears welled in our eyes, and she said yes. It was the best day of my life until our wedding day a year later." He zoned out as he told me, probably picturing it as it happened.

He wipes a tear from his eye. "We had been married for fifty-two years before God took her away five years ago."

"Sounds like you lived a long, beautiful life together," Mrs. Wilson chimes in.

"Oh, it was. It was," he replies.

"Guys," Finn says excitedly from behind the curtain. "They are pulling up now."

I straighten my jacket and walk to the tree, beside the sign. River dims the lights so that the tree and sign are illuminated. I hear the doors to the car close and footsteps on the porch stop behind the door. I wait for it to open, and Ginny leads the pack with Megan and Gina behind her. They hurry in and take their place, and Saige asks them what they are doing running until she stops in her tracks and sees everyone.

Tears well in her eyes when she sees the petals on the ground. Her eyes follow the trail and find my feet. I watch her eyes lift slowly and stop on the sign before raising to meet my eyes. Her warm brown eyes tell me my answer, but I wait to hear it.

She walks slowly towards me, ignoring everyone else but Leo. Knowing how much him being here means to her, she stops to hug him before continuing the walk to me. When she stands in front of me, I drop down to one knee.

Saige

Declan pulls out a black box and opens it to reveal the most beautiful princess cut diamond. It is surrounded by little diamonds on the band. I look back at him, meeting his eyes. Through my tears, I can see a single tear falling down his cheek.

"My love, I've had this ring in my pocket since we went to go to dinner, and you told me you were afraid something bad was going to happen. I was going to ask you that night in the restaurant, but I knew it wasn't wise because I wanted to make sure you knew in your heart that you and me, we were always endgame."

"You told me at the Christmas party that you weren't scared anymore, and you wanted to marry me and have my kids, and I was so elated. Everyone in this room has helped me prepare for this day since that evening. Everyone in this room is here for us, love."

"They know you are my better half, that you are stubborn, loving and give with your whole heart. You drive me wild but at the same time you calm my chaos. You are the light in the dark and the rainbow in the storm."

"You are the most beautiful woman I have ever set my eyes upon. I love you with every fiber of my being. Saige Rosaline Wilson, will you make me the happiest man in the world and be my wife?"

And now, a man I love kneels in front of me holding the most gorgeous ring I have ever seen. It could have been a ring pop for all I care because he just vowed in front of all our family and friends that he loves me unconditionally.

"Yes!" I exclaim. "Yes! Yes, Declan Alexander Wolfe! I will marry you! I can't wait to grow old with you and have children together. I want to watch you be the dad I know you can be. I can't wait to sit on the porch when we are old and gray, watching our grandchildren play in the yard. I want to spend every minute of my life with you because there is no one else."

He stands, and I jump into his arms. Our lips meet with such haste that I get half his lips and half his cheek in the kiss.

"I told you that you were someone's endgame. I just never told you that I planned on you being mine and me being yours. Hell, I fought it, but we were destined to be together," he says.

I don't know what my life will be like in a year, a month or even tomorrow. I do know, at this moment, I am blissfully happy because I found my endgame in Declan Wolfe.

Clara Moon

She lives in the country in Gibson County, Indiana with her long-suffering husband and their four wild boys. Throw in a cat named Tiger, a whole lot of hot wheel cars, monster trucks, a few derby cars, a TBR pile a mile long, and you have summed up her life.

When she is not writing you can find her losing her mind one child at a time, homeschooling, drowning in laundry, getting lost in between pages of a book and making wishes on the stars.